# Biopharmaceutical Case Studies: Engineering Challenges and Practical Solutions

By

Naveenganesh Muralidharan

Published by Book Writing Pioneer

Cover design by Book Writing Pioneer

ISBN: Printed in United States

BOOK WRITING PIONEER

# Dedication

Dedicated to:

*My parents* ***Swarnavalli*** *and* ***Muralidharan*** *for raising to me to believe in hard work; and to my wife* ***Malar*** *who believed in me; and my beloved children* ***Adhvay*** *and* ***Advika*** *who inspires me every single day,*

*Want to thank you.*

***Jason Bishop*** *Sr. Director Manufacturing and MSAT, at AGC Biologics for encouraging me and supporting me in the massive undertaking of writing this book.* ***Matthew Smith and Navneet Tyagi,*** *who inspired me as a knowledgeable engineer.*

*---- Naveenganesh Muralidharan ----*

# Editor & Author

**Naveenganesh Muralidharan**

Naveenganesh Muralidharan has done undergraduate in Bachelor of Technology in Biotechnology and Masters in Cell and Molecular biology. Naveen has 17+ years of progressive leadership experience in parenteral biologics and gene therapy platforms from leading global biopharmaceutical companies. Currently Naveen is a senior manager, Manufacturing science and Technology in AGC Biologics Boulder CO USA, leading a team of engineers and scientists responsible for process transfer to commercial manufacturing facility. He is a practicing engineer and subject matter expert in late-stage upstream process development, scale up, technology transfer, stage 2 process validation and stage-3 commercial ongoing process verification support. Naveen has published a substantial number of technical articles in peer-reviewed journals in the field of biopharmaceuticals.

# Co-Editor

**Mark Davis**

Mark Davis has been on a lifelong mission to enable production of new cancer treatments following the death of his mother at a young age. Having obtained a Master's degree in Biological Sciences, Mark moved in the field of biotech and has been involved in over 30 Development & Tech Transfers for new treatments. Mark is an SME in most areas of large scale protein purification, such as column packing, chromatography, UF/DF, virus removal filtration, etc. Currently acting as Director for MSAT for AGC Biologics in Boulder, CO, Mark is working to grow a team of highly effective MSAT Engineers to replace him when he retires. In 2020, Mark was selected as the "face of science research" in CO by the Scienceworks team for his dedication to new treatments.

# Contributors and Co-Authors


**Thatsinee Johnson**

MSAT Engineer

AGC Biologics, Boulder, CO USA

**Emma Bolduc**

MSAT Engineer

AGC Biologics, Boulder, CO USA

**Tyler Younger**

MSAT Engineer

AGC Biologics, Boulder, CO USA

**Grace Chan**

MSAT Engineer

AGC Biologics, Boulder, CO USA

**Leyla Saeednia Rose, PhD**

MSAT Senior Manager,

AGC Biologics, Boulder, CO USA

**Anthony Montedonico**

Director, Quality Control

AGC Biologics, Boulder, CO USA

# Table Of Contents

# Chapter 1: Mass transfer and Shear assessment of Bioreactor- A Case study

**Naveenganesh Muralidharan, Emma Bolduc, Mark Davis**

### Introduction

Increasing demands in the biologics industry and the limitations of single-use bioreactors up to 5000 L are pushing the industry to move to large-scale 20,000-L stainless-steel bioreactors. However, over decades of advancement in biologics manufacturing processes, industries have developed high-cell-density (HCD), upstream cell culture manufacturing processes. As these HCD processes are transferred from 2,000-L bioreactors to 20,000-L large-scale production bioreactors, the first concern for process engineers is assessing whether these 20,000-L bioreactors are capable of supporting HCD processes to meet the required oxygen demand. If so, the next concerns are whether the HCD process requires an aggressive impeller agitation rate and gas flow rate for oxygenation, which can introduce high shear to the cell culture process, and what scale-up methodologies can be adopted to ensure there are no adverse impacts on cell growth or productivity from excessive shear.

In cell culture operation, oxygen is one of the key rate-limiting substrates for cell growth and protein production. Cells consume oxygen from dissolved oxygen (DO) in liquid cell culture media. The primary function of a bioreactor is to maintain the DO concentration in order to support cell respiration through sparging and impeller agitation. Impeller agitation disperses sparged gas bubbles and promotes mass transfer of the gas bubbles through the gas-liquid (cell culture medium) interface. The rate of oxygen transfer (OTR) from gas to liquid is a function of the intrinsic properties of the cell culture growth medium and the design, and operating parameters of the bioreactor [1,2]. In this paper, we present a study on oxygen mass transfer performed in a 20,000-L-scale stirred-tank bioreactor (STBR) and discuss how data from mass transfer studies can be used to assess the maximum cell density that can be supported by a bioreactor. In addition, we also illustrate the **"shear-proof design space"** for bioreactor operating conditions.

## Methods for Studying Mass Transfer

### Pseudo-Medium Preparation and KLa Measurement

**KLa:** The volumetric oxygen transfer coefficient is a quantifiable measure of how efficiently oxygen can be transferred from a gas phase to a liquid medium. Here, "KL" is the mass transfer coefficient, and "a" is the interface area available for mass transfer. Because of the constantly varying dynamics of sparged gas bubbles inside a reactor, measuring "KL" and "a" independently is difficult. Thus, these terms are always measured together and reported as KLa in units of (1/h) [3]. For bioreactor operation, KLa is impacted by operating volume, impeller agitation rate, and gas flow rate through the sparger and overlay [4,5,6].

## Pseudo-Medium

**Effect of Salinity on KLa:** The solubility of DO decreases as salinity increases. Osmolality is a surrogate measurement of salinity. Most cell culture growth media are formulated at osmolality ranging from 290 to 320 mOsmol/kg [4]. Pseudo-medium is prepared by using a simple NaCl solution to mimic the osmolarity of the cell culture medium. When sodium chloride is dissolved in water, it completely dissociates into $Na^+$ and $Cl^-$. Thus, for every mole of sodium chloride per liter of medium, the osmolality increases by 2 Osmol/L [7]. Therefore, the amount of NaCl for pseudo-medium is calculated as 9 g/L according to Equation 1, shown in Box 1.

**Effect of Surfactant Concentration on KLa:** Pluronic F68 is one of the most widely used shear-protecting agents in cell culture medium formulation. As described in the literature, it is well known that such surface-active surfactants reduce the surface tension at the gas-liquid interface. Tharmalingam et al. (2015) showed the drop in liquid surface tension follows an exponential decay curve and plateaus after 1 g/L. Therefore, most commercially available off-the-shelf cell culture media are formulated at a Pluronic concentration of 1.0 g/L, as further increases do not have a considerable impact on liquid surface tension to further protect cells from shear [8]. Sieblist et al. (2013) reported a small to negligible impact on the mass transfer coefficient for Pluronic F68 concentrations of 0.1–1.0 g/L, determined by the usage of drilled hole spargers, as the bubble appearance and size are strongly dependent on sparger type. Therefore, no surfactant is used in preparing the pseudo-medium [29].

**Effect of Antifoam (Simethicone Emulsion C Concentration) on KLa:** Routledge (2012) reported that the addition of antifoam increases bubble coalescence in the cell culture medium, leading to a reduced mass transfer area and thereby reducing the KLa value [32]. McAndrew et al. (2021) modeled an empirical predictive equation showing a decrease of up to 50% in KLa at values beyond 30 ppm, as shown in Figure 1B (the expression for the percentage reduction in KLa according to the antifoam concentration is shown in Equation 2), for simethicone concentrations ranging from 1 to 100 ppm with Antifoam C emulsion solution in a drilled-hole sparger bioreactor system [31]. McAndrew et al. (2021) showed that the reduction in KLa follows an exponential decay curve and plateaus for antifoam concentrations exceeding 30 ppm. Because the amount of antifoam used in cell culture manufacturing processes can range from 0 to 30 ppm and the effect of antifoam concentration on KLa is predictable, no surfactant is used in preparing the pseudo-medium.

**Dynamics of Changes in Fluid Density and Viscosity in Bioreactors:** The magnitude and rate of change in the fluid viscosity and density of the culture medium in a bioreactor are affected by the viable cell density profile, culture duration, supplements in the formulated growth medium, feed additions, cell metabolism rate, base titrant consumed, etc. During cell culture fermentation, cells produce proteins, debris, metabolites, and growth factors, which increase the fluid density and viscosity. At the same time, cells also consume proteins, glucose, nutrients, and growth factors, which reduces the fluid density and viscosity, as described in [33]. In fed-batch mammalian cell culture, the fluid viscosity can range from 0.85 to 1.05 mPa.s, and the density can range from 1015 to 10007 kg/m$^3$ [16, 38] over a transition from a cell-free medium to a spent HCD harvest medium.

**Effect of Fluid Density and Viscosity on KLa:** Higbie's penetration theory for gas diffusion from gas bubbles rising in liquid is expressed as shown in Equation 3 [39]. Here, $D_L$ is the diffusion constant for oxygen, ϵ is the dissipation rate of turbulent kinetic energy per unit mass, μ is the liquid viscosity, and ρ is the liquid dynamic density. Equation 3 shows a proportional relationship between liquid density and mass transfer coefficient KL and an inverse relationship between liquid viscosity and coefficient KL.

In alignment with Higbie's penetration theory, Xu et al. (2019) and Solecki (2015) reported that increasing the viscosity results in a reduced KLa [34, 35]. Moreover, Koide et al. (1984) and Yoshida et al. (1965) reported that an increase in liquid density results in an increase in KLa [36, 37].

**Magnitude of Change in Density and Viscosity During Cell Culture Operation and Its Effect on KLa:** Pappenreiter et al. (2019) reported that no significant changes to KLa were observed between cell-free media and spent harvest media for a Chinese hamster ovary (CHO) fed-batch culture [40]. Therefore, changes in viscosity are considered to have a minimal overall impact on KLa. Hence, changes in viscosity and density are not implemented in the KLa predictive model study.

| Box 1: Effect of Medium Components on Kla | |
|---|---|
| Equation 1 | $S\left(\frac{g}{L}\right) = \frac{310\left(\frac{mOsmol}{kg}\right)\times\frac{1\ Osmol}{1000\ mOsmol}\times1\frac{kg}{L}}{\frac{1}{58.4}\left(\frac{mol}{g}\right).\times Species\ per\ mol\left(\frac{Osmol}{mol}\right).} = 9\ g/L$ |
| Equation 2 | % Decrease in KLa, $\%Dr_{KLa} = 52.74\ e^{(-0.14\times C_{Ant})} + 47.8$<br>Where $C_{Ant}$ is the Antifoam concentration in ppm |
| Equation 3 | Mass Transfer Coefficient $K_L = \frac{2}{\sqrt{\pi}}\sqrt{D_L}\left(\frac{\rho.\varepsilon_L}{\mu}\right)^{0.25}$ |

**Measurement Method:** An accurate method for measuring KLa in a large-scale bioreactor was proposed by Link et al. (1989), and it denoted the dynamic pressure method (DPM) [9]. In the DPM, when the measured dissolved oxygen (DO) value is stabilized for specific bioreactor operating parameters such as volume, impeller agitation rate, sparger gas flow rate, and pressure, the total pressure increases by 20%. According to Henry's law, an increase in reactor pressure leads to a simultaneous change in the oxygen concentration in all of the bubbles that are dispersed in the liquid and thereby reduces the influence of nonideal mixing of the gas phase on the KLa measurement. Once a step-change increase in the pressure is initiated in the bioreactor, the % DO value starts to increase and reaches a new saturation % DO value, as shown in Figure 1A. Plotting Ln [(C*-C) ÷(C*-$C_0$)] as a function of time, as shown in Figure 1B, yields a slope of (-KLa). Here, t is the time in seconds, C* is the saturation concentration of oxygen as a percentage, $C_0$ is the initial oxygen concentration as a percentage, and C is the oxygen concentration at any time as a percentage [5,9].

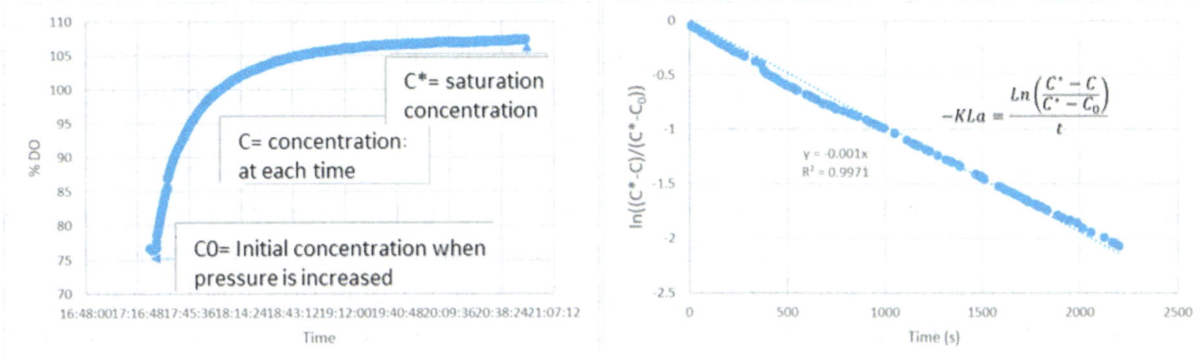


**Figure 1. DPM for KLa measurement.**

## Design of Experiment (DOE) and Power

A partial factorial design form is employed as the design of the experiment (DoE) to characterize and develop the KLa response surface predictive model. The input factors selected for the KLa characterization are impeller agitation rate (revolutions per minute [RPM]) at three levels (20, 30, and 40 RPM), Sparger air flow rate (liters per minute [LPM]) at three levels (250, 450, and 900 LPM), and vessel working volume (L) at two levels (10,000 and 16,800 L), as shown in Figure 2. Eight conditions with different combinations of volume, impeller agitation rate, and sparger gas flow rate were studied, as detailed in Figure 2.

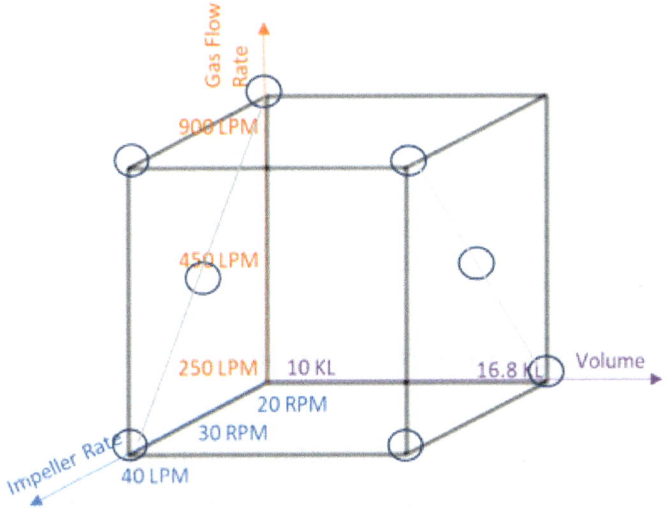


**Figure 2. Parameters and experimental conditions for the KLa study.**

## KLa Predictive Model

For each condition identified in Figure 3, the KLa value was measured and calculated using the DPM. A predictive model was developed based on a standard least-square regression model using JMP 14.2. The developed predictive expression is shown in Figure 3A. Figure 3B displays the actual values versus the predicted values. R-squared is a statistical measure of how well the prediction expression can fit the actual data. The obtained value of $R^2$=0.95 demonstrates that the predictive expression is reliable. Additionally, the p-value (0.0046) is less than 0.05, demonstrating that the measure of the strength of the association between the input and output variables is statistically significant. Figure 3C shows the prediction profiler, which displays the magnitude of change in the response variable (KLa) that occurs when only one input parameter is changed and all other parameters are held constant. As expected, Figure 3C shows an increase in KLa with increasing impeller agitation rate and decreasing working volume. Interestingly, Figure 4C also shows an increase in KLa with increasing gas flow rate up to a rate of 550 LPM; however, KLa starts decreasing for values beyond 550 LPM, which might be explained as an impeller flooding regime. At a certain combination of low impeller agitation speed and high gas flow rate, bubbles are not dispersed across the liquid by impeller agitation and simply escape out of the liquid [6].

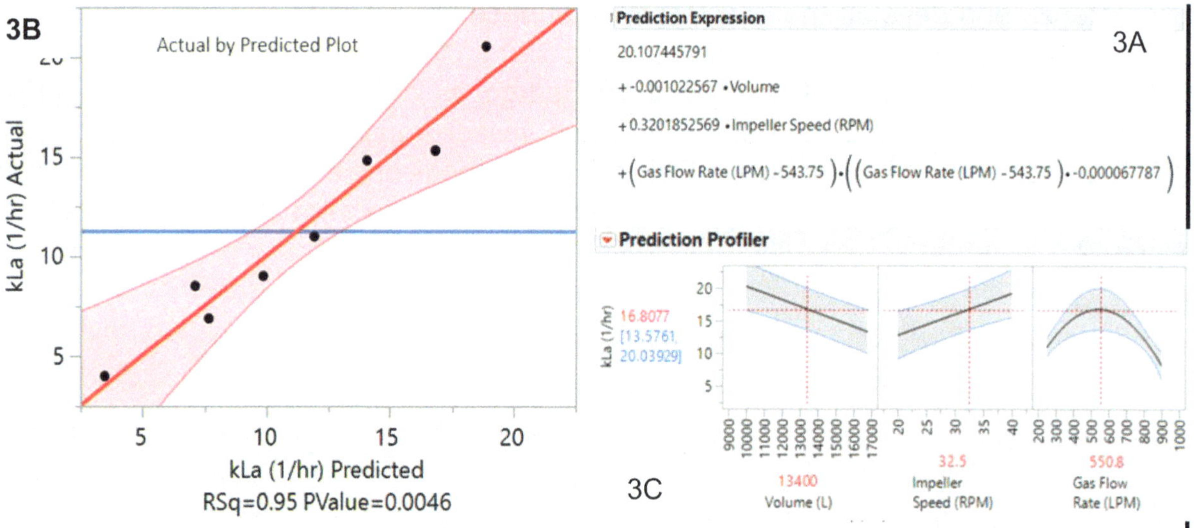


**Figure 3. KLa predictive model.**

## Maximum Cell Density That a Bioreactor Can Support Based on KLa

The OTR is a measure of how much oxygen can be transferred per unit of time in a bioreactor for a specific Kla at a specified fraction of oxygen in the gas phase. The OTR is calculated from Equations 4–6, as shown in Box 2. Here, KLa is the volumetric oxygen transfer coefficient (1/h), calculated from the predictive model expression shown in Figure 4A. C* is the saturation concentration of oxygen in mmol/L, calculated from Equation 4. H is Henry's coefficient for oxygen solubility in water; for typical culture operating conditions at 37°C, H=1.07 mmol/(L.atm) is a good approximation. P is the average pressure in the bioreactor in atm. A positive pressure above the atmospheric pressure of

1 atm is maintained in the bioreactor; the pressure in the headspace and additional pressure from the liquid height inside the bioreactor sum up to be greater than 1 atm. However, for simplicity in our calculation, P is assumed to be 1 atm. $F_{oxy}$ is the fraction of oxygen in the incoming gas. The fraction of oxygen in the air is 0.21; however, to assess the maximum capability of the bioreactor, we assume here that the bioreactor is sparged with pure oxygen. Therefore, we employed a value of $f_{oxy}$ = 1. $C_L$ is the set-point oxygen concentration maintained in the bioreactor in mmol/L, calculated from Equation 6. The oxygen concentration in the atmosphere is 21%. DO probes are calibrated to 100% through exposure to the atmospheric oxygen concentration. Therefore, a 50% DO set-point indicates 50% of the 21% atmospheric oxygen concentration.

| Box 2: OTR | |
|---|---|
| OTR | |
| Equation 4 | $OTR = KL_a(C^* - C_L) = KL_a\left(1.07\,\frac{mmol}{L} - 0.112\frac{mmol}{L}\right) = KL_a \times 0.96\,\frac{mmol}{L}$ |
| Equation 5 | $C^* = H \times P \times f_{oxy} = 1.07\frac{mmol}{L.atm} \times 1\,atm\ \times 1 = 1.07\,\frac{mmol}{L}$ |
| Equation 6 | $C_L = H \times P \times 0.21 \times DO_{st.pt} = 1.07\frac{mmol}{L.atm} \times 1\,atm \times 0.21 \times 0.50 = 0.112\,\frac{mmol}{L}$ |

**Oxygen Uptake Rate (OUR):** Oxygen is a key substrate in cell metabolism. In addition to maintaining sterility and homogeneity by mixing, the primary factor that determines the capability of a bioreactor is the ability to meet the oxygen respiration rate of cells or simply the OUR. As shown in Equation 9, the OUR is calculated as the product of the viable cell density and specific oxygen consumption rate of the cells [4]. Here, $Q_{o2}$ is the specific oxygen consumption rate of cells (pmol/(cell. day)), and Xi is the viable cell density ($10^6$ cells/mL).

**Specific OURs ($Q_{o2}$) Differ for Different Mammalian Cells:** The specific OUR is defined as the amount of oxygen consumed per cell per unit of time. For mammalian cells, $Q_{o2}$ is cell-line-specific. Jorjani et al. (1999) reported maximum specific oxygen consumption rates for three cell lines (baby hamster kidney [BHK], hybridoma, and CHO) at 37°C as 7.2, 5.28, and 7.44 (pmol/(cell. day)) [42].

**Effect of Temperature on the Specific OUR ($Q_{o2}$) of Mammalian Cells:** In cell culture operations, a downward temperature shift is often performed from 37°C to approximately 29°C–35°C to increase productivity and maintain product quality. This downward temperature shift has been shown to improve cell viability and specific productivity [43,44]. All biological and chemical reactions are temperature-dependent and can be modeled by the Arrhenius expression, as shown in equation 7. Here, A is the Arrhenius constant, and E is the activation energy (kJ/mol). R is the ideal gas constant (0.00831 kJ/mol.K), and T is the temperature in Kelvin. Equation 5 also shows the Arrhenius constant (A) and activation energy (E) values for three different cell lines (BHK, hybridoma, and CHO), as reported by Jorjani P et al. (1999)[42].

**Dynamic Change in Cell-Specific OUR ($Q_{o2}$) Inside Bioreactors:** The change in cell density per unit time is defined as the growth rate (cells/h), and the change in cell density per cell per unit time is defined as the specific cell growth rate (cells/(cell. h) ) or (1/h). In biologics protein manufacturing, bioreactors are often operated in fed-batch mode. Here, as the cells proliferate, the medium composition is constantly changing over the culture duration, which limits nutrients and accumulates toxic metabolites. This situation changes the physiological state of the cells and reduces the specific growth rate.

The viable cell density profile in batch mode or fed-batch mode is divided into the exponential growth phase, stationary phase, and declining phase. The cell growth rate is higher at the beginning of the culture time (exponential phase) and plateaus as the cells enter the stationary phase. The growth rate then falls as the cells enter the declining phase. It should be noted that the specific growth rate is a reflection of the physiological state of the cells to proliferate rather than the growth rate. In a fed-batch cell culture operation, it is typical to observe a decrease in the cell-specific growth rate; however, there is still an increase in the rate of cells produced.

**Effect of Culture Time on Cell-Specific OUR:** For a CHO cell culture, Ihling et al. (2022) reported that the specific OUR decreased from 5.7 to 2.4 pmol/cell.day at 96 h post-inoculation [46]. A similar observation of a specific OUR decrease from 7.7 to 4.8 pmol/cell.day as early as 50 h post-inoculation was reported by Deshpande et al. (2004) for a CHO cell culture [45].

**Effect of Specific Growth Rate on Cell-Specific OUR:** As cells actively proliferate, they require more oxygen for respiration. Therefore, the specific OUR is directly proportional to the specific growth rate [3]. An exponential correlation expression between the cell-specific growth rate and specific OUR was developed from the data reported by Deshpande et al. (2004) [45], as shown in Equation-9 and Figure-4.

**Effect of Cell Density on Cell-Specific OUR:** Over the culture duration, as the viable cell density increases, the metabolite concentration increases as a result of cell metabolism and feed additions, which reduces the specific OUR. This phenomenon was cited as a metabolic crowding effect in mammalian suspension cell culture by Sand et al. (1977) [49]. For a typical mammalian cell culture in a fed-batch bioreactor operation with a cell density of $0.5\times10^6$ to $50\times10^6$ cells/mL, the specific oxygen consumption rate ranges from 6.0 to 3.5 mmol/cell, as shown in Figure 6B.

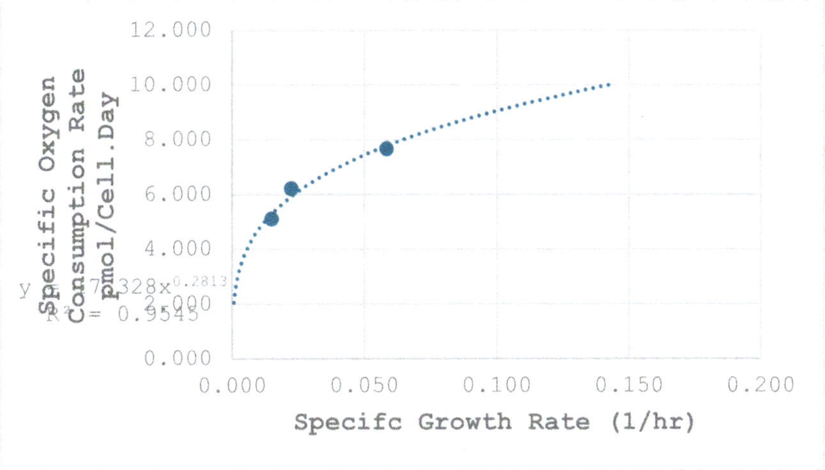


**Figure 4: Specific cell growth rate Vs. Specific oxygen consumption rate.**

For the purpose of illustration, a specific growth rate ranging from 0.03 to 0.001 (1/h) and a seeding density of $0.5\times10^6$ cells/mL are assumed [47], and the viable cell density profile and corresponding cell-specific OUR were simulated via Equations 8 and 9, as shown in Figure 5. The results show that $Q_{o2}$ =5.5 pmol/(cell. day) is a good approximation representing typical mammalian cell culture bioreactor operation to conservatively calculate the maximum viable cell density for assessing the bioreactor capability (1 pmol=$10^{-12}$ mol) [10, 41].

<table>
<tr><td colspan="2">Box 3: Dynamic Change in Specific OUR</td></tr>
<tr><td colspan="2">OTR</td></tr>
<tr><td>Equation 7</td><td>Temperature correction for $Q_{O2}$.<br>$$Q_{O2}\frac{pmol}{Cell.Day} = \left[A \times e^{-E/RT}\right] \times 24$$<br>

| Cell Line | BHK | Hybridoma | CHO |
|---|---|---|---|
| A, Arrhenius constant. | 6.08E+12 | 3.20E+14 | 1.28E+15 |
| E, Activation Energy kJ/mol.K | 79 | 90 | 93 |

R is Gas constant = 0.0083145 kJ/mol. K<br>T is the Temperature in Kelvin</td></tr>
<tr><td>Equation 8</td><td>Predicted viable cell density.<br>$$x_n = X_{n-1} \times e^{\Delta t \times \mu}$$<br>$\Delta t = t_n - t_{n-1}$ is the time duration (h)<br>μ is the assumed specific growth rate (1/h)<br>$X_{n-1}$ is the cell density at time $t_{n-1}$<br>$X_n$ is the cell density at time $t_n$</td></tr>
</table>

| | |
|---|---|
| Equation 9 | Specific OUR<br>$$Q_{o2} = 17.328 \times \mu^{0.2813}$$<br>μ is the assumed specific growth rate (1/h) |

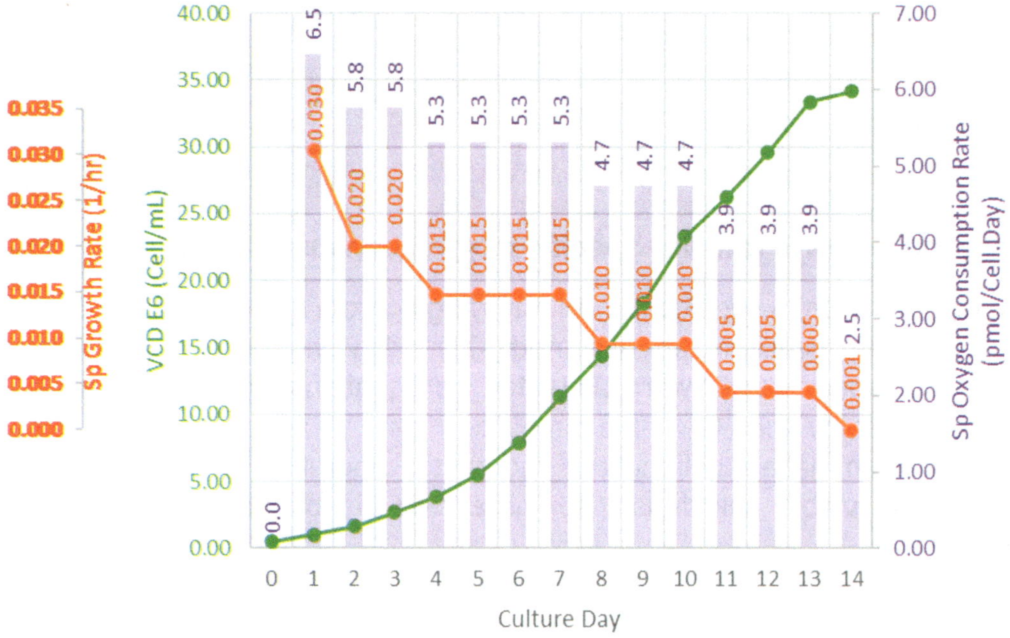


**Figure 5: Illustrative example (Simulated) of typical cell growth, specific cell growth rate, and specific oxygen consumption rate.**

During cell culture operations, the OTR of the bioreactor should be equal to the OUR, expressed as OTR=OUR. By setting Equations 4 and 10 equals to each other, we can calculate the maximum cell count that can be supported by KLa, as expressed in Equation 11. Equation 11 indicates that approximately 4×10$^6$ cells/mL can be supported for a KLa value of 1 (1/h) when pure oxygen is used as the sparge gas.

| Box 4: OTR, OUR, and Maximum Cell Density | |
|---|---|
| OUR | |
| Equation 10 | $$OUR = x_i \times Q_{o2} = x \frac{10^6 cells}{mL} \times 10^3 \frac{mL}{1L} \times 5.5 \frac{10^{-12} mol}{cell.day} \times \frac{10^3 mmol}{mol} \times \frac{1 day}{24\ h}$$<br>$$= 0.23 \times x_i \frac{mmol}{L}$$ |
| Maximum Cell Density | |

| | |
|---|---|
| Equation 11 | $x_{i,max} = \dfrac{KL_a \frac{1}{hr} \times 0.96 \frac{mmol}{mL}}{0.23\left(\frac{mmol}{L.hr} \Big/ \frac{10^6 cells}{mL}\right)} = KL_a \frac{1}{hr} \times 4.18 \frac{cells}{mL}$ |

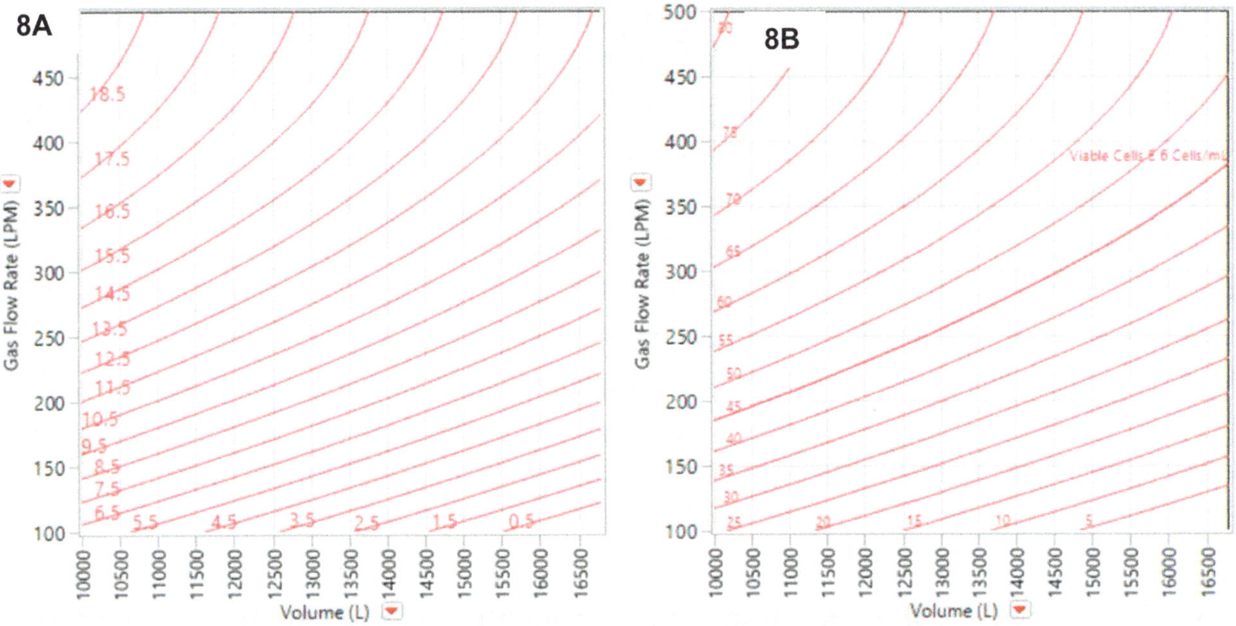


**Figure 6. A) Contour profile showing the predicted KLa (1/h) obtained by using the prediction expression shown in Figure 4A as a function of volume (L) and gas flow rate (LPM) at a set impeller agitation rate of 30 RPM. B) Contour profile showing the maximum viable cell density (10⁶ cells/mL) predicted by Equation 9, for each KLa value shown in Figure 6A.**

## Bioreactor Mixing Time Assessment

The impeller discharge rate ($m^3/s$) is the volume pumped from the impeller blade per unit of time and is calculated according to Equation 12, where $N_F$ is the impeller flow number, n is the impeller agitation rate in RPM, and $d_i$ is the impeller diameter in meters. The circulation time is defined as the ratio of liquid volume in $m^3$ to impeller discharge rate in $m^3/s$, as shown in Equation 13. The bioreactor mixing time is the time required to achieve a given degree of homogeneity when starting from a completely segregated state. After several circulations, the desired degree of homogeneity is reached [11]. For a stirred tank with several baffles and a small impeller-to-tank-diameter ratio, Doran (2013) reported that the mixing time is approximately four times the circulation time, as shown in Equation 14 [11]. In our 20,000-L bioreactor, the agitation system is built with two Chemineer LIGHTNIN A320 impellers with flow number $N_F$ = 0.62. The calculated mixing time for different impeller agitation values is shown in Figure 7A. Figure 7A shows that there is no significant improvement in the mixing time for values beyond 30 RPM.

| Box 5: Impeller Mixing Time | |
|---|---|
| Equation 12 | Impeller discharge rate ($m^3/s$), $Q_{imp} = N_F \times n \times d_i^3$ |
| Equation 13 | Impeller circulation time (s), $t_{cir} = \frac{V}{Q_{imp}}$ |
| Equation 14 | Impeller mixing time (s), $t_{mix} = 4 \times t_{cir}$ |

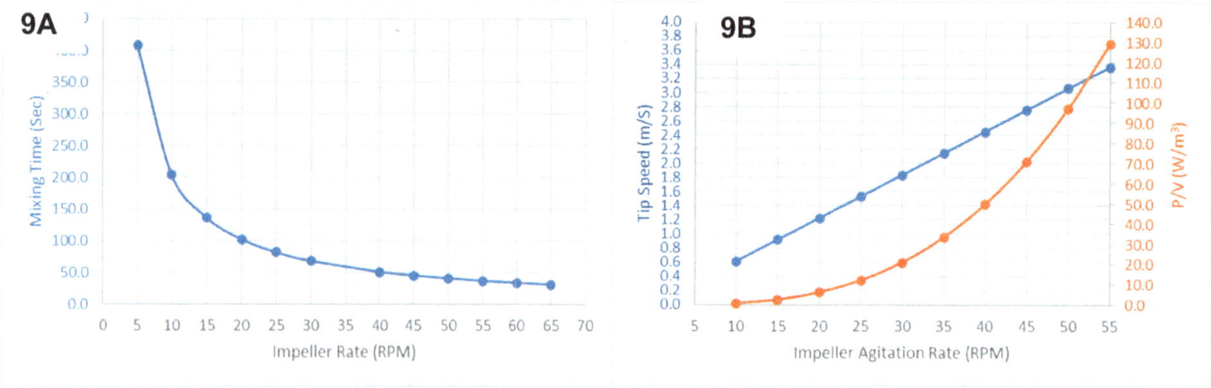


**Figure 7. A) Mixing time (s) versus impeller agitation rate (RPM). B) Tip speed (m/s) and P/V ($W/m^3$) versus impeller agitation rate.**

## Shear Assessment for the Impeller Agitation Rate

Once the KLa predictive model is established, the next step is to identify any limitations on the impeller agitation rate. The most widely used parameters for scaling up the impeller agitation rate are the power over volume (P/V), expressed in $W/m^3$, and impeller tip speed, expressed in m/s.

Power indicates energy consumed over time. The power consumed by the impeller averaged over the entire volume of the bioreactor is denoted as P/V. The P/V approach is used not only to scale the impeller speed for different sizes of a given impeller design but also to scale between different impeller designs and geometries, as impeller power calculations accommodate design differences between various impeller configurations [12,13,14]. Commercial-scale bioreactors are typically operated at P/V values of up to 50 $W/m^3$ to avoid any deleterious impacts on cell health [15]. P/V is calculated from Equation 15, where $N_p$ is the impeller power number provided by the manufacturer and ρ is the density of the liquid. For ρ, 1015 $kg/m^3$ is a good approximation for cell culture medium [16].

Although the average P/V is widely used as a scaling parameter in the biopharmaceutical industry for determining impeller speed across a range of STBR scales, it does not account for the scale-dependent shear heterogeneity that is normally present inside a bioreactor. Heterogeneity is prevalent in large-scale STBRs. For example, Hu et al. (2011) reported that 70.5% of the total power consumed by a pitched-blade impeller dissipates in the liquid volume near the impeller zone [17]. Impeller tip speed is a surrogate measure of the maximum shear inside a bioreactor. The shear rate is defined as the change in fluid velocity over distance. In an impeller-based STBR, the maximum fluid velocity is observed at the tip of the impeller blade as it revolves in the fluid [14]. For a constant P/V maintained across different sizes of bioreactors, the impeller tip velocity increases as the bioreactor scale increases [4]. Hence, the impeller tip velocity is often viewed as a critical parameter to be assessed when scaling the impeller speed. Such assessments consider only the impeller diameter and agitation speed, not the impeller design. The impeller tip speed is calculated from Equation 16. For a typical cell culture process, maintaining an impeller tip velocity of 0.6–1.8 m/s has been recommended to prevent adverse effects on cell growth [18]. Figure 7B shows the impeller tip speed and P/V for different impeller agitation rates for an operation volume of 16,800 L. We observe a limitation in the impeller agitation rate at 30 RPM for a maximum acceptable impeller tip velocity of 1.8 m/s and at 40 RPM based on the maximum acceptable P/V limit of 50 W/m$^3$. Therefore, we conservatively set 30 RPM as the impeller rate based on the maximum tip speed of 1.8 m/s to avoid any lethal effects on the cell culture.

| Box 6: Shear According to Impeller Agitation Rate | |
|---|---|
| Equation 15 | Power by volume (W/m$^3$), $\left(\frac{P}{V}\right) = \rho\left(\frac{N_p d_i^5 n^3}{V}\right)$ |
| Equation 16 | Impeller tip speed $\vartheta_{Imp,Tip} = \frac{\pi d_i n}{60}$ |

## Shear Assessment for the Gas Flow Rate

**The average shear introduced by sparging gas** into a cell culture STBR is commonly assessed by the energy dissipation rate (EDR) for sparged bioreactors, as reported by Bhavaraju et al. (1978). The average EDR from gas sparging is calculated per Equation 17, where $Q_g$ is the gas flow rate in m$^3$/s, $d_T$ is the bioreactor tank diameter, g is the acceleration rate (9.8 m/s$^2$), P1 and P2 are the pressure on the surface of the bioreactor liquid and at the sparging point, respectively (in kg·m$^{-1}$·s$^{-2}$ or Pascals), and $h_T$ is the bioreactor liquid height (m). Hu et al. (2011) summarized 24 different studies on shear assessment and reported an EDR of 10$^4$ W/m$^3$ as sublethal for most mammalian cells [23].

Another widely used parameter that is assessed for scaling the gas flow rate in cell culture bioreactor operations is the gas volumetric rate per bioreactor unit volume, expressed as the volume of air per unit volume of liquid per minute (VVM). The VVM directly influences shear across different bioreactor scales, and holding this parameter constant does not account for differences in sparger configurations and designs that are often unique to bioreactor models and manufacturers. Chisti (2000) reported a decrease in the specific cell growth rate for gas flow rates >0.04 VVM [19]. Another parameter used for scaling up the bioreactor gas flow rate in an STBR is the superficial gas velocity, defined as the ratio of the volumetric gas flow rate to the bioreactor cross-sectional area. However, this superficial gas velocity calculation is a part of the average EDR equation for gas sparging, as shown in Equation 17. Therefore, the superficial gas velocity is not further discussed.

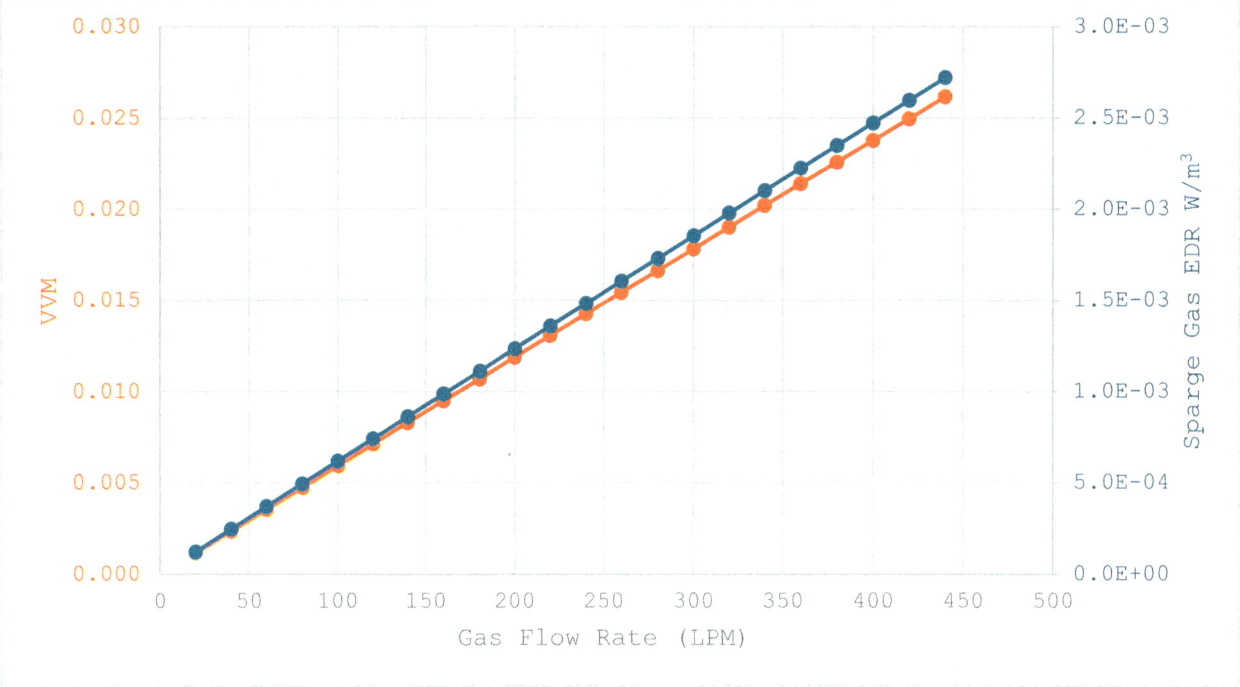


**Figure 8: VVM and sparge gas EDR (W/m$^3$) versus gas sparge flow rate (LPM).**

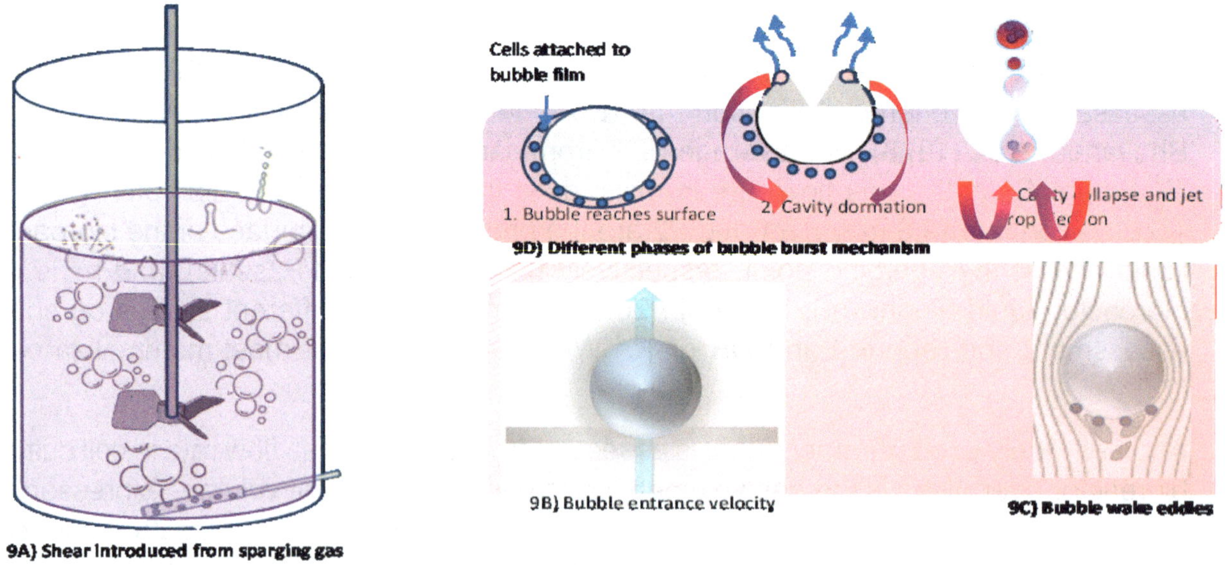


**Figure 9: Localized shear from gas sparging.**

**The localized shear introduced by sparging gas** into a cell culture STBR is assessed in three phases: 1) when a gas bubble is generated by the sparger holes, 2) when the bubble rises upward across the liquid height in the bioreactor, and 3) when the bubble reaches the surface and bursts at the gas–liquid surface interface [19].

**When bubbles are generated at the sparger hole**: At this point, the shear is assessed based on the gas-entrance velocity (GEV) at the sparger orifice. The GEV is defined as the ratio of the volumetric gas flow rate to the total area available for gas to exit, calculated per Equation 18. Here, $Q_g$ is the gas flow rate in L/s, $d_o$ is the diameter of a single hole in the sparger (m), and $n_0$ is the number of holes in the sparger. Chaudhary et al. (2020) reported GEV values of >30 m/s and >60 m/s as critical GEV values for NS0 [non-secreting murine myeloma] cells and CHO cells, respectively, to avoid any adverse impacts on cell growth or productivity [20,28]. Figure 9B shows that the critical GEV of 60 m/s for CHO cells is reached at a sparge gas flow rate of 200 LPM.

**When bubbles rise through the bioreactor liquid height**: In this case, the shear is assessed based on bubble wake eddy length. As bubbles rise through a bioreactor, the circulating fluid carried behind them experiences the greatest drag force, as shown in Figure 11C. For bubble rise, shear assessment is performed by calculating the bubble wake micro-eddy length. The bubble wake eddy length is calculated from Equations 19–24 [19]. A bubble wake micro-eddy length that is less than or equal to the size of the cells in a culture is detrimental to cell viability. Hence, that length should be maintained at >20 µm for most mammalian cell culture operations to prevent negative effects on cell growth due to associated shear [4,19]. Figure 9C shows that for sparge gas flow rates up to 450 LPM, the bubble wake eddy length is above 34 µm.

**When bubbles burst at the gas–liquid interface:** As a bubble rises, cells become trapped in the film around the gas bubble. As the bubble reaches the gas–liquid interface, a cavity is formed on the bubble surface; then, the cavity collapses, and a liquid jet is formed as the bubble bursts and disappears. The cells carried in the bubble film volume will undergo lethal shear when the bubble film volume forms a jet as the bubble disintegrates, as shown in Figure 9D. This bubble burst shear is assessed from the EDR at the bubble burst, calculated as a function of bubble diameter according to Equation 25. Equation 25 is derived from data reported by Boulton-Stone and Blake (1993); the data were obtained by using a nonlinear exponential model with JMP14 software [17,21,22,23]. Wall et al. (2017) reported a lethal response from CHO cells when exposed to EDR levels above $10^6$–$10^8$ W/m$^3$ [24]. Conservatively, as reported by Hu et al. (2011), EDR levels above $10^4$ W/m$^3$ can be considered sublethal for most cell culture operations [23].

The above method of calculating the EDR when a bubble burst depends on the bubble diameter only; however, this method does not account for the total amount of bubbles generated or the rate of bubble generation. Tramper et al. (1988) presented a first-order cell-specific death rate constant calculation as a function of bubble size, rate of bubble generation per unit volume of culture, and bubble film volume or bubble kill volume. The bubble kill volume is the volume over which cells are carried, and experience shear as the bubble bursts in the gas–liquid interface, or simply the bubble film volume [26]. The death rate constant can be calculated from Equations 26–28 in Box 7. For shear-proof control conditions, Tramper et al. (1988) and Chisti (2000) showed that the death rate constant is approximately 0.032 (1/h). Therefore, a gas sparge design yielding a $K_d$ value below 0.032 (1/h) is considered to ensure shear-proof conditions for the cells. Figure 10C shows that for sparge gas flow rates up to 450 LPM, the bubble burst EDR is below $10^4$ $W/m^3$, and the death rate constant is below 0.032 (1/h).

| Box 7: Shear From Sparging Gas | |
|---|---|
| Shear when a bubble forms at the sparger hole: Bubble entrance velocity | |
| Equation 17 | $Average\ EDR\ from\ gas\ sparging = \frac{Q_g \times P2}{\left(\frac{\pi d_T^2}{4}\right)} \times \frac{ln\left(\frac{P1}{P2}\right)}{(P1 - P2)}$<br>where $P2 = P1 + (\rho \times g \times h_T)$ |
| Equation 18 | $Gas\ entance\ velocity, GEV = \frac{Q_g}{n_O\left(\frac{\pi d_O^2}{4}\right)}$ |
| Shear when a bubble rises though the bioreactor liquid height: Bubble rise eddy length per Chisti (2000) | |
| Equation 19 | $Bubble\ area\ (m^2),\ A_b = \frac{\pi d_b^2}{4}$ |
| Equation 20 | $Bubble\ velocity\ (\frac{m}{S}),\ \vartheta_b = \left(\frac{2\sigma}{d_b\rho} + \frac{0.5d_b}{g}\right)^{1/2}$<br>Where σ is the liquid surface tension (0.65 N/m), ρ is the liquid density (1015 $kg/m^3$), and g is the acceleration due to gravity (9.8 $m/s^2$) |
| Equation 21 | $Drag\ force\ from\ bubble\left(\frac{kg.m}{s^{-2}}\right), F_b = \frac{C_{d,B}\,\vartheta_b^2 A_b \rho}{2}$<br>Where $C_d$ is the drag coefficient coefficient for rising bubbles, assumed to be 2.6 (dimensionless) [19,25] |
| Equation 22 | Bubble EDR ($W/m^3$ or $\frac{kg.m^2}{s^{-3}}$), $EDR = F_b.\vartheta_b$ |
| Equation 23 | EDR (W/kg), $\varepsilon_b = (EDR) \div 1000$ |
| Equation 24 | $Bubble\ eddy\ length,\ \eta b = 10^6\left(\frac{v^3}{\varepsilon_{b,}}\right)^{1/4}$<br>v is the kinematic viscosity of the fluid (9.8x$10^{-7}$ $m^2/s$) |
| Shear when a bubble bursts at the gas-liquid interface: Bubble burst eddy length | |

| | |
|---|---|
| Equation 25 | $EDR_{Bub,}burst = e^{\left[-194.43\times(Log(d_b))^3\right]-\left[217.02\times(Log(d_b))^2\right]-\left[129.07\times Log(d_b)\right]-19.599}$<br><br>For the above empirical bubble burst relationship, the bubble diameter $d_b$ has units of cm. |
| Death rate constant | |
| Equation 26 | Rate of bubble generation, $R_b = \frac{Q_g}{V_{b.}} \div V = \frac{Q_g}{\left(\frac{\pi.d_b{}^3}{6}\right)} \div V$ |
| Equation 27 | Kill volume, $V_{Kill,B} = \left[\left(\frac{\pi.d_b{}^3}{6}\right) - \left(\frac{\pi.(d_b+\delta)^3}{6}\right)\right]$<br><br>δ: Film thickness of a bubble = 50 μm [19] |
| Equation 28 | First-order bubble death rate constant, $K_{d,Bubble} = V_{Kill,B} \times R_b$ |

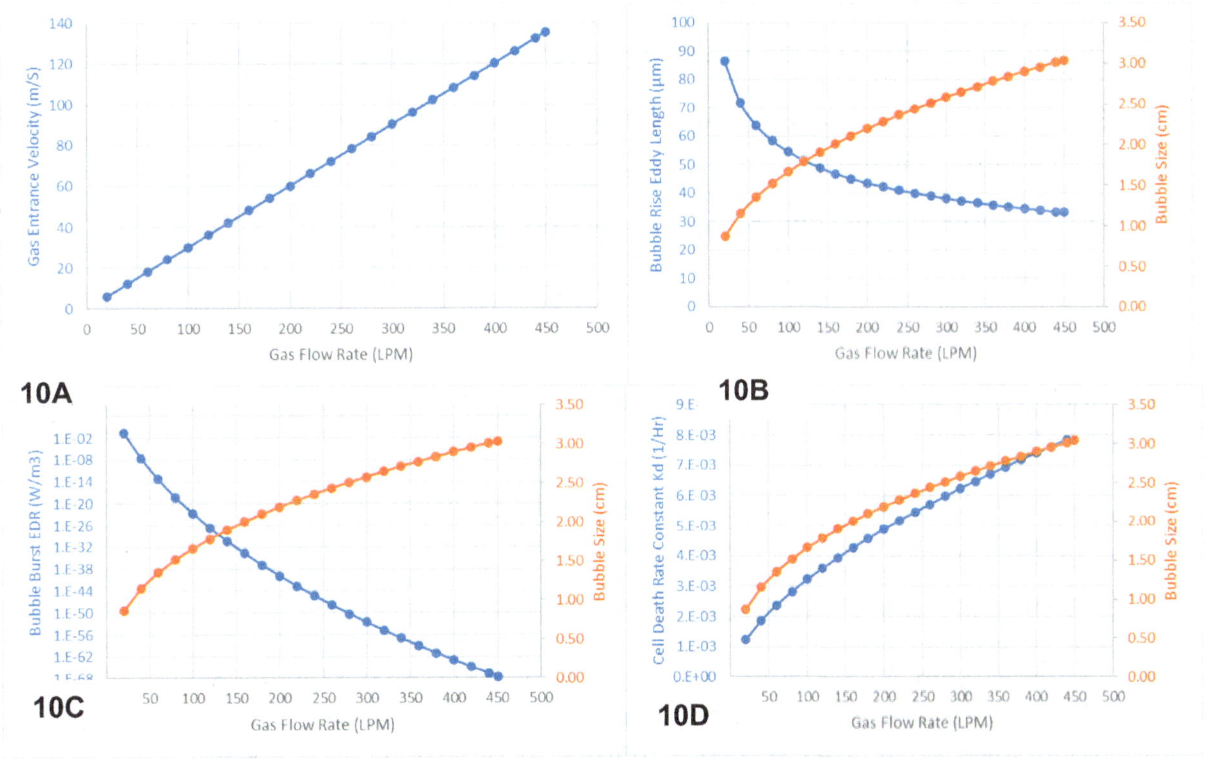


**Figure 10. A) GEV (m/s) versus gas flow rate (LPM). B) Bubble diameter (cm) and bubble rise eddy length (μm) versus gas flow rate (LPM). C) Bubble diameter (cm) and the bubble burst EDR (W/m³) at the gas–liquid interface versus gas flow rate. D) Bubble diameter (cm) and sparging death rate constant (1/h) versus gas flow rate.**

## Conclusion

The presented assessment for determining the maximum cell density that can be supported for a KLa value is based on the assumption of 5.5 mmol/(cell. day); this assumption is appropriate for most fed-batch mammalian cell culture operations. However, Goudar et al. (2011) reported that some clones of CHO cells have cell-specific OURs of up to 10 pg/(cell. day) [27]; therefore, readers should carefully evaluate the assumption of a specific OUR in such instances. Additionally, for shear assessment, the maximum tip speed, GEV, and the bubble burst EDR represent the region of shear-proof design based on previously reported studies and do not necessarily indicate the edge of failure. Therefore, if necessary, a marginal increase in any of the above shear assessments could be explored with an appropriate scale-down model or detailed risk assessment.

## References

1. Shuler, M. L., Kargi, F., & DeLisa, M. (2017). Bioprocess engineering: Basic concepts. Prentice Hall.

2. Doran, P. M. (2013). Bioprocess engineering principles. Academic Press.

3. Stanbury, P. F., Whitaker, A., & Hall, S. J. (2013). Principles of fermentation technology. Elsevier.

4. Hu, W. (2020). Cell culture Bioprocess engineering (2nd ed.). CRC Press.

5. Clark, D. S., & Blanch, H. W. (1997). Biochemical engineering (2nd ed.). CRC Press.

6. Benz, G. T. (2021). Agitator design for gas-liquid Fermenters and bioreactors. John Wiley & Sons.

7. Rasouli, M.(2016).Basic concepts and practical equations on osmolality: Biochemical approach. Clinical Biochemistry,

49(12), 936-941. doi:10.1016/j.clinbiochem.2016.06.001

8. Tharmalingam, T., & Goudar, C. T. (2015). Evaluating the impact of high Pluronic® F68 concentrations on antibody-producing CHO cell lines. Biotechnology and bioengineering, 112(4), 832–837. https://doi.org/10.1002/bit.25491

9. Linek, V., Benes, P., & Vacek, V. (1989). Dynamic pressure method for kla measurement in large-scale bioreactors. Biotechnology and bioengineering, 33(11), 1406–1412. https://doi.org/10.1002/bit.260331107

10. Xiu, Z. L., Deckwer, W. D., & Zeng, A. P. (1999). Estimation of rates of oxygen uptake and carbon dioxide evolution of animal cell culture using material and energy balances. Cytotechnology,

29(3), 159–166. https://doi.org/10.1023/A:1008004618163

11. Doran, P. M. (2013). Bioprocess engineering principles. Academic Press.

12. Pérez JS, et al. Shear Rate in Stirred Tank and Bubble Column Bioreactors. Chem. Eng. J. 124(1–3) 2006: 1–5; https://doi.org/10.1016/J.CEJ.2006.07.002.

13. Nienow AW. Reactor Engineering in Large Scale Animal Cell Culture. Cytotechnol. 42(1) 2003: 21–33; https://doi.org/10.1007/s10616-006-9005-8.

14. Muralidharan, N. (2023, February 9). Shear-Proof Design Space: Scaling Stirred-Tank Bioreactors for Cell Culture Processes. Bioprocess International, 21(1-2), 36-38.

https://bioprocessintl.com/upstream-processing/bioreactors/shear-proof-design-space-scaling-stirred-tank-bioreactors-for-cell-culture-processes/

15. 7 Nyberg G, et al. Modeling of Biopharmaceutical Processes — Part 1: Microbial and Mammalian Unit Operations. BioPharm Int. 21(6) 2008;

https://www.biopharminternational.com/view/modeling-biopharmaceutical-processes-part-1-microbial-and-mammalian-unit-operations.

16. Poon, C. (2020). Measuring the density and viscosity of culture media for the optimized computational fluid dynamics analysis of microdevices.

https://doi.org/10.1101/2020.08.25.266221

17. 6 Hu W, Berdugo C, Chalmers JJ. The Potential of Hydrodynamic Damage to Animal Cells of Industrial Relevance: Current Understanding. Cytotechnol. 63(5) 2011: 445–460; https://doi.org/10.1007/s10616-011-9368-3.

18. Wilde, D. D., Dreher, T., Zahnow, C., Husemann, U., Greller, G., Adams, T., & Fenge, C. (2014, September 23). Superior scalability of single-use bioreactors. BioProcess International.

https://bioprocessintl.com/upstream-processing/upstream-single-use-technologies/superior-scalability-single-use-bioreactors/

19. Chisti Y. Animal-Cell Damage in Sparged Bioreactors. Trends Biotechnol. 18(10) 2000: 420–432; https://doi.org/10.1016/s0167-7799(00)01474-8.

20. Chaudhary, G., Luo, R., George, M., Tescione, L., Khetan, A., & Lin, H. (2020). Understanding the effect of high gas entrance velocity on Chinese hamster ovary

(CHO) cell culture performance and its implications on bioreactor scale-up and sparger design. Biotechnology and bioengineering, 117(6), 1684–1695. https://doi.org/10.1002/bit.27314

21. Boulton-Stone, J. M., & Blake, J. R. (1993). Gas bubbles bursting at a free surface. Journal of Fluid Mechanics, 254, 437-466.

https://doi.org/10.1017/s0022112093002216

22. Boulton-Stone, J. M. (1995). The effect of surfactant on bursting gas bubbles. Journal of Fluid Mechanics, 302, 231-257.

https://doi.org/10.1017/s0022112095004083

23. Hu, W., Berdugo, C., & Chalmers, J. J. (2011). The potential of hydrodynamic damage to animal cells of industrial relevance: current understanding. Cytotechnology, 63(5), 445–460. https://doi.org/10.1007/s10616-011-9368-3

24. Walls, P. L., McRae, O., Natarajan, V., Johnson, C., Antoniou, C., & Bird, J. C. (2017). Quantifying the potential for bursting bubbles to damage suspended cells. Scientific Reports, 7(1). https://doi.org/10.1038/s41598-017-14531-5

25. Kulkarni, A. A., & Joshi, J. B. (2005). Bubble formation and bubble rise velocity in Gas−Liquid Systems: a review. Industrial & Engineering Chemistry Research, 44(16), 5873-5931. https://doi.org/10.1021/ie049131p

26. Tramper, J., Smit, D., Straatman, J., & Vlak, J. M. (1988). Bubble-column design for the growth of fragile insect cells. Bioprocess Engineering, 3(1), 37-41. https://doi.org/10.1007/bf00372858

27. Goudar, C. T., Piret, J. M., & Konstantinov, K. B. (2011). Estimating cell-specific oxygen uptake and carbon dioxide production rates for mammalian cells in perfusion culture. Biotechnology progress, 27(5), 1347–1357.

https://doi.org/10.1002/btpr.646

28. Zhu, Y., Cuenca, J. V., Zhou, W., & Varma, A. (2008). NS0 cell damage by high gas velocity sparging in protein-free and cholesterol-free cultures. Biotechnology and bioengineering, 101(4), 751–760. https://doi.org/10.1002/bit.21950

29. Sieblist, C., Jenzsch, M., & Pohlscheidt, M. (2013). Influence of pluronic F68 on oxygen mass transfer. Biotechnology Progress, 29(5), 1278-1288.

https://doi.org/10.1002/btpr.1770

30. Murhammer, D. W., & Pfalzgraf, E. C. (1992). Effects of pluronic F-68 on oxygen transport in an agitated, sparged bioreactor. Biotechnology Techniques, 6(3), 199-202. https://doi.org/10.1007/bf02439343

31. McAndrew, J., & Kauffman, G. (2021, April 6). Characterizing the Effects of Antifoam C Emulsion on Oxygen Mass Transfer within the BIOne Drilled-Hole Sparger and Microsparger Single-Use Bioreactor Systems. American Pharmaceutical Review.

https://www.americanpharmaceuticalreview.com/Featured-Articles/575447-Characterizing-the-Effects-of-Antifoam-C-Emulsion-on-Oxygen-Mass-Transfer-within-the-BIOne-Drilled-Hole-Sparger-and-Microsparger-Single-Use-Bioreactor-Systems/

32. Routledge, S. J. (2012). Beyond De-Foaming: The effects of antifoams on bioprocess productivity. Computational and Structural Biotechnology Journal, 3(4). doi:10.5936/ csbj.201210014

33. Poon, C. (2020). Measuring the density and viscosity of culture media for optimized computational fluid dynamics analysis of in vitro devices.

https://doi.org/10.1101/2020.08.25.266221

34. Xu, Z., Singh, R. K., Bao, J., & Wang, C. (2019). The direct effect of solvent viscosity on the physical mass transfer for wavy film flow in a packed column. Industrial & Engineering Chemistry Research, 58(37), 17524-17539.

https://doi.org/10.1021/acs.iecr.9b01226

35. Solecki, M. (2015). Mass transfer: Advancement in process modeling. BoD – Books on Demand.

36. KOIDE, K., TAKAZAWA, A., KOMURA, M., & MATSUNAGA, H. (1984). Gas holdup and volumetric liquid-phase mass transfer coefficient in solid-suspended bubble columns. JOURNAL OF CHEMICAL ENGINEERING OF JAPAN, 17(5), 459-466. https://doi.org/10.1252/jcej.17.459

37. Yoshida, F., & Akita, K. (1965). Performance of gas bubble columns: Volumetric liquid-phase mass transfer coefficient and gas holdup. AIChE Journal, 11(1), 9-13. https://doi.org/10.1002/aic.690110106

38. Pham, C. Y. (2005, February 17). USE OF DEPTH FILTRATION IN SERIES Related WITH CONTINUOUS ENTRIFUGATION TO CLARIFY MAMMALIAN CELL CULTURES. U.S. Patent No. 20050037333A1.

https://patentimages.storage.googleapis.com/ed/88/30/64d8ed92c98458/US20050037333A1.pdf

39. Werner, S., Kaiser, S. C., Kraume, M., & Eibl, D. (2014). Computational fluid dynamics as a modern tool for engineering characterization of bioreactors. Pharmaceutical Bioprocessing, 2(1), 85-99. https://doi.org/10.4155/pbp.13.60

40. Pappenreiter, M., Sissolak, B., Sommeregger, W., & Striedner, G. (2019). Oxygen uptake rate soft-sensing via dynamic kLa computation: Cell volume and metabolic transition prediction in mammalian Bioprocesses. Frontiers in Bioengineering and Biotechnology, 7. https://doi.org/10.3389/fbioe.2019.00195

41. Goudar, C. T., Piret, J. M., & Konstantinov, K. B. (2011). Estimating cell-specific oxygen uptake and carbon dioxide production rates for mammalian cells in perfusion culture. Biotechnology progress, 27(5), 1347–1357.

https://doi.org/10.1002/btpr.646

42. Jorjani, P., & Ozturk, S. S. (1999). Effects of cell density and temperature on oxygen consumption rate for different mammalian cell lines. Biotechnology and bioengineering, 64(3), 349–356.

https://doi.org/10.1002/(sic)1097-0290(19990805)64:3<349::aid-bit11>3.0.co;2-v

43. Wang, Z., Wang, C., & Chen, G. (2022). Kinetic modeling: A tool for temperature shift and feeding optimization in cell culture process development. Protein expression and purification, 198, 106130.

https://doi.org/10.1016/j.pep.2022.106130

44. McHugh, K. P., Xu, J., Aron, K. L., Borys, M. C., & Li, Z. J. (2020). Effective temperature shift strategy development and scale confirmation for simultaneous optimization of protein productivity and quality in Chinese hamster ovary cells. Biotechnology progress, 36(3), e2959. https://doi.org/10.1002/btpr.2959

45. Deshpande, R. R., & Heinzle, E. (2004). On-line oxygen uptake rate and culture viability measurement of animal cell culture using microplates with integrated oxygen sensors. Biotechnology Letters, 26(9), 763-767.

https://doi.org/10.1023/b:bile.0000024101.57683.6d

46. Ihling, N., Munkler, L. P., Paul, R., Berg, C., Reichenbächer, B., Kadisch, M., Lang, D., & Büchs, J. (2022). Non- invasive and time- resolved measurement of the respiration activity of Chinese hamster ovary cells enables prediction of key culture parameters in shake flasks. Biotechnology Journal, 17(8).

https://doi.org/10.1002/biot.202100677

47. Jang, J.D., Barford, J.P. (2000). Effect of feed rate on growth rate and antibody production in the fed-batch culture of murine hybridoma cells. Cytotechnology 32, 229–242. https://doi.org/10.1023/A:1008169417980

48. Wohlpart, D., Kirwan, D., & Gainer, J. (1990). Effects of cell density and glucose and glutamine levels on the respiration rates of hybridoma cells. Biotechnology and bioengineering, 36(6), 630–635. https://doi.org/10.1002/bit.260360611

49. Sand, T., Condie, R., & Rosenberg, A. (1977). Metabolic crowding effect in suspension of cultured lymphocytes. Blood, 50(2), 337-346.

https://doi.org/10.1182/blood.v50.2.337.337

# Chapter 2: $CO_2$ control strategy in large-scale cell culture bioreactors

*Naveenganesh Muralidharan, Thatsinee Johnson, Emma Bolduc, and Mark Davis.*

## Introduction

Elevated $CO_2$ concentrations have adverse impacts on cell health, causing changes in metabolic state, decreased cell productivity, and altering the glycosylation profile of therapeutic proteins [1]. Inhibitory effects on cell growth and productivity start at $CO_2$ concentrations 15% that of atmospheric pressure (760 mmHg), i.e., 115 mmHg [1]. Therefore, in biologics production, the $CO_2$ concentration in a cell culture bioreactor must be maintained below 115 mmHg. However, during the scale-up of bioreactor operations, maintaining the $CO_2$ profile below this maximum limit is considered challenging. The simplest methodology that is most frequently used by process engineers to control $CO_2$ concentrations is manual feedback control. In this method, the dissolved $CO_2$ level in the cell culture liquid is measured, and if it exceeds a threshold value (i.e., the action limit), the overall gas flow rate is increased by a certain amount [2]. However, a problem in manual feedback $CO_2$ control is identifying the correct increment for the total gas flow rate. This increment is often determined by trial-and-error, exposing the process to the risk of uncertainty. Accordingly, in the present study, we derived a sound mathematical model to predict and control the dissolved $CO_2$ concentration in a cell culture bioreactor as a function of KLa, pH set point, viable cell density, lactate, and the bicarbonate profile of the culture. The models have been verified in a 20,000L bioreactor scale. This simplified model should help readers predict and control $CO_2$ profiles in manufacturing-scale bioreactors easily. Furthermore, we discuss the current state of understanding of factors impacting excessive dissolved $CO_2$ accumulation in large-scale bioreactors in terms of geometrical bioreactor design and sparger configuration.

## Impact of excessive $CO_2$ concentration on cell culture performance:

For a typical fed-batch cell culture, $CO_2$ is produced by cellular respiration as cells metabolize glucose, which plays a major role in energy production to support cell growth rate and productivity. Transport of polar and charged molecules like sugars and ions occurs through the restrictive, selective process in the lipid bilayer membranes of the cells. However, uncharged molecules like $CO_2$ can freely diffuse through the lipid bilayer membrane. When excessive $CO_2$ enters the cytoplasm, it reacts with water to produce hydrogen ions, which changes the intracellular pH. This causes cells to spend energy on maintaining the pH rather than cell growth and protein expression, as shown in Figure 1. In addition, $CO_2$ can react with ions in the media, lowering the culture pH [3, 4, 5]. In turn, the bioreactor's pH control cascade demands more base titrant, the consumption of which increases osmolality, leading to inhibition of cell growth and productivity [6].

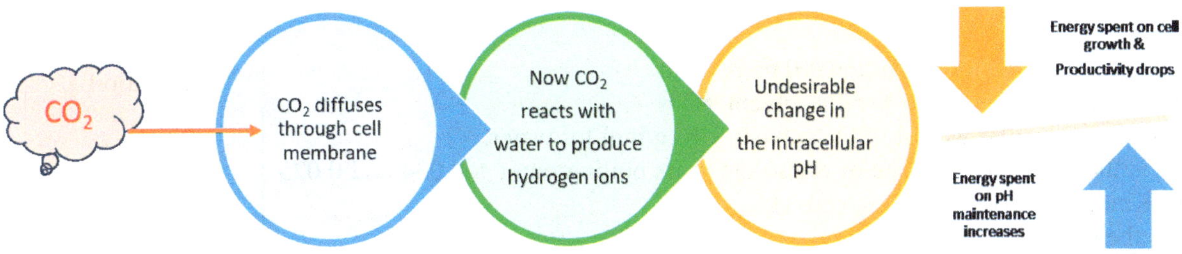


**Figure 1: Impact of excessive $CO_2$ concentration on cell culture performance.**

## Effect of $CO_2$ mass transfer coefficient on excessive $CO_2$ accumulation

Early in the culture, it is necessary to sparge $CO_2$ to maintain the pH. However, as the cell density increases in the bioreactor, the accumulation of $CO_2$ occurs due to cellular respiration. For a typical cell culture process, for every mole of oxygen consumed, one mole of $CO_2$ is produced (Respiratory Quotient [RQ] = 1) [7]. Therefore, to maintain an optimal $CO_2$ concentration inside a bioreactor, oxygen transfer and $CO_2$ removal should be balanced. In other words, the $O_2$ transfer rate should be equal to the $CO_2$ transfer rate, as expressed in Equation 1. Here, *KLa* is the volumetric oxygen transfer coefficient, and $C_B$* and $C_L$ are the molar concentrations of $O_2$ or $CO_2$ in the purged gas bubble and liquid, respectively.

*KLa* is the product of *KL* (the film transfer coefficient) and *a*, i.e., the interfacial surface area per volume of the culture ($m^2/m^3$). Both $CO_2$ and $O_2$ experience the same interfacial surface area and hydrodynamic conditions inside the bioreactor, but *KL* differs for $CO_2$ and $O_2$, and it is proportional to the liquid phase diffusivity of the respective gases, as shown in Equation 2. Here, *D* is the diffusivity, $\vartheta_B$ is the bubble velocity, and $d_b$ is the bubble diameter. The diffusion constants for $O_2$ and $CO_2$ at 37 °C are calculated as 3.4 × $10^{-9}$ and 2.9 × $10^{-9}$ $m^2/s$, respectively, using Wilke and Chang's (1955) method, as shown in Equation 3 [8]. Applying the diffusivities of $CO_2$ and $O_2$ in Equation 2, the mass transfer coefficient ratio of $CO_2$ to $O_2$ ($\Phi$) is 0.90. This is in alignment with previously reported $\Phi$ values for large bubbles under laminar flow equal to 0. 90. [9, 20].

| **Equations 1 to 3: Effect of $CO_2$ mass transfer coefficient on excessive $CO_2$ accumulation** | |
|---|---|
| $OTR = CTR => KLa_{O2}(C^*_{BO2} - C_{L,O2}) = -KLa_{CO2}\,(C^*_{B,CO2} - C_{L,CO2})$ | Equation 1 |

| | |
|---|---|
| $K_L = \sqrt{\dfrac{4.D.\vartheta_B}{\pi.d_B}}$ | Equation 2 |
| $D_L = \dfrac{1.173 \times 10^{-13} \times (\forall.M)^{0.5}.T}{\mu \times V_m^{0.6}}$<br><br>Here,<br>μ is the viscosity of the solution = 0.66 $mNs/m^2$<br>∀ is the association factor for the solvent = 2.6.<br>M is the molecular weight of the solvent = 18 g/mol for water.<br>$V_m$ is the molecular volume of the solute at its boiling point = 0.034 and 0.025 $m^3$/Kmol for $CO_2$ and $O_2$, respectively.<br>T is the temperature in Kelvin. | Equation 3 |

*Φ* values below 0.90 have also been reported for micro spargers and at aggressively high gas flow rates using drilled hole spargers. The gas flow conditions for laminar flow can be assessed based on the bubble Reynolds number satisfying the condition of being less than 2000 (bubble Reynolds number is calculated per Equation 18) [10]. Reduced *Φ* values far below 0.90 at aggressive turbulent gas flow rates or while using micro spargers will reduce the $CO_2$ *Kla* in comparison to $O_2$ *Kla* and thereby increase excessive $CO_2$ accumulation. For gas flow rates to support up to 20 × $10^6$ cells/mL in our 20,000-L bioreactor sparger configuration , we satisfy the condition for laminar flow (i.e., Bubble Reynolds number < 2000). Therefore, the assumption of *Φ* = 0.90 is valid for our bioreactor operating conditions. Readers must carefully evaluate their sparger configuration and bubble Reynolds number using Equation 18 before assuming *Φ* value of 0.90. It is also recommended to perform a separate *Kla* study specifically for $CO_2$ when gas flow rate Reynolds numbers are> 2000 and do not satisfy the conditions for laminar gas flow.

## Effect of $CO_2$ bubble saturation time

The changes in the concentrations of $CO_2$ and $O_2$ inside a gas bubble that is rising in a liquid column can be expressed as shown in Equations 4 and 5 [12]. Here, $K_{G,O2}$ and $K_{G,CO2}$ are the overall gas phase mass transfer coefficients for $O_2$ and $CO_2$, respectively; $D_{O2}$ and $D_{CO2}$ are the diffusion coefficients for $O_2$ and $CO_2$, respectively; $\delta$ is the thickness of the bubble film ($\delta$ = 50 µm is a good approximation [17]), $A_b$ is the surface area of a single bubble in $m^2$, $V_b$ is the volume of a single bubble in $m^3$, $C_B$ stands for the $O_2$ or $CO_2$ concentration of a bulk gas-phase bubble expressed in mmHg, $C_L$ is the liquid phase concentration that is in equilibrium with the gas phase. *m* is defined as the partition constant. "*m*" is the function of the solubility of a gas. $CO_2$ and $O_2$ have different solubilities in a fluid, as given by Henry's coefficient expressed as the amount of gas that is solubilized per unit volume of the liquid per unit pressure in mmol/L.atm. The values of Henry's coefficient (*H*) are 25 × $10^{-3}$ and 1 × $10^{-3}$ mol/L.atm for $CO_2$ and $O_2$, respectively. Therefore, $CO_2$ is 25 times more soluble in liquid than oxygen at atmospheric pressure.

| **Equations 4 and 5: Bubble saturation time for $O_2$ and $CO_2$** | |
|---|---|
| For changes in $O_2$ concentration in a bubble: $$\frac{dC_{O2}}{dt} = m_{O2}.K_{G,O2} \times \left(\frac{A_b}{V_b}\right) \times \left(C_{b,O2} - C_{L,O2}{}^{*}\right)$$ Here, $m_{O2} = H_{O2}.R.T = 1.07 \times 10^{-3}.R.T = 0.03;\ K_{G,O2} = \left(\frac{D_{O2}}{\delta}\right)\ ;\ V_b = \frac{4}{3}\pi R^3\ , A_b = 4\pi R^2$ | Equation 4 |
| For changes in $CO_2$ concentration in a bubble: $$\frac{dC_{CO2}}{dt} = m_{CO2}.K_{G,CO2} \times \left(\frac{A_b}{V_b}\right) \times \left(C_{L,CO2}{}^{*} - C_{b,CO2}\right)$$ Here, $$m_{CO2} = H_{CO2}.R.T = 25 \times 10^{-3}.R.T = 0.64;\ \ K_{G,CO2} = \left(\frac{D_{CO2}}{\delta}\right)$$ | Equation 5 |

For illustration, assume a 0.5-mm-diameter air bubble is rising in a liquid, and the size of the bubble remains constant with no shrinkage throughout its lifetime. Assuming air is purged through the sparger at atmospheric pressure (760 mmHg), and the mole faction of $O_2$ in the air is 0.21, then the $O_2$ concentration in the sparged air bubble is 159 mmHg (0.21 × 760 mmHg). For dissolved oxygen (DO), the set point of 40% is equal to 64 mmHg (0.40 × 0.21 × 760 mmHg). Then, the $O_2$ and $CO_2$ concentrations in the bubble at time zero are 159 and 0 mmHg, respectively, and the liquid $O_2$ and $CO_2$ concentrations are 64 and 115 mmHg, respectively. A sample calculation for changes in the $O_2$ and $CO_2$ concentrations in the bubble is shown in Figures 2A and 2B. Figure 2C shows the change in the concentration of $O_2$ and $CO_2$ in the bubble, demonstrating that the bubble attains 95% saturation for $CO_2$ between 5 to 6 s. This value is in alignment with previously reported experimental values of between 5 and 9 s [3 and 13]. Therefore, the driving force for $CO_2$ drops to zero after 6 s, and no further $CO_2$ can be transferred into the bubble. On the other hand, for $O_2$ transfer, bubble $O_2$ concentration falls relatively slowly, and the bubble continues to supply $O_2$ to the liquid as it rises. In summary, as the bubble attains $CO_2$ saturation in a short period, it is effective for $CO_2$ removal for only a small portion of its lifetime.

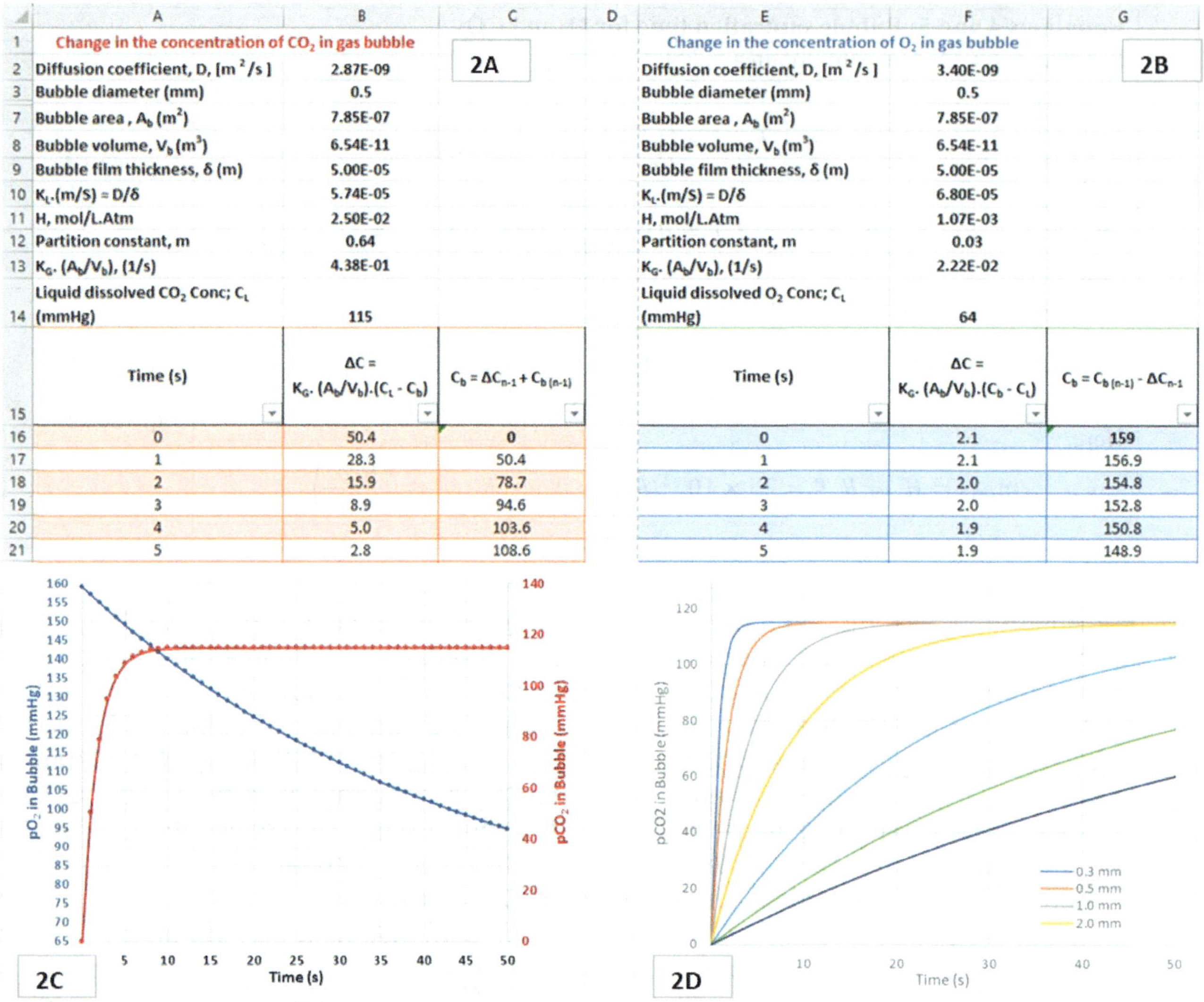

2A

| | A | B | C |
|---|---|---|---|
| 1 | Change in the concentration of $CO_2$ in gas bubble | | |
| 2 | Diffusion coefficient, D, [$m^2/s$] | 2.87E-09 | |
| 3 | Bubble diameter (mm) | 0.5 | |
| 7 | Bubble area , $A_b$ ($m^2$) | 7.85E-07 | |
| 8 | Bubble volume, $V_b$ ($m^3$) | 6.54E-11 | |
| 9 | Bubble film thickness, δ (m) | 5.00E-05 | |
| 10 | $K_L$.(m/S) = D/δ | 5.74E-05 | |
| 11 | H, mol/L.Atm | 2.50E-02 | |
| 12 | Partition constant, m | 0.64 | |
| 13 | $K_G$. ($A_b/V_b$), (1/s) | 4.38E-01 | |
| 14 | Liquid dissolved $CO_2$ Conc; $C_L$ (mmHg) | 115 | |
| 15 | Time (s) | ΔC = $K_G$. ($A_b/V_b$).($C_L$ - $C_b$) | $C_b = \Delta C_{n-1} + C_{b(n-1)}$ |
| 16 | 0 | 50.4 | 0 |
| 17 | 1 | 28.3 | 50.4 |
| 18 | 2 | 15.9 | 78.7 |
| 19 | 3 | 8.9 | 94.6 |
| 20 | 4 | 5.0 | 103.6 |
| 21 | 5 | 2.8 | 108.6 |

2B

| | E | F | G |
|---|---|---|---|
| 1 | Change in the concentration of $O_2$ in gas bubble | | |
| 2 | Diffusion coefficient, D, [$m^2/s$] | 3.40E-09 | |
| 3 | Bubble diameter (mm) | 0.5 | |
| 7 | Bubble area , $A_b$ ($m^2$) | 7.85E-07 | |
| 8 | Bubble volume, $V_b$ ($m^3$) | 6.54E-11 | |
| 9 | Bubble film thickness, δ (m) | 5.00E-05 | |
| 10 | $K_L$.(m/S) = D/δ | 6.80E-05 | |
| 11 | H, mol/L.Atm | 1.07E-03 | |
| 12 | Partition constant, m | 0.03 | |
| 13 | $K_G$. ($A_b/V_b$), (1/s) | 2.22E-02 | |
| 14 | Liquid dissolved $O_2$ Conc; $C_L$ (mmHg) | 64 | |
| 15 | Time (s) | ΔC = $K_G$. ($A_b/V_b$).($C_b$ - $C_L$) | $C_b = C_{b(n-1)} - \Delta C_{n-1}$ |
| 16 | 0 | 2.1 | 159 |
| 17 | 1 | 2.1 | 156.9 |
| 18 | 2 | 2.0 | 154.8 |
| 19 | 3 | 2.0 | 152.8 |
| 20 | 4 | 1.9 | 150.8 |
| 21 | 5 | 1.9 | 148.9 |



**Figure 2: Bubble saturation time.**

## Effect of bioreactor liquid hydrostatic pressure on excessive $CO_2$ accumulation

Bioreactor aspect ratio, defined as liquid height to tank diameter (H/D), is typically maintained between 1.0 to 1.5 [14, 15]. While scaling up the operational volume of the bioreactor, the liquid height increases (per Equation 6) and thereby increases the hydrostatic pressure *P* (per Equation 7). Fuller et al. (1966) developed an empirical correlation for the diffusivity coefficient that shows an inverse relationship to pressure, as shown in Equation 8 [16]. Equations 6 to 8 show as bioreactor height increases, thereby total pressure increases and diffusion coefficient deceases, making $CO_2$ removal from a culture more challenging.

Figure 2 shows the increase in the liquid height and corresponding solubility of $CO_2$ for different bioreactor volumes with an assumed aspect ratio of 1.5.

| Equations 6 to 8: Bioreactor height and increase in pressure on diffusivity | |
|---|---|
| $V = \frac{\pi \times D^2}{4} \times H; Assume\ H = 1.5 \times D, Rearranging, H = \left(\frac{4 \times V}{\pi \times 1.5^2}\right)^{1/3}$ | Equation 6 |
| $P = 1\ atm + \left[\rho_L \times g \times H \times \frac{(9.87e-6)atm}{1\ pascal}\right]$ Here, $\rho_L$ is the liquid density (1000 Kg/m$^3$), $g$ is gravity (9.8 Kg/m$^3$), and 1 atm is atmospheric pressure. | Equation 7 |
| Diffusivity as a function of pressure and temperature. $D_{A,B} = \frac{1.013 \times 10^{-7}.T^{1.75}\left(\frac{1}{M_A}+\frac{1}{M_B}\right)^{1/2}}{P\left[v_A^{1/3}+v_B^{1/3}\right]^2}$ $M_A$ and $M_B$ are the molecular weights of the solute and solvent in g/mol ($M_{CO2}$ = 44, $M_{O2}$ = 32, $M_{H2O}$ = 18). $v_A$ and $v_B$ are the diffusion volume coefficients of the solute and solvent ($v_{CO2}$ = 26.9, $v_{O2}$ = 16.6, $v_{H2O}$ = 10.73). $P$ is the pressure in Atm, and $T$ is the temperature is K (370 K) | Equation 8 |

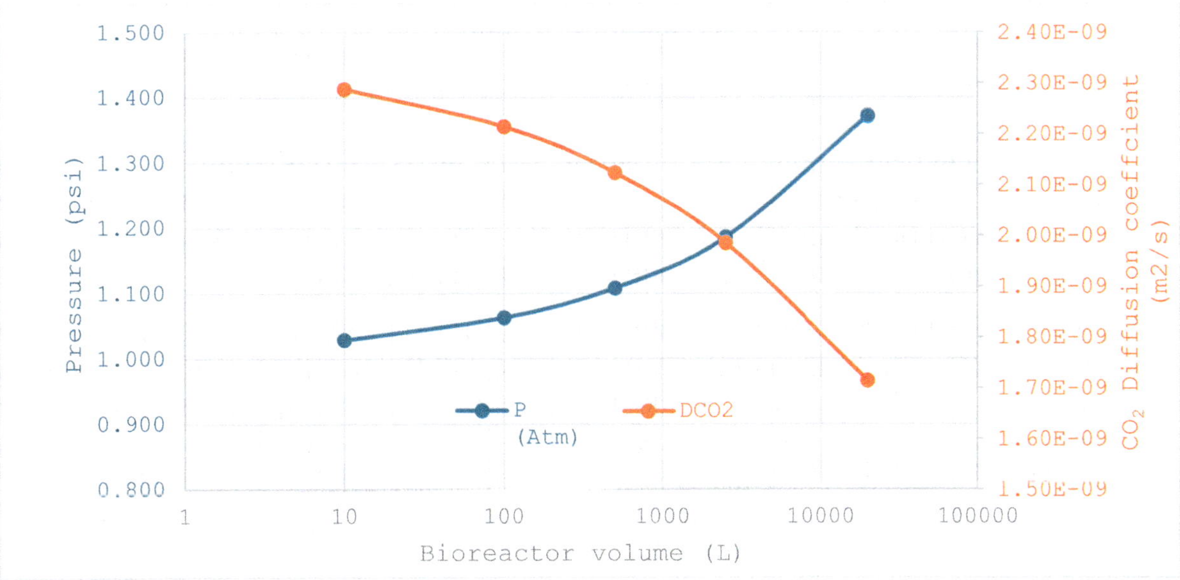


**Figure 3: Impact of bioreactor height.**

## Effect of difference in $O_2$ and $CO_2$ driving force on excessive $CO_2$ accumulation

As the bubble germinates and rises through the liquid, the period of time from bubble generation to the bubble reaching the gas–liquid surface and disappearing is defined as bubble residence time ($T_{B,\ R}$). During its lifetime in the liquid, a bubble serves two purposes for cell culture operation: 1) transferring $O_2$ from the bubble into the liquid, and 2) removing dissolved $CO_2$ from the liquid to the bubble. The rate of both $O_2$ transfer and $CO_2$ removal depends on the driving force, $\Delta C = C_s - C_T$. Here, $C_S$ and $C_T$ are the starting and target concentrations of the gas species in the bubble. ΔC dictates the rate of gas mass transfer. **For $O_2$ transfer**: Assuming air is purged through the sparger at atmospheric, the $O_2$ concentration in the sparged air bubble $C_{S,\ O2}$ is 159 mmHg (0.21 × 760 mmHg). % DO set point ($C_{T,\ O2}$) of 40% is equal to 64 mmHg (0.40 × 0.21 × 760 mmHg). The driving force for $O_2$ transfer is calculated to be 96 mmHg, as shown in Equation 9 [1]. **For $CO_2$ transfer**: The driving force for the $CO_2$ is expressed in Equation 10. Here, $C_{T,\ CO2}$ is the **desired maximum $pCO_2$ limit (115 mmHg), and** $C_{Equl,\ CO2}$ is dissolved $CO_2$ concentration in equilibrium with the gas stream. To remove $CO_2$ from the liquid at the same rate as the transfer of $O_2$ to the liquid, we need driving force $\Delta_{CO2}$ equal to $\Delta_{O2}$. Hence, equating Equation 9 and Equation 10 and solving for $C_{Equl,\ CO2}$ will yield a value of 19 mmHg, as expressed in Equation 11.

| **Equations 9 and 10: Effect of $CO_2$ driving force on excessive $CO_2$ accumulation** | |
|---|---|
| $\Delta C_{O2} = (C_{s,O2} - C_{T,O2}) = 160 - 64\ mmHg = 96\ mmHg$ | Equation 9 |
| $\Delta C_{CO2} = (C_{T,O2} - C_{Equi,O2}) = (115\ mmHg - C_{Equil,O2})$ | Equation 10 |
| $C_{Equil,O2} = (115 - 96)\ mmHg = 19\ mmHg$ | Equation 11 |

This value of 19 mmHg is only 2.5% of atmospheric pressure (760 mmHg). This means that as the bubble rises when the $CO_2$ concentration in the bubble reaches 19 mmHg, the $CO_2$ removal rate drops below the $O_2$ transfer rate. Therefore, we define 19 mmHg as the rate-limiting maximum bubble $CO_2$ concentration, [$C_{CO2,\ RL}$], and

the time for the bubble to reach the maximum rate-limiting $CO_2$ concentration is defined as the bubble $CO_2$ rate-limiting equilibrium time $T_{B,RL}$. If the bubble residence time $T_{BR}$ is less than $T_{B,\ RL}$, then the bubble is efficient in removing $CO_2$ throughout its lifetime. If $T_{BR}$ is larger than $T_{B,\ RL}$, then the bubble is efficient in $CO_2$ removal equivalent to $O_2$ transfer only until time $T_{B,\ RL}$. Hence, larger fast-rising bubbles with shorter residence times are more efficient than smaller bubbles with longer residence times [1, 7].

For a typical cell culture bioreactor process, $O_2$ KLa is enhanced by using micro spargers and/or a blend of pure $O_2$ and air to increase the driving force ΔC. Both lead to sufficient $O_2$ transfer rates using low gas flow rates, which further enhances the accumulation of $CO_2$ at a large scale.

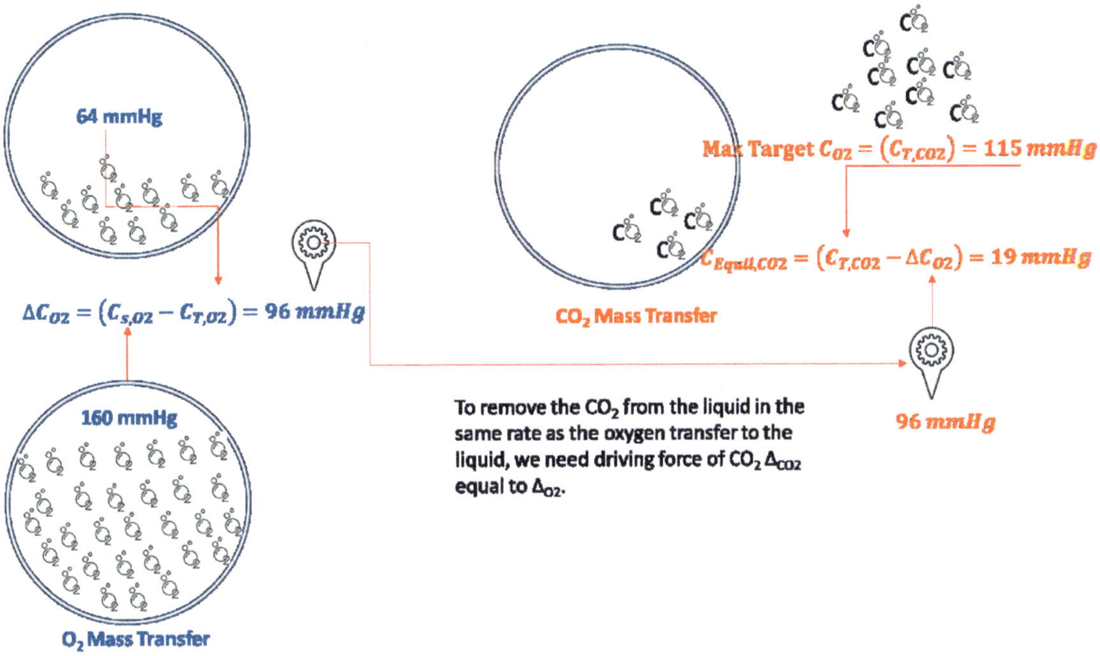


**Figure 4: Difference in $O_2$ and $CO_2$ driving forces on excessive $CO_2$ accumulation.**

## Effect of sparger design and gas entrance on excessive $CO_2$ accumulation

As discussed before, bubble residence time plays a critical role in the dissolved $CO_2$ concentration in a culture broth. The faster the bubble travels through the liquid column, the more efficient the $CO_2$ transfer rate. The bubble velocity is a function of bubble size. The bubble size and bubble velocity can be calculated using Equations 12 to 17 [17, 18].

Figure 4 shows the bubble rise velocity as a function of bubble diameter. Bubbles with sizes less than 0.1 mm (or 100 µm), called microbubbles, have low rising velocities. Here, the bubble movement is dominated by liquid surface tension, leading to reduced bubble rising velocity, causing longer bubble residency time in the bioreactor and poor $CO_2$ removal from the cell culture. Smaller bubbles give higher mass transfer areas but also have slow-rising velocities and reduced $CO_2$ driving force. Therefore, the optimum operating conditions for effective $CO_2$ removal is a sparger flow rate that maintains the ratio of bubble residence time to bubble saturation time ≥ 1.0.

| **Equations 12 to 18: Bubble size and bubble velocity** | |
|---|---|
| $$Gas\ Entance\ Velocity, GEV = \frac{Q_g}{n_O\left(\frac{\pi d_O^2}{4}\right)}$$ | Equation 12 |
| | Equation 13 |

| **Equations 12 to 18: Bubble size and bubble velocity** | |
|---|---|
| $d_b = 1.17.GEV^{0.4}.d_O^{0.8}.g^{0.2}$ | |
| $V_1 = \frac{1}{36} \times \frac{(\rho_L - \rho_g).g.d_b^2}{\mu_L}$ | Equation 14 |
| $V_2 = V_1 \left[1 + 0.73667 \frac{(g.d_b)^{1/2}}{V_1}\right]^{1/2}$ | Equation 15 |
| $V_3 = \left(\frac{3.\sigma}{\rho_L.d_b} + \frac{g.d_b.(\rho_L - \rho_g)}{2.\rho_L}\right)^{1/2}$ | Equation 16 |
| $\vartheta_b = 1 \div \sqrt{\frac{1}{{V_2}^2} + \frac{1}{{V_3}^2}}$ | Equation 17 |
| $N_{Bubble,Re} = \frac{d_O \vartheta_O \rho}{\mu}$ | Equation 18 |

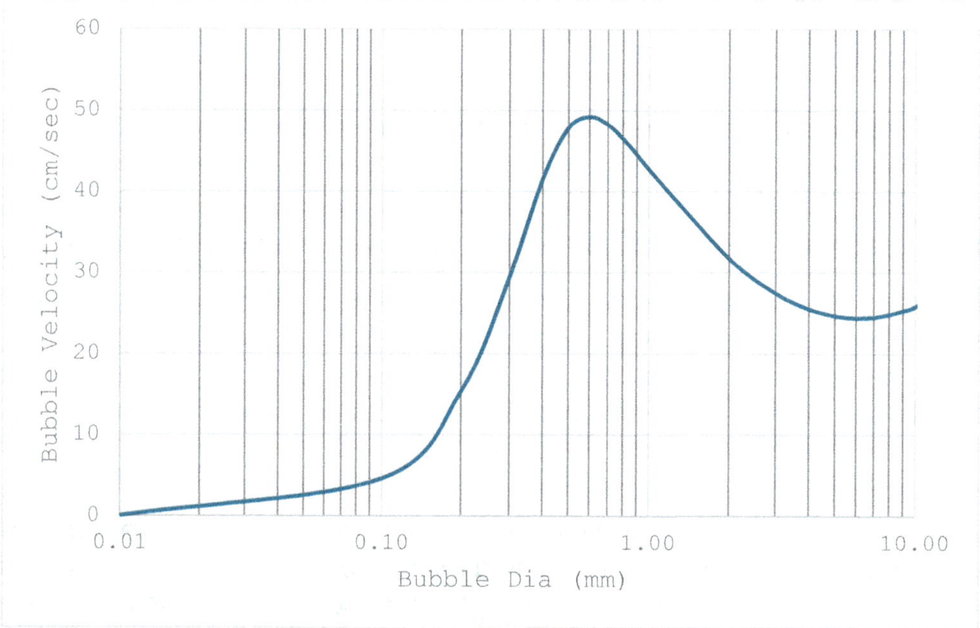


**Figure 5: Bubble diameter vs. bubble rise velocity.**

## $CO_2$ predictive model assumptions and limitations

### Assumptions:

- The rate of mass transfer is much faster than the $O_2$ uptake rate and $CO_2$ evolution rate of cells. Therefore, the mass balance governing equations: $O_2$ transfer rate equals $O_2$ uptake rate, and $CO_2$ transfer rate equals $CO_2$ evolution rate.
- The bioreactor mass transfer system is assumed to be at a pseudo-steady state. This means over the very short period of bubble residence time in the bioreactor, the $O_2$ and $CO_2$ concentration in the

liquid does not change, while the $CO_2$ concentration in bubbles is dynamic and changing continuously.

- The cell culture performance attributes, like viable cell density, oxygen uptake rate, lactate profile, and bicarbonate profile, are known from previous at-scale or small-scale runs.
- This model also assumes the biological metabolite consumption and production rate of cells is conserved across different scales of bioreactor operation and from batch to batch.
- The sparge rate is sufficiently low to prevent bubble coalescence.
- As the bubbles rise through the liquid, the drop in the $O_2$ mole fraction from the bubbles is compensated by an increase in the $CO_2$ mole fraction in the bubbles.

## Limitations:

- This model can only be used when the bioreactor mass transfer co-efficient (*Kla*) is characterized.
- The model assumes that the *Kla* from the surface gas–liquid interface is small and insignificant compared to the mass transfer from sparging gas bubbles and is therefore applicable only for large manufacturing-scale bioreactors.
- The assumption that $CO_2$ *KLa* = 0.90 times $O_2$ *KLa* is applicable only for bubbles generated under laminar conditions using drilled hole spargers and does not apply to bubbles generated using micro spargers or when gas flow rates using drilled hole spargers are operated under turbulent conditions.
- This model only accounts for major metabolites like $CO_2$, lactate, and bicarbonate for pH control that are most frequently measured in the cell culture process. Therefore, it does not include other organic acids or base components produced by cells during fermentation.

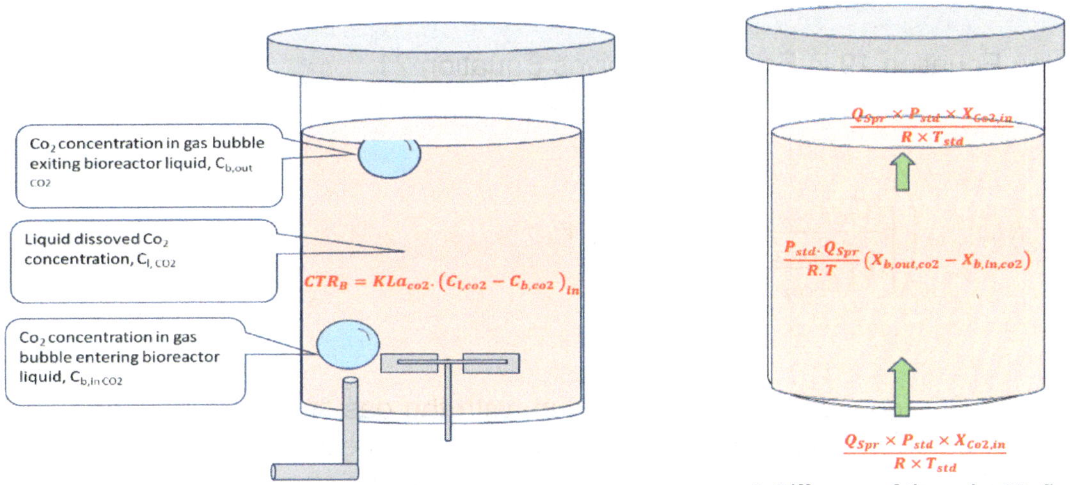


**A: $CO_2$ Mass Balance from Bubble to Liquid.**

**B. Difference of the molar $CO_2$ flow rate in the entering and leaving bubbles.**

**Figure 6: $CO_2$ Mass balance for the liquid in a bioreactor system.**

## $CO_2$ predictive model

As shown in Figure 6A, the $CO_2$ transfer rate from the liquid to sparged gas bubbles can be expressed as shown in Equation 19. Here, $C_{,b,\ co2}$ represents the $CO_2$ concentration in the bubble (mmol/L), $C_{l,CO2}$ represents the liquid dissolved $CO_2$ concentration (mmol/L), and $KLa_{CO2}$ represents the $CO_2$ mass transfer coefficient (1/h). The suffix (ln) indicates the logarithmic mean for driving force. In large-scale bioreactors, because of the gradient of increasing hydrostatic pressure from the surface of the liquid to the bottom of the vessel, the composition of a gas phase bubble is dynamic. Accordingly, the driving force is expressed as a logarithmic mean driving force [11].

$$CTR_B.V = KLa_{co2}.V.\left(C_{l,co2} - C_{b,co2}\right)_{ln} \qquad \text{Equation 19}$$

The logarithmic mean gas bubble $CO_2$ concentration can be expressed as the function of bubble $CO_2$ concentration entering and leaving the culture liquid in the bioreactor, as shown in Equation 20 [11]. Here, the suffixes b, in, CO2 and b, out, CO2 indicate $CO_2$ concentration in the bubble going into the liquid and exiting the liquid, respectively.

$$\left(C_{l,co2} - C_{b,co2}\right)_{ln} = \left[\frac{\left(C_{b,in,co2} - C_{b,out,co2}\right)}{ln\left(\frac{C_{l,co2} - C_{b,in,co2}}{C_{l,co2} - C_{b,out,co2}}\right)}\right] \qquad \text{Equation 20}$$

Substituting Equation 19 in Equation 20 gives Equation 21:

$$CTR_B.V = KLa_{b,co2}\left(\left[\frac{\left(C_{b,in,co2} - C_{b,out,co2}\right)}{ln\left(\frac{C_{l,co2} - C_{b,in,co2}}{C_{l,co2} - C_{b,out,co2}}\right)}\right]\right).V \qquad \text{Equation 21}$$

The dissolved $CO_2$ concentration in equilibrium with the gas stream in Equation 21 can be expressed as a function of Henry's constant, system pressure, and mole fraction of $CO_2$ (Concentration, C = P.H.X) by applying Henry's law, as shown in Equation 22 [11]. Here, $P_l$ is pressure (atm), H is the henry coefficient (mol/L.atm), and X is the mole fraction of gas. Suffixes b, in, CO2 and b, out, CO2 represent $CO_2$ concentration in a bubble going into the liquid and exiting the liquid, respectively.

$$CTR_B.V = KLa_{b,co2}.V\left(\frac{\left(X_{b,out,co2}.P_{l,co2}.H_{co2} - X_{b,in,co2}.P_{l,co2}.H_{co2}\right)}{ln\left(\frac{C_{l,co2} - C_{b,in,co2}}{C_{l,co2} - C_{b,out,co2}}\right)}\right) \qquad \text{Equation 22}$$

As shown in Figure 6B, the moles of $CO_2$ transferred from the sparge stream can also be determined from the difference in the molar $CO_2$ flow rate in the entering and leaving bubbles. If we assume that the gas hold-up volume is constant, then the $CO_2$ transfer rate from the sparger can be expressed as shown in Equation 23. Here, $P_{std}$ is the standard pressure (Atm), $Q_{spr}$ represents the sparger flow rate, R is the relative gas constant, and T is the temperature in K.

| **Equations 23 to 33: Derivation of dissolved $CO_2$** | |
|---|---|
| $CTR_B.V = \frac{P_{std}.Q_{Spr}}{R.T}\left(X_{b,out,co2} - X_{b,in,co2}\right)$ | Equation 23 |
| Now, equating Equation 22 and Equation 23 will yield Equation 24 <br> $KLa_{b,co2}.V\left(\frac{\left(X_{b,out,co2} - X_{b,in,co2}\right)p_l.H_{co2}}{ln\left(\frac{C_{l,co2} - C_{b,in,co2}}{C_{l,co2} - C_{b,out,co2}}\right)}\right) = \frac{P_{std}.Q_{Spr}}{R.T}(X_{b,out,co2} - X_{b,in,co2})$ | Equation 24 |
| Simplification of Equation 24 will yield Equation 25. <br> $ln\left(\frac{C_{l,co2} - C_{b,in,co2}}{C_{l,co2} - C_{b,out,co2}}\right) = \frac{KLa_{b,co2}.V.R.T.P_l.H_{Co2}}{P_{std}.Q_{Spr}}$ | Equation 25 |
| For simplification in further calculation, the right-hand side of Equation 25 is termed as a constant named $A_{CO2}$, as this term has no unit all together. <br> $\frac{KLa_{b,co2}.V.R.T.P_l.H_{Co2}}{P_{std}.Q_{Spr}} = A_{co2}$ | Equation 26 |
| $ln\left(\frac{C_{l,co2} - C_{b,in,co2}}{C_{l,co2} - C_{b,out,co2}}\right) = A_{co2} \Rightarrow \left(\frac{C_{l,co2} - C_{b,in,co2}}{C_{l,co2} - C_{b,out,co2}}\right) = Exp\ (A_{co2})$ | Equation 27 |
| Re-arranging the numerator and denominator in Equation 27, the right-hand side of Equation 28 takes a negative sign: <br> $\left(\frac{C_{l,co2} - C_{b,out,co2}}{C_{l,co2} \quad C_{b,in,co2}}\right) = Exp\ (-A_{co2})$ | Equation 28 |

| Equations 23 to 33: Derivation of dissolved $CO_2$ | |
|---|---|
| Expressing dissolved $CO_2$ concentration in equilibrium with the gas stream in Equation 28, as a function of Henry's constant, system pressure, and mole fraction of $CO_2$ (Concentration, C= P.H.X) by Applying Henry's law will yield Equation 29. [6, 8]. $$\left(\frac{C_{l,co2} - X_{b,out,CO2}.P_l.H_{Co2}}{C_{l,co2} - X_{b,in,CO2}.P_l.H_{Co2}}\right) = Exp\ (-A_{co2})$$ | Equation 29 |
| Rearranging Equation 29 and solving for the concentration of $CO_2$ in the bubble exiting the liquid is given by Equation 30: $$X_{b,out,Co2}.P_l.H_{Co2} = C_{l,co2}\left(1 - Exp(-A_{co2})\right) + X_{b,in,Co2}.P_l.H_{Co2}.Exp(-A_{co2})$$ | Equation 30 |
| Now, substituting Equation 26 and Equation 30 in Equation 22 and solving for dissolved $C_{l,\ CO2}$ will yield Equation 31 to predict the liquid dissolved $CO_2$ concentration. Refer to Appendix A for details of algebraic mathematical simplification. $$C_{l,co2} = \frac{CTR_T.A_{co2} + KLa_{b,co2}.X_{b,in,co2}.P_l.H_{Co2}.(1 - Exp(-A_{co2}))}{KLa_{b,co2}(1 - Exp(-A_{co2}))}$$ | Equation 31 |
| Often, In cell culture bioreactor operation, liquid dissolved $CO_2$ is measured as partial pressure of $CO_2$ ($pCO_2$) in millimeter mercury (mmHg). The $CO_2$ concentration calculated using Equation 32 is converted to pCO2 in mmHg using the ideal gas law (P × V = n × R × T). Rearranging the ideal gas expression will yield dissolved pCO2 as follows: Here, T is the temperature expressed in Kelvin. $$pCO_2 = C_{l,CO2} \times R \times T$$ | Equation 32 |

In Equation 31, there are two unknown terms: $CO_2$ transfer rate (CTR in the equation) and mole fraction of $CO_2$ ($X_{b,\ inCO2}$). The $CO_2$ transfer rate can be calculated from the $CO_2$ evolution rate (CER in the equation), which in turn is dependent on the oxygen uptake rate (OUR in the equation) of the cells and respiratory quotient (RQ). CER is calculated as shown in Equation 33. Here, RQ is defined as the moles of $CO_2$ released for every mole of $O_2$ consumed. Hu (2020) reported an RQ value of 1.0 for mammalian cells [7].

$$CTR = CER = RQ.OUR \qquad \text{Equation 33}$$

Mole fraction of **$CO_2$ ($X_{b, inCO2}$) from m**edium chemistry

Typical cell culture media buffering is achieved using a $CO_2$-bicarbonate-based buffer. Because the pH of the medium is dependent on the fine balance of dissolved carbon dioxide ($CO_2$) and bicarbonate ($HCO_3^-$). Often, cell culture carbonate buffered media is operated around neutral pH. $CO_2$ reacts with water to form carbonic acid, as shown in Equation 34 [19]. Assuming the amount of dissolved $CO_2$ in the culture medium is equal to the amount of $CO_2$ in the gas phase at equilibrium and applying the Henderson–Hasselbalch principle, the cell culture medium buffer can be expressed as shown in Equation 35 [19]. In mammalian cell culture fermentation, one other metabolite, lactate, plays a critical role in medium buffer chemistry. Lactate is a predominant metabolite produced by cells that brings the pH into the acidic range in bioreactor environments. Lactate has an equilibrium constant pKa of 5.5. Because a typical cell culture is maintained around a neutral pH of 7.0, one mole of lactate produced by cells will demand one mole of base titrant for neutralization. Due to this neutralization, the culture broth now displaces the acidic component of the buffer in the form of $CO_2$ gas. So, the effective concentration of base in the culture will be [$HCO_3$] − [Lactate] [19]. Based on this reaction in the culture, we can now introduce lactate into the Henderson–Hasselbalch equation and Equation 35 can be rewritten as shown in Equation 36. Gramer et al. (2007) showed an empirical relationship between pH, $CO_2$, lactate, and bicarbonate concentration, as shown in Equation 37, and verified the application of the model in Equation 37 using actual cell culture runs [19]. Here, lactate and bicarbonate concentrations are expressed in mmol/L, and $CO_2$ concentration is expressed in %.

| **Equations 35 to 38: Medium buffer chemistry** | |
|---|---|
| $CO_2 + H_2O \leftrightarrow [HCO_3^-] + [H^+]$ | Equation 34 |
| $pH = pKa + \frac{[HCO3]}{[CO_2]}$ | Equation 35 |
| $pH = pKa + \frac{[HCO3] - [Lactate]}{[CO_2]}$ | Equation 36 |
| $[Lacate] = [BiCarbonate] - 0.88.[CO_2\%]^{0.79}.10^{(pH-6.38)}$ | Equation 37 |

Based on the correlation expression shown in Equation 37, a contour plot was created showing the lactate concentration in g/L as a function of $pCO_2$ in % and bicarbonate concentration in mMol for four different pH values ranging from 6.90 to 7.05 typically used for cell culture, as shown in Figure 7. The mole fraction of $CO_2$ in the gas purge can be calculated based on the cell culture lactate and bicarbonate concentrations. In some cell culture platform processes, post-inoculation, rather than calling $CO_2$ under pH control, CO2 is sparged between 5 to 10% for a specific short period of time between 24 to 48 hours to ensure a specific amount of CO2 is maintained in the culture, in such instances, mole fraction sparged $CO_2$ gas is substituted for the value of $X_{b,\ in,\ CO2}$ instead of using Figure 6.

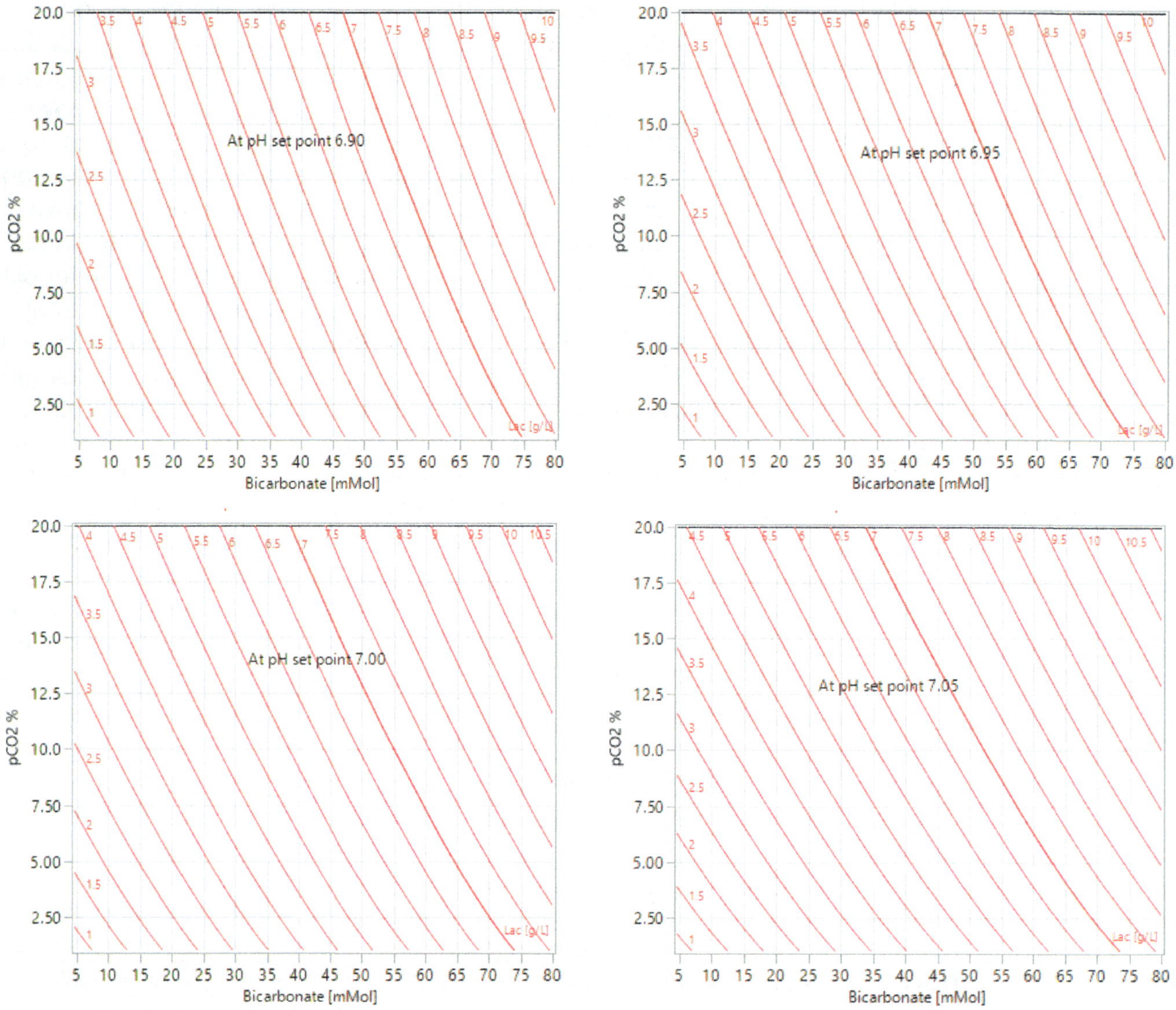


**Figure 6: Correlation between pH, pCO2, lactate, and bicarbonate to determine the mole fraction of** $CO_2$ ($X_{b,\ inCO_2}$)**.**

At Scale Model Verification and Successful implication of predictive model.

At 20,000L production bioreactor, we ran a high cell density CHO cell culture process up to 20 × $10^6$ cell/mL peak cell density. The pCO2 concentration was measured using Nova Flex 2 metabolite analyzer. 23 actual measured pCO2 values are plotted against the predicted values as shown in Figure 7A, linear regression of predicted over measured $CO_2$ values gave an $R^2 = 0.87$ demonstrates, that the predictive expression is reliable. Additionally, the p-value less than 0.001 demonstrates the measure of strength of association between the predicted and actual values is statistically significant. Figure 7B shows Density Ellipse fit. The density ellipse shows the degree of correlation between the predictive and explanatory variable using correlation coefficient and its p value. The correlation coefficient shown in Figure 7 is the Pearson correlation coefficient (r) and it is the most common way of measuring a linear correlation. It is a number ranging between –1 and 1 that measures the strength and direction of the linear relationship between two variables. r = 0.93 demonstrates, that there is a linear relationship between predicted and actual pCO2 values is strong and p value of <0.0001 for regression coefficient "r" signifies that the linear relationship is statistically significant. Figure 7C shows the residual plot at different measured actual CO2 concentration. Figure 7C, demonstrates for 19 out of 23 data points the absolute difference between the measured and predicted CO2 values are within ± 10 mmHg which is the expected range for QC level-1 standard check with the mean pCO2 value of 70 mmHg for NovaFlex2 metabolite analyzer. Furthermore, as the measurement range increases, the acceptable expected range also increases that explains the higher residual values at measured pCO2 above 100 mmHg. NovaFlex2 analyzer used for this study does not have any QC standard checks above 70 mmHg.

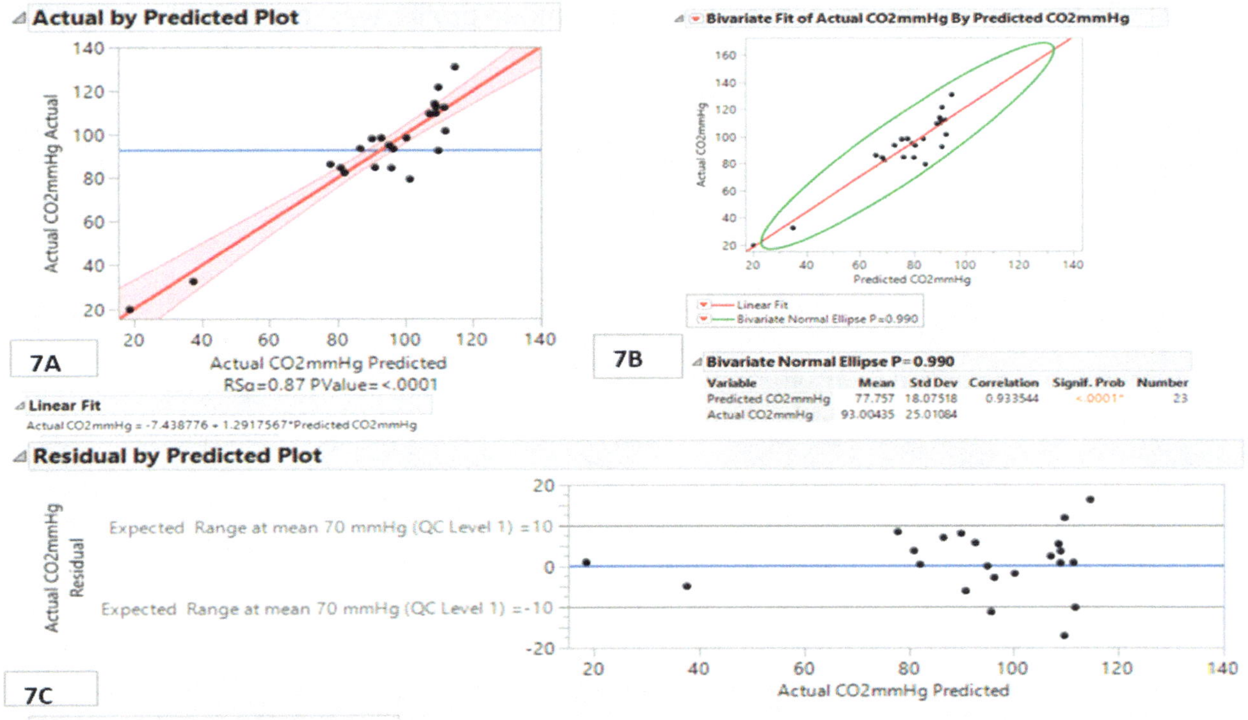


**Figure 7: pCO2 predictive model validation.**

Sample **design space for Bioreactor operation to control $pCO_2$.**

A contour plot was drawn to predict the dissolved $CO_2$ concentration using Equation 31 with sparger total gas flow rate and viable cell density as explanatory variables, as shown in Figure 6. The assumptions for the parameters in the predictive model are summarized in Table 6, based on the values reported by Hu (2022), to represent typical production bioreactor operating conditions [1, 7].

| Box 1: pCO2 Predictive Model Assumptions |
|---|
| Henry Coefficient H = 25 mmol/L. Atm |
| Temperature 37 °C |
| pH set point = 7.00 |
| Bicarbonate concentration = 35 mmol/L |
| Lactate concentration = 4.0 g/L. |
| Bioreactor Volume = 15,000 L |
| Impeller Agitation Rate = 30 RPM |

Additionally, Equation 31 demands two more input values, that is $CO_2$ mole fraction and *Kla*. For $CO_2$ mole fraction, Figure 6C is used with the assumptions in Box 1; A $CO_2$ mole fraction of 5% is calculated. 4 to 7 % is a good approximation to cover a wide range of cell culture operation. For *KLa* value, a predictive expression created by experimental studies is used, as reported in our previous published article Muralidharan et al. (2024) [17]. Based on the above assumptions, a contour profile was created showing $pCO_2$ profile as a function of gas flow rate and viable cell density, as shown in Figure 8.

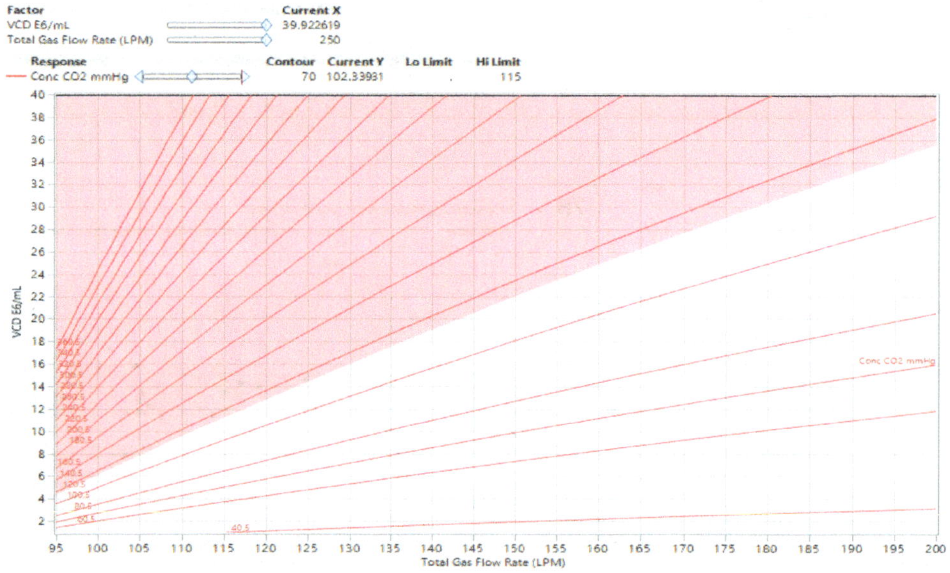


**Figure 8: pCO2, design space for bioreactor operating conditions.**

## Conclusions

This article summarizes the impact of excessive $CO_2$ accumulation in cell culture operation, considering factors in scaling up that cause $CO_2$ accumulation. A predictive model to predict and control $CO_2$ accumulation in large manufacturing-scale bioreactors is presented. Readers are encouraged to carefully weigh the limitations of this model to assess its suitability before applying it to their systems. As shown in Figure 7, there is an offset between the predicted to actual pCO2 values. This could be due to the variability of measurement instruments and the limitations of the assumptions in the model. However, the application of this model is to estimate the ballpark of increment in total gas flow rate required to control excessive $CO_2$ accumulation and not necessarily to precisely predict the $CO_2$ concentration with accuracy.

## References

1. Hu, W. "SCALING UP AND SCALING DOWN ON CELL CULTURE BIOREACTORS." In Cell Culture Bioprocess Engineering, 2nd ed., 281. CRC Press, 2020.

2. Muralidharan, N., Johnson, T., & Davis, M. (2023, November 16). Identifying False Metabolite Measurements During Cell-Culture Monitoring Effective Application of the Multivariate Hotelling's T2 Statistic. Bioprocess International, 21(11-12), 29-31. Retrieved from

https://bioprocessintl.com/2023/november-december-2023/identifying-false-metabolite-measurements-during-cell-culture-monitoring-effective-application-of-the-multivariate-hotellings-t2-statistic/

3. Xing, Z., Lewis, A. M., Borys, M. C., & Li, Z. J. (2017). A carbon dioxide stripping model for mammalian cell culture in manufacturing scale bioreactors. Biotechnology and Bioengineering, 114(6), 1184-1194.

https://doi.org/10.1002/bit.26232

4. DeZengotita, V. M., Schmelzer, A. E., & Miller, W. M. (2002). Characterization of hybridoma cell responses to elevated pCO2 and osmolality: Intracellular pH, cell size, apoptosis, and metabolism. Biotechnology and Bioengineering, 77(4), 369-380. https://doi.org/10.1002/bit.10176

5. Mostafa, S. S., & Gu, X. (2003). Strategies for improved dCO2 removal in large-scale fed-batch cultures. Biotechnology Progress, 19(1), 45-51.

https://doi.org/10.1021/bp0256263

6. Xing, Z., Kenty, B. M., Li, Z. J., & Lee, S. S. (2009). Scale-up analysis for a CHO cell culture process in large-scale bioreactors. Biotechnology and Bioengineering, 103(4), 733-746. https://doi.org/10.1002/bit.22287

7. Hu, W. " OXYGEN TRANSFER IN CELL CULTURE BIOREACTORS." In Cell Culture Bioprocess Engineering, 2nd ed., 219. CRC Press, 2020.

8. Wilke, C. R., & Chang, P. (1955). Correlation of diffusion coefficients in dilute solutions. AIChE Journal, 1(2), 264-270. doi:10.1002/aic.690010222

9. Royce, P. N., & Thornhill, N. F. (1991). Estimation of dissolved carbon dioxide concentrations in aerobic fermentations. AIChE Journal, 37(11), 1680-1686. https://doi.org/10.1002/aic.690371111

10. Muralidharan, N. (2023, February 9). Shear-Proof Design Space: Scaling Stirred-Tank Bioreactors for Cell Culture Processes. Bioprocess International, 21(1-2), 36-38.

https://bioprocessintl.com/upstream-processing/bioreactors/shear-proof-design-space-scaling-stirred-tank-bioreactors-for-cell-culture-processes/

11. Doran, P. M. (1995). Mass Transfer. In Bioprocess Engineering Principles (1st ed., p. 210- 213). Elsevier Science & Technology Books.

12. Katoh, S., Horiuchi, J., & Yoshida, F. (2015). Mass Transfer. In Biochemical engineering: A textbook for engineers, chemists and biologists (2nd ed., p. 73- 77). John Wiley & Sons.

13. Sieblist, C., Hägeholz, O., Aehle, M., Jenzsch, M., Pohlscheidt, M., & Lübbert, A. (2011). Insights into large-scale cell-culture reactors: II. gas-phase mixing and $CO_2$ stripping. Biotechnology Journal, 6(12), 1547-1556.

https://doi.org/10.1002/biot.201100153

14. Liow, K. Y., Thouas, G. A., Tan, B. T., Thompson, M. C., & Hourigan, K. (2009). Modeling the transport of momentum and oxygen in an aerial-disk-driven bioreactor used for animal tissue or cell culture. IFMBE Proceedings, 1672-1675. https://doi.org/10.1007/978-3-540-92841-6_415

15. Stadler, E. L., & B. Braun Biotech Inc. (2001, October). Fermentor / Bioreactor Design Lecture [Paper presentation]. Bioprocess Equipment Design Seminar, Atlanta, GA.

16. Fuller, E. N., Schettler, P. D., & Giddings, J. C. (1966). New method for prediction of binary gas-phase diffusion coefficients. Industrial & Engineering Chemistry, 58(5), 18-27. https://doi.org/10.1021/ie50677a007

17. Muralidharan, N., Bolduc, E., & Davis, M. (2024, January/February). Characterizing Oxygen Mass Transfer and Shear During Cell Culture Calculating the Maximum Cell Density Supported By a 20,000-liter Stirred-Tank Bioreactor. Bioprocess International, 22(1-2), 2-10.

18. Baz-Rodr'ıguez, S., Aguilar-Corona, A., & Soria, A. (2012). RISING VELOCITY FOR SINGLE BUBBLES IN PURE LIQUIDS. Revista Mexicana de Ingenier'ıa Qu'ımica, 11(2), 269-278. https://www.scielo.org.mx/pdf/rmiq/v11n2/v11n2a6.pdf

19. Gramer, M. J., & Ogorzalek, T. (2007). A semi-empirical mathematical model is useful for describing the relationship between carbon dioxide, pH, lactate, and base in a bicarbonate-buffered cell-culture process. Biotechnology and Applied Biochemistry, 47(4), 197-204. https://doi.org/10.1042/ba20070001

20. Calderbank, P., & Moo-Young, M. (1961). The continuous phase heat and mass-transfer properties of dispersions. Chemical Engineering Science, 16(1-2), 39-54. https://doi.org/10.1016/0009-2509(61)87005-x

## Appendix

| Appendix A- Algebraic mathematical simplification from Equation 31 to Equation 32. | |
|---|---|
| **Step-1** | $CTR_T. = KLa_{b,co2}.\left(\frac{\left(C_{l,co2}(1-Exp(-A_{co2})\right) + X_{b,in,Co2}.P_l.H_{Co2}.Exp(-A_{co2}) - X_{b,in,co2}.P_l.H_{Co2})}{A_{co2}}\right)$ |
| **Step-2** | $CTR_T. = KLa_{b,co2}.\left(\frac{\left(C_{l,co2}(1-Exp(-A_{co2})) + X_{b,in,Co2}.P_l.H_{Co2}.(Exp(-A_{co2})-1)\right)}{A_{co2}}\right)$ |
| **Step-3** | $CTR_T. = KLa_{b,co2}.\left(\frac{\left(C_{l,co2}(1-Exp(-A_{co2})) - X_{b,in,co2}.P_l.H_{Co2}.(1-Exp(-A_{co2}))\right)}{A_{co2}}\right)$ |
| **Step-4** | $CTR_T = KLa_{b,co2}\left(\frac{\left(C_{l,co2}(1-Exp(-A_{co2})) - X_{b,in,co2}.P_l.H_{Co2}.(1-Exp(-A_{co2}))\right)}{A_{co2}}\right)$ |
| **Step-5** | $CTR_T.A_{co2} = KLa_{b,co2}\left(\left(C_{l,co2}(1-Exp(-A_{co2})) - X_{b,in,co2}.P_l.H_{Co2}.(1-Exp(-A_{co2}))\right)\right)$ |
| **Step-6** | $CTR_T.A_{co2} = \left(KLa_{b,co2}.C_{l,co2}(1-Exp(-A_{co2})) - \left(KLa_{b,co2}.X_{b,in,co2}.P_l.H_{Co2}.(1-Exp(-A_{co2}))\right)\right)$ |
| **Step-7** | $CTR_T.A_{co2} + KLa_{b,co2}.X_{b,in,co2}.P_l.H_{Co2}.(1-Exp(-A_{co2})) = \left(KLa_{b,co2}.C_{l,co2}(1-Exp(-A_{co2}))\right)$ |
| **Step-8** | $CTR_T.A_{co2} + KLa_{b,co2}.X_{b,in,co2}.P_l.H_{Co2}.(1-Exp(-A_{co2})) = KLa_{b,co2}.C_{l,co2} - KLa_{b,co2}.C_{l,co2}.Exp(-A_{co2})$ |
| **Step-9** | $CTR_T.A_{co2} + KLa_{b,co2}.X_{b,in,co2}.P_l.H_{Co2}.(1-Exp(-A_{co2})) = C_{l,co2}(KLa_{b,co2}.-KLa_{b,co2}.Exp(-A_{co2})$ |
| **Step-10** | $\frac{CTR_T.A_{co2} + KLa_{b,co2}.X_{b,in,co2}.P_l.H_{Co2}.(1-Exp(-A_{co2}))}{(KLa_{b,co2}.-KLa_{b,co2}.Exp(-A_{co2})} = C_{l,co2}$ |
| **Step-11** | $C_{l,co2} = \frac{CTR_T.A_{co2} + KLa_{b,co2}.X_{b,in,co2}.P_l.H_{Co2}.(1-Exp(-A_{co2}))}{KLa_{b,co2}(1-Exp(-A_{co2})}$ |

# Chapter 3: Manufacturing Process Control Strategy to drive the Mammalian Cells to undergo metabolic Shift.

**Naveenganesh Muralidharan*, Emma Bolduc, Mark Davis**

## Introduction

Mammalian cells used for biologics production initially consume glucose as the primary carbon source and will produce lactate during early exponential phase growth. Once the culture approaches the stationary phase, the cells will begin to consume lactate as their main carbon source. The shift from glucose to lactate as the main energy source is known as the lactate metabolic shift. This shift is desirable during upstream operations in biologics production as it typically results in higher protein yields. A review of basic cellular metabolism is shown in Figure 1. As part of this process, glucose is converted to pyruvate which is then transferred to the mitochondria, where it enters the tricarboxylic acid (TCA) cycle. In this way, pyruvate is oxidized to $H_2O$ and $CO_2$, and energy is produced. However, if the mitochondrial oxidative potential is insufficient, pyruvate will be converted to lactate, which will accumulate in the culture broth. High concentrations of lactate will result in a reduction in pH; this will signal the automatic addition of additional base titrant by the bioreactor's pH control mechanism. The addition of base titrant increases the osmolality of the culture broth; this will ultimately inhibit cell growth, reduce protein productivity, and alter the glycosylation profile of the therapeutic protein produced [1]. Although largely considered a desirable response, the lactate metabolic shift is frequently inconsistent between batches, even in controlled commercial-scale operations [2]. The mechanisms underlying the control of this metabolic shift remain poorly understood and have been reported piecemeal with no systemic overview. To address this important concern, we review the current literature focused on the parameters that may affect the lactate metabolic shift in mammalian cell culture manufacturing processes. We provide a consolidated summary of factors believed to control metabolic behavior in cell culture leading to the desired lactate metabolic shift.

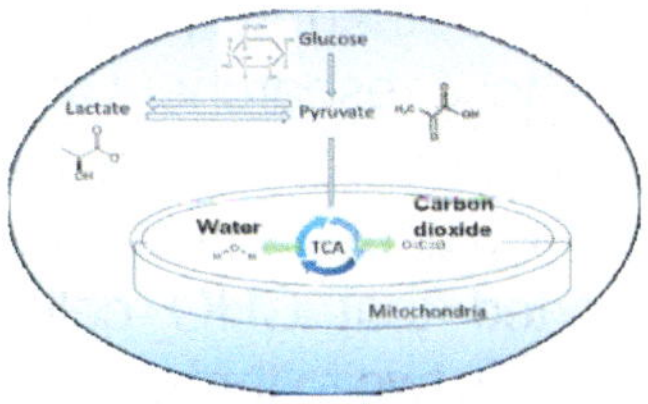


**Figure 1. Lactate metabolic shift.**

## Factors Influencing the Lactate Shift

### Effect of $CO_2$ concentration

In a typical fed-batch culture, $CO_2$ is produced by cellular respiration as glucose is metabolized. This process plays a major role in energy production needed to support cell growth and productivity. During the early phases of culture growth under standard bioreactor conditions, $CO_2$ sparging is required to maintain the pH. As the cell density increases, the concentration of $CO_2$ also increases. In a typical cell culture, one mole of $CO_2$ is produced for every mole of $O_2$ consumed. Under these conditions, the Respiratory Quotient [RQ] = 1 [1]. Therefore, to maintain an optimal $CO_2$ concentration inside the bioreactor, $O_2$ transfer and $CO_2$ removal must be balanced. Bioreactor operating conditions, including sparger gas flow rate, agitation, and pressure, can all have an impact on $CO_2$ accumulation in the culture broth. For example, increasing the flow rate of the sparger gas may result in the removal of too much $CO_2$. A $pCO_2$ concentration below 25 mmHg during the first three days may alter cell culture performance by inhibiting the lactate metabolic shift [3].

By contrast, low rates of gas flow can lead to an increase in the concentration of dissolved $CO_2$. Inappropriately elevated levels of $CO_2$ may delay or even prevent cells from undergoing the desired lactate metabolic shift and lead to lactate accumulation. For example, Brunner et al. [4] reported that $pCO_2$ concentrations >95 mmHg can prevent the desired lactate metabolic shift. Therefore, ensuring the $pCO_2$ concentration between 25 and 95 mmHg during the early stages of cell growth in culture may be critical to ensure a consistent lactate metabolic lactate shift across multiple batches.

### Effects of glucose and lactate concentration

The density profile of viable cells grown in batch or fed-batch mode can be divided into exponential growth, stationary, and declining phases. The cell growth rate is highest during the first (exponential) phase and plateaus as the cells enter the stationary phase. The cell growth rate then falls as the cells enter the declining phase. Mulukutla et al. [5] reported that cells can be pushed toward a lactate metabolic shift by limiting the concentration of available glucose during the follow-up to the initial lactate production phase. Under these conditions, cells can consume glucose and produce lactate until the glucose concentration falls below a threshold value (0.5 mM or 0.1 g/L) and lactate has accumulated to 15 to 40 mM (1.4 to 3.4 g/L). The cells are then maintained under glucose limitation for a specific duration. When the glucose limitation period has been completed, cells are then re-fed to achieve an extracellular glucose concentration of no more than 2 g/L. These researchers also noted that a change in the duration of glucose limitation might prevent the cells from achieving the desired lactate metabolic shift [5]. It is critical to note that cells under glucose limitation still need a trace amount to prevent starvation. Acosta et al. [6] reported that CHO cells undergo lactate shift at glucose concentrations 1.0 to 1.5 mM; this value is two to three times higher than the previously reported value by Mulukutla et al. [5]. Furthermore, Acosta et al. [6] also demonstrated monitoring the molar ratio of lactate to glucose against glucose concentration over the period of glucose limitation as an effective explanatory tool to monitor metabolic shifts. Therefore, it is recommended that maintaining the consistent molar ratio of lactate to glucose over the duration of glucose limitation is more critical than the absolute concentrations.

Liste-Calleja et al. [7] reported that HEK293 cells responded to a reduction in pH by undergoing a lactate metabolic shift. This group also noted that a reduction in pH accompanied by lactate supplementation resulted in the co-consumption of both glucose and lactate.

In summary, it will be important to consider the interactive effects and the overall impact of pH, $pCO_2$, glucose and lactate concentrations, and the duration of glucose limitation. These parameters might be maintained as uniformly as possible across all batches to achieve a consistent lactate metabolic shift across multiple batches.

## Effect of seeding density and glucose concentration per cell

Viable cell seeding density and the cell growth profile frequently vary between batches in commercial cell culture operations. This variability may be introduced either from raw material, inherent error from cell counting machines, and/or from the manufacturing operation itself. Thus, if the system is designed as a constant continuous or bolus glucose feeding strategy independent of bioreactor cell count, different batches will have different glucose concentrations per cell. Drapeau D et al. [8] reported that lactate production by mammalian cells is controlled by feeding glucose at the rate of glucose consumed by cells rather than constant fed-batch or continuous rate of glucose addition based on bioreactor sample glucose concentration. Here, the rate of glucose consumed is a function of the viable cell density profile. Therefore, it is recommended to monitor and control glucose concentration per cell to achieve consistency in lactate metabolic shifts between batches.

## Effect of bioreactor mixing time and the pH gradient

The bioreactor's automated pH control signals the addition of a base titrant whenever the pH hits a lower deadband. In large-scale bioreactors, the base titrant is frequently added to the surface of the culture liquid. Mixing time will increase as the scale of operation increases. Longer bioreactor mixing times can create pH gradients of ≥ 9.0 units over 5% of the volume of large-scale bioreactors. This localized region of the high pH zone is often called the alkaline zone. Brunner et al. [9] identified a 5% alkaline zone in a stirred tank bioreactor with operating volume of 10,000 to 12,000 L. Langheinrich and Nienow [10] demonstrated that intracellular pH ($pH_i$) increases by ~2 units as the cells enter the alkaline zone even with a very short exposure time. Xu et al. [11] showed that the addition of base titrant in response to an increase in $pCO_2$ in large-scale bioreactors with long mixing times causes stress to fed-batch CHO cultures and prevents them from undergoing a lactate metabolic shift. Therefore, when scaling up a bioreactor manufacturing process, it is imperative to consider the bioreactor mixing time and/or ensure that the base titrant is introduced at a point close to the impeller zone.

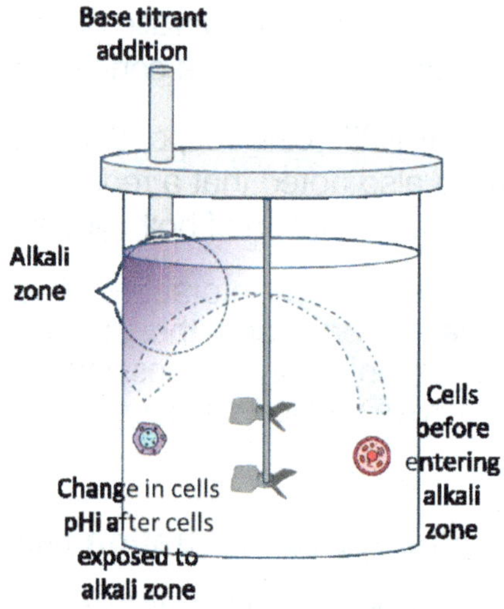


**Figure 2. pH gradient inside large manufacturing scale bioreactor**

## Effect of bioreactor mixing time and the dissolved $O_2$ gradient

$O_2$ characteristic time (TC) is defined as the ratio of $O_2$ concentration (C*) in the incoming gas (in mM) to the rate of $O_2$ consumption by the cells (in mM/sec). In other words, $O_2$ $t_c$ is a measure of how fast the delivered $O_2$ is consumed, as expressed in Equation (1) [12]. C* is the molar concentration of $O_2$ in a purged gas bubble, as calculated in Equation (2). H is Henry's coefficient for $O_2$ solubility in liquid. For typical culture conditions at 37 °C, H=1.07 mmol/(L.atm) is a good approximation, with P representing the average pressure in the bioreactor in atm. A positive pressure above atmospheric pressure (1 atm) is maintained in the bioreactor; thus, the pressure in the headspace added to the pressure from liquid height inside the bioreactor will be > 1 atm. However, for simplicity in our calculation, P is assumed to be 1 atm. $F_{oxy}$ is the fraction of $O_2$ in the incoming gas. The fraction of $O_2$ in air is 0.21. The rate of $O_2$ consumed is expressed as the $O_2$ Uptake Rate (OUR). As shown in Equation (3), the OUR is calculated as the product of the viable cell density and their rate of $O_2$ consumption [1]. Here, we approximate the specific $O_2$ consumption rate of cells ($Q_{O2}$) at 5.5 pmol/cell. Day [13]. $X_i$ is the viable cell density (VCD; × $10^6$ cells/mL). Thus:

$$t_C = C^* \div OUR \qquad (1)$$

$$C^* = H \times P \times f_{oxy} = 1.07 \frac{mmol}{L.atm} \times 1\,atm \times 0.21 = 0.225 \frac{mmol}{L} \qquad (2)$$

$$OUR = x_i \times Q_{o2} = x \frac{10^6 cells}{mL} \times 10^3 \frac{mL}{1L} \times 5.5 \frac{10^{-12} mol}{cell.day} \times \frac{10^3 mmol}{mol} \times \frac{1day}{24\,h} = 0.23 \times x_i \frac{mmol}{L.h} \qquad (3)$$

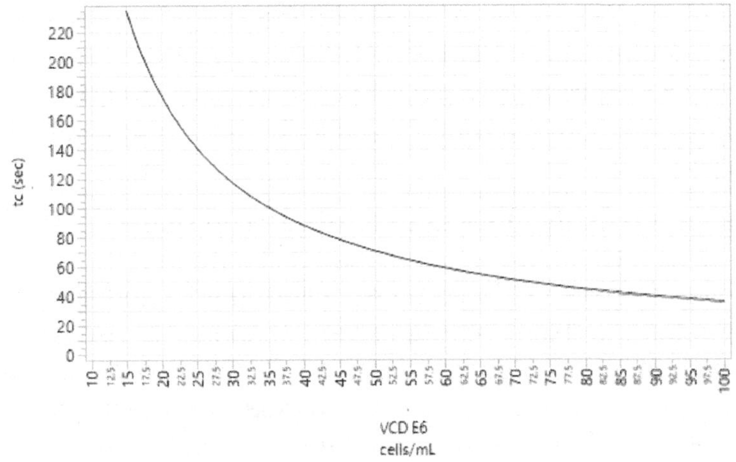


**Figure 3. $O_2$ characteristic time ($t_c$) *vs.* viable cell density (VCD)**

## Effect of media preparation, filtration, and equilibration

**Media Preparation:** Typically, one needs to accommodate uncertainties (e.g., equipment downtime and availability) in large-scale commercial production suites. The flexibility in media composition is incorporated in process design, for example, taking into consideration whether cell culture media is filtered directly into the receiving bioreactor or into to storage tank and then transferred into the receiving bioreactor at a later time. Forte T et al. [14] reported that the stability of a liquid cell culture medium depends on various factors that affect storage conditions, such as temperature, exposure to light, and time. Forte T also showed improper storage conditions have led to the degradation of organic components precipitate of amino acids in formulated medium, leading to poor cell culture performance. Furthermore, Neutsch L et al. [15] showed exposing cell culture media and feeds to an ambient light source only for a short period resulted in photo-degradation of vital nutrients in media, impacting cell culture performance. Typical biomanufacturing platforms do include intermediate storage of feeds and media in transparent plastic bottles or transparent bags, which do not guarantee the exclusion of light over a prolonged duration without light protection. Hence, the option of using transparent storage containers without proper shielding from exposure to light does have the potential to impact media stability and, thereby, cell culture performance and metabolic shift. Therefore, one's specific procedural choice on filtration of media directly in a bioreactor or filtration into a storage tank and then transfer into a bioreactor can lead to differences in cell culture performance between the batches. Thus, to maintain consistency between batches, it is recommended to carefully characterize all possible media storage conditions as cited by Forte T [14].

**Media Filtration**: During the scale-up operation, an oversized filter is typically selected to avoid the possibility of clogging or as an extra safety factor to facilitate microbial control. The risks associated with the use of oversized filter membranes generally go unnoticed. Growth media contain a metabolically balanced composition of basal nutrients, such as amino acids, carbohydrates, inorganic salts, and vitamins in water, which are necessary for cell growth and proliferation [2]. Loss of nutrients from cell culture media is expected to have an adverse impact on cell culture performance. Na J et al. [16] reported the loss of organic components from cell culture media using 0.2 μm sterile filtration. Therefore, as a simplified best practice, it is recommended to maintain the filtration volume to effective filter area ratio as close as possible to the receiving site, which is commonly employed in the biopharmaceutical industry for sizing normal flow filtration [17].

**Media Equilibration and dissolved $O_2$ standardization process**: Cell culture media pH is typically maintained using a $CO_2$-bicarbonate-based buffer system. Hoshan et al. [18] reported that air sparge removes dissolved $CO_2$ from cell culture media and spontaneously increases the medium pH. Therefore, problems can emerge secondary to excess gassing using only processed air over a short duration during dissolved $O_2$ (DO) probe standardization or even from mild airflow over a long duration when the media has been added to the bioreactor substantially before the time of inoculation. Both processes can remove $CO_2$ from the culture media and increase the pH; Brantley et al. [19] reported that an increase in pH resulted in the precipitation of critical components (trace elements) from the cell culture media and thus impart differences in cell culture performance. Therefore, for consistent cell culture performance, it is recommended to use 5– 7% $CO_2$ along with air based on bi-carbonate concentration in the growth media to avoid excessive removal of $CO_2$ from cell culture media and the resulting increase in pH [2].

## Discussion

The rates of natural reactions depend on duration, the availability of substrates, and environmental conditions. With these three factors as the inception of an idea to explore, we reviewed the different manufacturing and operating parameters that can influence the lactate metabolic shift in mammalian cell culture. Future work will need to focus on a multivariable analysis of these parameters to understand their potential additive and synergistic impact on cell culture performance.

## Acknowledgment

None

## Conflict of Interest

None

## Disclaimer

The views and opinions expressed in this document are those of the authors only and do not necessarily reflect the official policy or position of AGC Biologics.

## References


1. Muralidharan N, Johnson T, Bolduc E, et al. CO2 Control Strategy for Large-Scale Cell Culture Bioreactor Operation. Adv. BioSci. Bioeng. 2024, 12(1), 1-13.

2. Hu, Wei-Shou. "Cell Culture Data Analysis." In Cell Culture Bioprocess Engineering. 2nd ed., CRC P, 2020, 172-174.

3. Zhao L, Wang C, Wang J, et al. Low CO2 partial pressure steers CHO cells into a defective metabolic state. Biotechnol Lett. 2023;45(9):1103-1115.

4. Brunner M, Doppler P, Klein T, et al. Elevated pCO2 affects the lactate metabolic shift in CHO cell culture processes. Eng Life Sci. 2017;18(3):204-214.

5. Mulukutla BC, Yongky A, Grimm S, et al. Multiplicity of steady states in glycolysis and shift of metabolic state in cultured mammalian cells. PLoS One. 2015;10(3):1-20.

6. Acosta ML, Sánchez A, García F, et al. Analysis of kinetic, stoichiometry, and regulation of glucose and glutamine metabolism in hybridoma batch cultures using logistic equations. Cytotechnology. 2007;54(3):189-200.

7. Liste-Calleja L, Lecina M, Lopez-Repullo J, et al. Lactate and glucose concomitant consumption as a self-regulated pH detoxification mechanism in HEK293 cell cultures. Appl Microbiol Biotechnol. 2015;99(23):9951-9960.

8. Drapeau D, Stanek T, Luan Y-T; Wyeth, assignee. Restricted glucose feed for animal cell culture. US patent. US7429491B2. September 30, 2008.

9. Brunner M, Braun P, Doppler P, et al. The impact of pH inhomogeneities on CHO cell physiology and fed-batch process performance - two-compartment scale-down modeling and intracellular pH excursion. Biotechnol J. 2017;12(7).

10. Langheinrich C, Nienow AW. Control of pH in large-scale, free suspension animal cell bioreactors: alkali addition and pH excursions. Biotechnol Bioeng. 1999;66(3):171-179.

11. Xu S, Jiang R, Mueller R, et al. Probing lactate metabolism variations in large-scale bioreactors. Biotechnol Prog. 2018;34(3):756-766.

12. Lara AR, Galindo E, Ramírez OT, et al. Living with heterogeneities in bioreactors: understanding the effects of environmental gradients on cells. Mol Biotechnol. 2006;34(3):355-381.

13. Muralidharan, N, Bolduc E, Davis M. Characterizing Oxygen Mass Transfer, and Shear During Cell Culture Calculating the Maximum Cell Density Supported By a 20,000-liter Stirred-Tank Bioreactor. Bioprocess International. 2024; 22(1-2): 2-10.

14. Forte T, Grinnell C, Zhang A, Polilli B, et al. Methods for identifying precipitates and improving the stability of chemically defined highly concentrated cell culture media. Biotechnol Prog. 2023;39(4): e3345.

15. Neutsch L, Kroll P, Brunner M, et al. Media photo-degradation in pharmaceutical biotechnology - the impact of ambient light on media quality, cell physiology, and IgG production in CHO cultures. J Chem Technol Biotechnol. 2018;93(8):2141-2151

16. Na J, Suh D, Cho YH, Baek Y. Comparative Evaluation of the Performance of Sterile Filters for Bioburden Protection and Final Fill in Biopharmaceutical Processes. Membranes (Basel). 2022;12(5):524.

17. Haindl, S., Stark, J., Dippel, J., et al. Scale-up of Microfiltration processes. Chemie Ingenieur Technik. 2020; 92(6): 746-758.

18. Hoshan L, Jiang R, Moroney J, et al. Effective bioreactor pH control using only sparging gases. Biotechnol Prog. 2019;35(1):e2743.

19. Brantley T, Moore B, Grinnell C, Khattak S. Investigating trace metal precipitation in highly concentrated cell culture media with Pourbaix diagrams. Biotechnol Bioeng. 2021;118(10):3888-3897.

# Chapter 4: Shear Assessment for Mammalian Cell Culture Clarification Using a Disc Stack Centrifuge

**Naveenganesh Muralidharan, Tyler Younger, Grace Chan, and Mark Davis**

## Introduction

In biologics manufacturing, the clarification of unprocessed bulk cell broth is the first step of purification. In the clarification process or the primary recovery step, solid particles, including cells and cell debris, are removed and filtered through 0.2-µm polish filters prior to subsequent downstream purification processing. Typically, cell culture clarification is performed by using either a two-stage depth filter or centrifugation followed by a one-stage depth filter setup. Although the use of two-stage cellulose-based depth filters has been established as an effective approach for cell culture clarification, Beckett (2014) reported that cost and space constraints associated with depth filter capacity limit the usage of depth-filter-only clarification to bioreactor capacities of up to 4000 L. For larger capacities, biomanufacturers prefer to use a disc stack centrifuge (DSC) as the first clarification step [1].

Over the past two decades, DSCs have been well-established for the primary clarification of cell culture material. The scale-up of DSCs can be performed based on the well-known concept of maintaining a constant $Q/\Sigma$ ratio across scales. $Q/\Sigma$ is defined as the ratio of centrifuge feed flow rate (Q) to the gravity equivalent setting area ($\Sigma$), which is equivalent to the area required for settling under gravity for specific operation conditions and equipment designs [2]. $Q/\Sigma$ is a surrogate measure of the particle settling capacity of the centrifuge. Application of the $Q/\Sigma$ ratio concept comes with the assumption that the solid particles subjected to the centrifugal force are shear-resistant and that the particles remain intact during centrifugation. However, mammalian cells are sensitive to shear, and damage to cells may result in the release of intracellular compounds, including host cell proteins, DNA, and proteases, which may reduce the level of the therapeutic target protein product and increase the impurity load in the clarified harvest material [3, 4].

As companies move biologics production from single-use facilities to large-scale manufacturing to meet market demands, they must consider the effect of shear when using DSCs. The operating conditions for a DSC should be selected based on a design space that balances both particle settling capacity ($Q/\Sigma$) and shear. Although extensive discussions on $Q/\Sigma$ are available in the literature, there is no straightforward scale-up methodology for DSC shear assessment. Hence, in this article, we discuss three methods for shear assessment in a DSC as a function of centrifuge design and operational parameters, namely, (1) the Eddy length model (ELM), (2) the tip speed model (TSM), and (3) the power dissipation model (PDM). Furthermore, we present an illustration of the operational design space for a DSC, showing the balance between particle settling capacity and shear.

## Method 1: Particle Eddy Length

**Fluid flow velocity ($\vartheta_L$):** Under the conditions of DSC operation, it is assumed that the fluid flow between the disc spacing is laminar, the flow is evenly divided between all available disc spaces, and the settled particles do not return to the annular space between discs [9]. With these assumptions, for a fluid flowing through the annular space between discs, as shown in Figure 1A, the fluid velocity is given by Equation 1 [9]. Here, Q is the centrifuge feed flow rate in $m^3/s$, $n_{ds}$ is the number of disc spaces and $A_{avg}$ is the average cross-sectional area for the flow of fluid between the disc spacing. $R_o$ and $R_i$ are the outer and inner radii of the conical discs of the centrifuge, and h is the distance or spacing between the discs.

**Particle velocity under centrifugal force ($\vartheta_{pcf}$) in static fluid conditions:** Under centrifugation, as the bowl rotates, the centrifugal force accelerates the particles outward from the center axis of rotation. The centrifugal velocity of a particle in a static liquid is given by Equation 2 [9]. Here, $\rho_L$ and $\mu_L$ are the dynamic density and dynamic viscosity of the fluid, respectively, where $\rho_L = 1015\ kg/m^3$ and $\mu_L = 1.05 \times 10^{-3}$ P.s are good approximations for a typical cell culture broth at harvest [4, 8]. $D_p$ is the particle diameter. For Chinese hamster ovary (CHO) cells, Maschke (2022) reported that the cell size follows a Gaussian normal distribution with an expected average size of approximately 14.45 µm. Therefore, $d_p$ is assumed to be 14.5 µm for applications of cell culture harvest [4]. However, in DSC applications for cell recirculation to bioreactors operating in perfusion mode, a more stringent value of 20 µm is recommended, as most viable mammalian cells have a range of up to 20 µm in diameter. N is the centrifuge bowl speed in rotations per minute (RPM), ω is the angular velocity in 1/s, and R is the radius of rotation. For the shear assessment, R is assumed to be $R_o$ as a conservative approach.

**Drag force ($F_d$):** The force of friction on a particle that resists its motion through a fluid is called the drag force. In the settling process under centrifugation, where the motion of the bulk fluid flow is opposite to the particle settling direction, particles experience a drag force due to the relative motion between the fluid and particles. Drag acts in the direction opposite to the particle motion, i.e., in the same direction as the fluid flow. Therefore, the relative particle velocity, also referred to as the slip velocity ($\vartheta_p$ ), is the difference between the particle centrifugal settling velocity for a static liquid ( $\vartheta_{pcf}$) and the fluid velocity between the disc space ($\vartheta_f$), as shown in Figure 1B. The balance between the drag force and centrifugal force acting on the particles enables the particles to achieve a constant velocity $\vartheta_p$ [10].

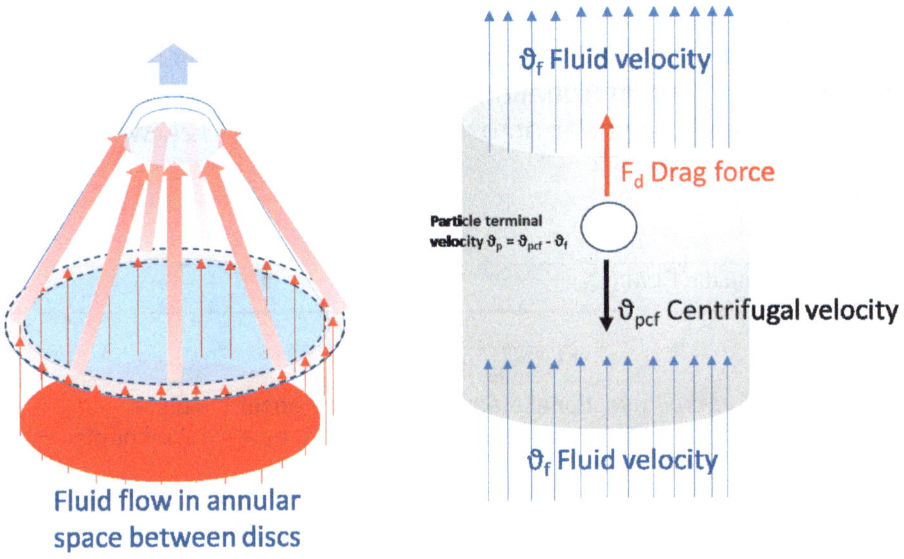


**Figure 1: Fluid and particle flow between the discs.**

Based on Stokes' law, the drag force acting on a moving particle when placed in a fluid flowing in the opposite direction is given by Equation 3 [12] with the following assumptions: 1) As the particles pass through the centrifuge, the particles do not aggregate or break and are spherical in shape. 2) The particle concentration in the suspension is low enough to avoid any settling hindrances. 3) The particles move in the radial direction and do not have a tangential motion component at any time. 4) The settling velocity of the particles is in the laminar or Stokes flow region; thus, the Reynolds number should be less than 0.4 at all times.

**Drag coefficient ($C_d$):** For spherical particles in the Stokes flow regime, $C_d$ is calculated as a function of the Reynolds number, as shown in Equation 3 [5, 11, 15].

**Reynolds number (Re):** The Reynolds number is a dimensionless quantity calculated as the ratio of inertial to viscous forces within a fluid flow, where the inertial force causes the fluid to flow and the viscous force acts as a resistance to flow. Therefore, flows with a low Re value are characterized as laminar and smooth, whereas flows with a high Re value are characterized as turbulent. Clark et al. (1997) cited Re < 0.4 as the laminar flow or Stokes regime, Re = 0.4–500 as the transition flow or Allen regime, and Re > 500 as the turbulent or Newton flow regime. Clark also reported that the settling of whole cells and protein under centrifugation typically falls under the laminar or Stokes regime [5]. Mei (1992) presented an expression for the particle Reynolds number for a moving particle in a flowing liquid, as shown in Equation 4 [6, 7], where $\vartheta_p$ is the particle slip velocity (m/s).

**Energy dissipation rate (EDR):** In the centrifugation settling process, the rate at which the kinetic energy of the fluid is lost as the particle moves and drags through a flowing fluid is defined as the EDR. This dissipation rate depends on the particle speed and the magnitude of the drag force. The EDR is calculated as shown in Equation 5 [12]. The **specific EDR ($\epsilon_p$) per cell particle** is given by the EDR divided by the cell particle volume, as shown in Equation 6 [12].

**Kolmogorov eddy length ($\ell_{eddy}$):** During centrifugation, the kinetic energy from the fluid dissipates from large eddies and cascades into smaller eddies. The smallest eddy length below the cell particle size is considered to be lethal to cells. The smallest or Kolmogorov eddy length ($\ell_{eddy}$) is calculated as shown in Equation 7, and this $\ell_{eddy}$ value is used as a scalable parameter to maintain the same shear across different DSCs [12], where Υ is the kinematic viscosity of the fluid ($m^2/s$).

| Box A: Method 1: Shear assessment based on the ELM ($\ell_{eddy}$) | |
|---|---|
| Equation 1 | $$\vartheta_L = \frac{Q}{n_{ds}.A_{avg}}$$ Where $A_{avg}$ is the average cross-sectional area between the concentric discs, determined as the average over the cross-section between the outer and inner disc radii. $$A_{avg} = 2.\pi\left(\left(R_o + h\right)^2 - R_o^{\,2}\right) + \left(\left(R_i + h\right)^2 - R_i^{\,2}\right)$$ |
| Equation 2 | $$\vartheta_{pcf} = \frac{d_p^2\left(\rho_p - \rho_L\right)\omega^2 R}{18\mu_L};\ \omega = \frac{2\pi N}{60}$$ |
| Equation 3 | $F_d = C_d \frac{\rho_L}{2}\vartheta_p^2\left(\frac{\pi d_p^2}{4}\right);\ \vartheta_p = \left(\vartheta_{pcf} - \vartheta_f\right);$ and $C_d = \frac{24}{Re}$ for the Stokes region |
| Equation 4 | $$Re_p = \frac{\rho_L \times d_p \times \left(\vartheta_p\right)}{\mu_L}$$ |
| Equation 5 | $$EDR = F_d \times \vartheta_p$$ |
| Equation 6 | $$\epsilon_p = \left[EDR \div \left(\frac{\pi d_p^{\,3}}{6}\right)\right] \div \rho_L$$ |
| Equation 7 | $$\ell_{eddy} = \left(\frac{\gamma^3}{\varepsilon_p}\right)^{1/4}$$ |

## Cell Damage Index and Model Fitting for the ELM

Lactate dehydrogenase (LDH) is an intracellular component in mammalian cells. Because it is released during cell rupture, LDH is often used in shear assessments as an indicator of cell damage [7]. Shekhawata et al. (2018) presented shear stress values for cell culture clarification using a DSC (Culturefuge 100™ [BTPX305H], Alfa Laval, Sweden) based on computational fluid dynamics and verified the predicted shear stress using measured LDH values for different combinations of centrifuge bowl speed and feed flow rate. Using the LDH values reported by Shekhawata et al. (2018) as response variables and $\ell_{eddy}$ values calculated from Equation 7 as explanatory variables, we applied the Standard Least-Square Model Fit function in JMP version 16.0 to demonstrate the predictability of shear in a DSC system based on the ELM, as shown in Figure 2.

Figure 2 shows the linear relationship between LDH concentration and calculated Kolmogorov eddy length with a prediction expression. Figure 2 shows p-values of 0.0008 and <0.0001 for the eddy length and intercept, respectively, which are both less than 0.05, demonstrating that the strength of association between the input variable (eddy length, $\ell_{eddy}$) and output prediction (LDH concentration) has a high degree of statistical significance. Therefore, the application of a constant $\ell_{eddy}$ may be an effective method of shear assessment for scaling DSC operations.

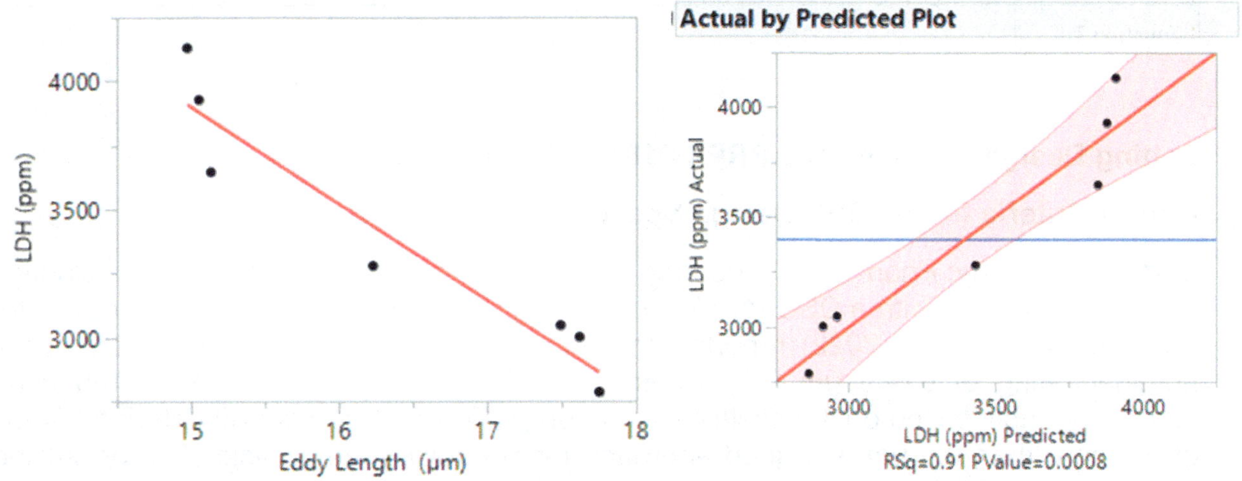


**Prediction Expression**

9550.8311119 + -376.7076933 • Eddy Length (μm)

**Parameter Estimates**

| Term | Estimate | Std Error | t Ratio | Prob>\|t\| |
|---|---|---|---|---|
| Intercept | 9550.8311 | 862.7162 | 11.07 | 0.0001* |
| Eddy Length (μm) | -376.7077 | 52.70765 | -7.15 | 0.0008* |

**Figure 2: Demonstration of shear prediction for a DSC using the Kolmogorov ELM.**

## Particle Settling Capacity of the Centrifuge

To maintain the same settling capacity across different makes and models of centrifuges, a constant Q/Σ ratio is applied. For a DSC, the Q/Σ ratio is calculated from Equation 8 [4, 5]. Here, g is the acceleration from gravity (9.8 $m/s^2$), and Θ is the half-cone angle of the centrifuge discs in radians. Centrifuge manufacturers typically report the half-cone angle in degrees (°); thus, the half-cone angle is converted from degrees to radians by multiplying the angle in degrees by a factor of π/180°.

The smallest particle that can be removed under centrifugation can be calculated from Stokes' law for the settling of solid particles, as presented by Stokes in 1851 and shown in Equation 9 [4, 5]. Ambler (1959) reported that the smallest separation particle size calculation is based on the sigma theory and thus gives only a nominal value rather than an absolute value. Pham (2010) reported that only 50% separation efficiency is achieved for the calculated particle size ($d_{p,\,min}$) for a given Q/Σ ratio [5].

| Box B: Particle settling capacity | |
|---|---|
| Equation 8 | $Q/_{\Sigma} = Q \div \left(\frac{2\pi n\omega^2(R_o{}^3 - R_i{}^3)}{3g\ tan\theta}\right)$ |
| Equation 9 | $\frac{(\rho_p - \rho_L) \times g \times d_p^2}{18\mu_L} = Q/_{\Sigma} => d_{p,min} = \left[(Q/_{\Sigma})\frac{18\mu_L}{(\rho_p - \rho_L) \times g}\right]^{1/2}$ |
| Equation 10 | $G, Force = \frac{R_o . \omega^2}{g}$ |

## Setting Design Space for the BRPX 618 HGV-34 Centrifuge

## Cut-off Criteria for the DSC Design Space

**Settling capacity:** Pham (2010) reported an average particle size of 0.5 μm for a clarified cell culture harvest with a DSC [4]. For a two-stage cellulose-based Millipore depth filter harvest, Parau et al. (2022) reported that the first-stage Millistak DOHC filter has a nominal rating of 0.6–9 μm [17]. Millistak DOHC filters and DSCs are often used interchangeably based on the scale of operation [1]. Therefore, a cut-off criterion ($d_{p,\ min}$) of no more than 0.6 μm is a good approach for controlling the particle size for settling capacity in the DSC operation design space.

**Eddy length:** For CHO cells in the stationary phase of cell growth, Maschke (2022) measured an average cell size and standard deviation of 13.57 μm ± 1.02 μm [18]. Nienow (2020) reported that keeping the eddy size larger than 18 μm should prevent fluid dynamic damage for most CHO cell cultures [20]. As most mammalian cells are less than 20 μm in diameter [12], the criterion for $\ell_{eddy}$ values to be less than 20 μm should ensure that the centrifuge operates in a shear-proof zone. However, in a study on cell damage index using LDH values, Shekhawata et al. (2018) cited an LDH concentration of approximately 1,200 ppm for a shear-proof design, which is equivalent to an eddy length of 22 μm. Therefore, $\ell_{eddy}$ is conservatively set as less than 22 μm.

**G-force:** The G-force or relative centrifugal force is the radial force generated by the rotation of the centrifuge, expressed relative to the gravitational force. The G-force is calculated from Equation 10 [4]. Doran (2013) reported that DSCs are designed to generate high G-forces ranging from 5,000 to 15,000 g in order to minimize the settling time and centrifuge processing time [22]. The harvest operation is a clean, but not sterile, process. Therefore, for large-scale (20,000-L) biologics productions, DSC harvest operations are often targeted to be completed within 4–6 hours to avoid excessive microbial proliferation. Aktiengesellschaft (2002) and Pham (2010) reported 6,500–7,500 g and 8,000–9,000 g, respectively, for cell culture harvest with a DSC. Therefore, we set the G-force to be greater than 5,000 g for the timely completion of the harvest operation.

A contour plot showing $\ell_{eddy}$, G-force, Q/Σ, and $d_{p,\ min}$ was created as a function of the centrifuge feed flow rate and bowl speed for the 60 L DSC used in our 20,000-L bioreactor facility, as shown in Figure 3 along with the geometric design parameters. The contour plot in Figure 3 displays the risk zones related to shear and settling capacity and indicates the desired operational space for a low shear that avoids cell damage while maintaining a reasonable settling capacity. Figure 3 identifies a narrow range for the $Q/\Sigma$ value from $3.1\times10^{-9}$ to $4.1\times10^{-9}$ m/s as the preferred operating zone. For cell culture clarification with a DSC, Pham (2010) recommended a $Q/\Sigma$ value ranging from $1.0\times10^{-9}$ to $2.6\times10^{-8}$ m/s. However, Maybury et al. (2000) and Iammarino et al. (2007) experimentally observed a 6%–10% reduction in clarification efficiency based on the culture viability as the $Q/\Sigma$ value increased from $3.4\times10^{-9}$ m/s to $1.35\times10^{-8}$ m/s [13, 14]. This observation by Maybury and Iammarino is in alignment with the centrifuge design space in Figure 3, which also shows a reduction in clarification efficiency with increasing $Q/\Sigma$.

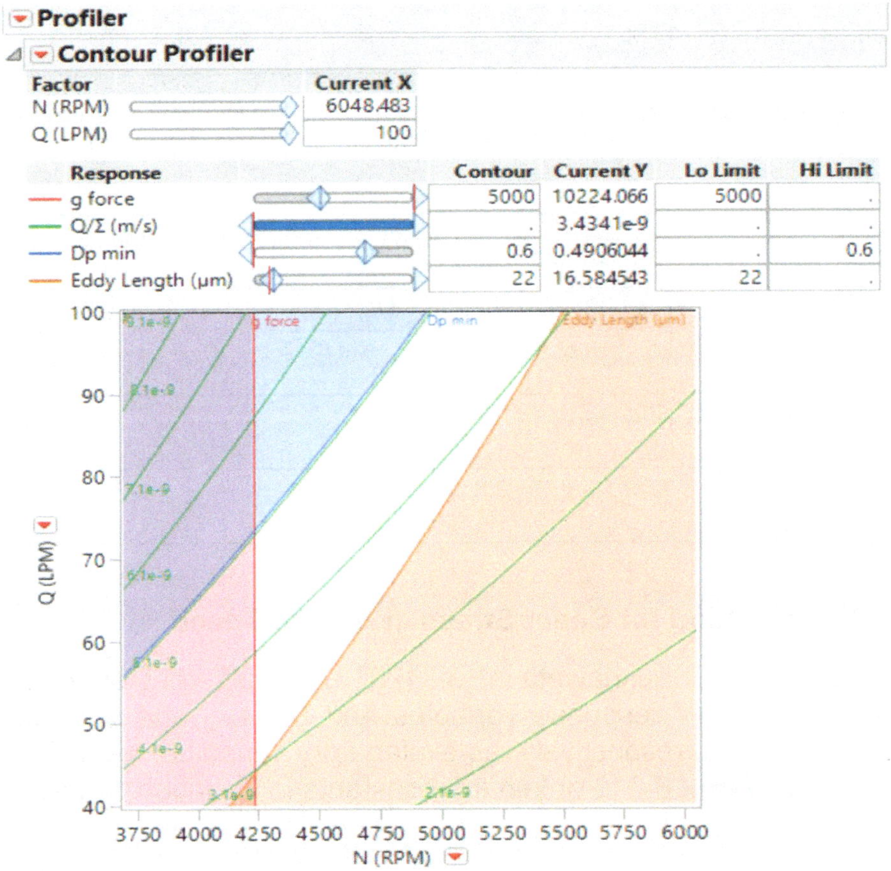


**Figure 3: Operational design space DSC.**

**Method 2: Tip Speed Model (TSM)**

**Average shear stress:** Schlichting (1979) reported that the maximum shear stress ($\tau_{max}$) for a fluid flow over the rotating surface of a disc can be obtained from Equation 11 [20]. Here, $\vartheta_{tip}$ is the tip velocity of the disc at radius R. The average shear across the disc is given by the average between the shear stress at $R_o$ and $R_i$, as shown in Equation 12.

**Shear stress exposure time:** The impact of shear on mammalian cells depends not only on the magnitude of the shear stress but also on the shear stress exposure time. Ludwig et al. (1992) reported that the critical shear stress at which cell morphology is impacted ranges from 0.75 to 1.0 $N/m^2$ over a duration of 24 h. For shorter exposure durations up to 1 h, Ludwig reported that cells can tolerate higher stresses, up to 20 $N/m^2$ [21]. Bae et al. (2016) reported that shear stress greater than 250 $N/m^2$ is required to induce mechanical damage in CHO cells [23]. Therefore, the duration of exposure to a shear field is an important component to consider when modeling cell damage. The residence time of a cell particle along the axial distance in the annular space between the discs of a DSC is given by Equation 13 [4]. Pham et al. (2022) reported on cell damage as a function of both shear stress and the duration of shear field exposure using a power-law model, as shown in Equation 14 [24].

| Box C: Method 2: Shear assessment based on the TSM | |
|---|---|
| Equation 11 | $\tau_{max} = 0.322.\mu_L.\vartheta_{tip}.\left(\frac{\rho_L.\vartheta_{tip}}{\mu_L.R}\right)^{1/2}$ ; $\vartheta_{tip} = \frac{2.\pi.R_o.N}{60}$ ; $R = R_0\ for\ \tau_{max}\ at\ R_o$, $R = R_i\ for\ \tau_{max}\ at\ R_i$ |
| Equation 12 | $\tau_{Avg} = \frac{\tau_{max,o} + \tau_{max,i}}{2}$ |
| Equation 13 | $t_s = \frac{\pi.(R_o^2 - R_i^2).d_a}{Q}$; $d_a = \frac{(R_o - R_i)}{\sin\theta}$ |
| Equation 14 | $Cell\ damage\ index\ = k.\tau_{avg}{}^{\alpha}.t_s{}^{\beta}$ |
| Equation 15 | $LDH\ (ppm) = 3.8\ \tau_{avg}{}^{1.3}.t_s{}^{0.43}$ |

## Cell Damage Index and Model Fitting for Shear Stress at the Tip Speed

Using the LDH values reported by Shekhawata et al. (2018) for different operating conditions in a Culturefuge 100™ as response variables and the $\tau_{avg}$ and $t_s$ values calculated from Equations 12 and 13, respectively, as explanatory variables, we utilized the Model Fit function in JMP version 16.0 to obtain the constants in Equation 14 as k = 3.8, α = 1.3, and β = 0.43.

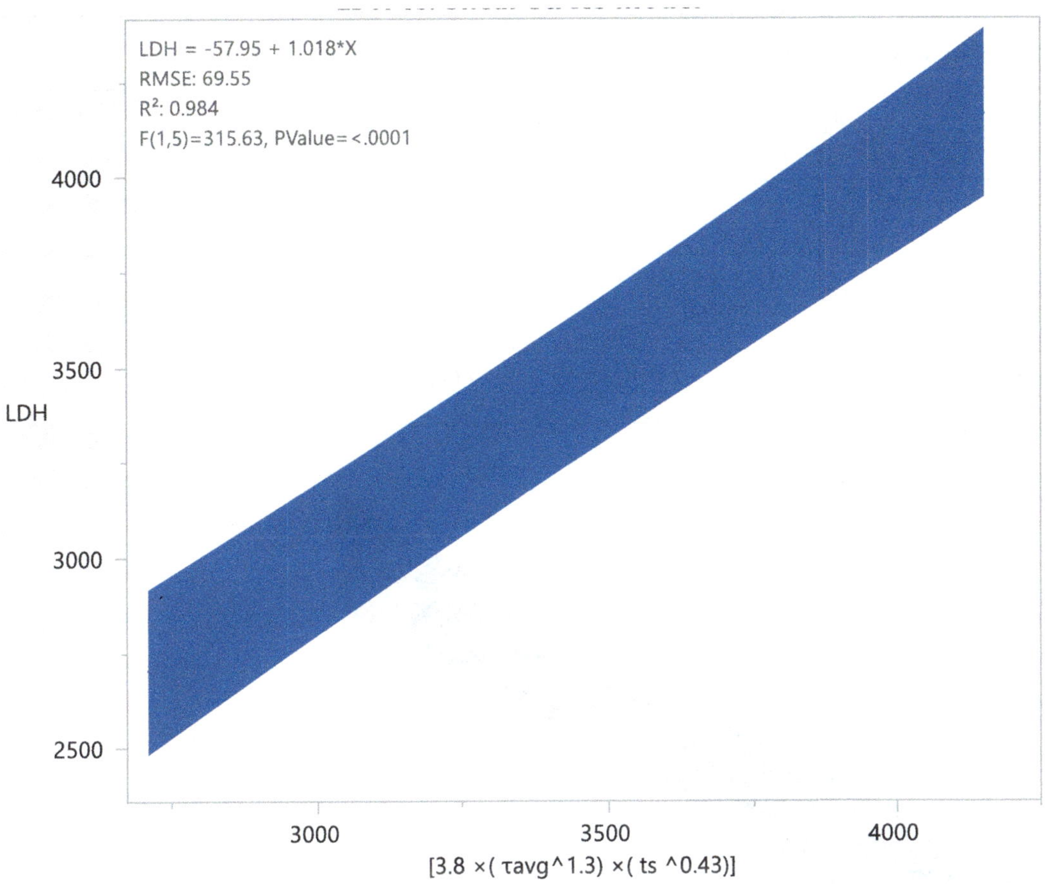


**Figure 4: Predictability of shear produced in a DSC according to the TSM.**

Figure 4 shows the linear relationship between LDH concentration and Equation 15. The $R^2$ value for the prediction expression is a statistical measure of how well the prediction expression can fit the actual data. The $R^2$ value of 0.98 demonstrates that the predictive expression is reliable. Additionally, the p-value of <0.0001 demonstrates that the strength of association between the input variable ($3.8 \times \tau_{avg}^{1.3} \times t_s^{0.43}$) and output prediction (LDH concentration) has a high degree of statistical significance. The p-value of <0.0001 also indicates that 99.99% of the variability in the LDH concentration is explained by ($3.8 \times \tau_{avg}^{1.3} \times t_s^{0.43}$). Therefore, holding ($3.8 \times \tau_{avg}^{1.3} \times t_s^{0.43}$) as a constant may be an effective method for maintaining a similar shear across different scales of DSC operation.

## Method 3: Power Dissipation Model (PDM)

**Average shear stress:** Murrell (1998) demonstrated that the power dissipated in the feed zone of a DSC can be calculated via Equation 16. Here, $\omega$ is the angular velocity in 1/s. Similar to the TSM, the impact of the dissipated power on the cells depends on the duration over which the cells are exposed to the power, calculated as the centrifuge bowl residence time ($t_{Rb}$) by Equation 17. Here, $V_b$ is the centrifuge bowl volume. Now, the cell damage index can be expressed by a power law as a function of both the dissipated power and the bowl residence time, as shown in Equation 18. The constants in Equation 18 are identified as $k = 0.16$, $\alpha = 0.98$, and $\beta = 1.4$ based on the same cell damage index and model fitting method described above.

| Box D: Method 3: Shear assessment based on the PDM | |
|---|---|
| Equation 16 | $P_{dis} = \frac{1}{2}.Q.\rho_L.R_o^2.\omega^2 + \frac{1}{2}.Q.\rho_L.(R_o^2 - R_i^2).\omega^2, where\ \omega = \frac{2\pi N}{60}$ |
| Equation 17 | $t_{RB} = \frac{V_b}{Q}$ |
| Equation 18 | $Cell\ damage\ index\ = LDH\ (ppm) = k\ P_{Dis}{}^{\alpha}.t_{RB}{}^{\beta}$ |
| Equation 19 | $LDH\ (ppm) = 0.16\ P_{Dis}{}^{0.98}.t_{RB}{}^{1.4}$ |

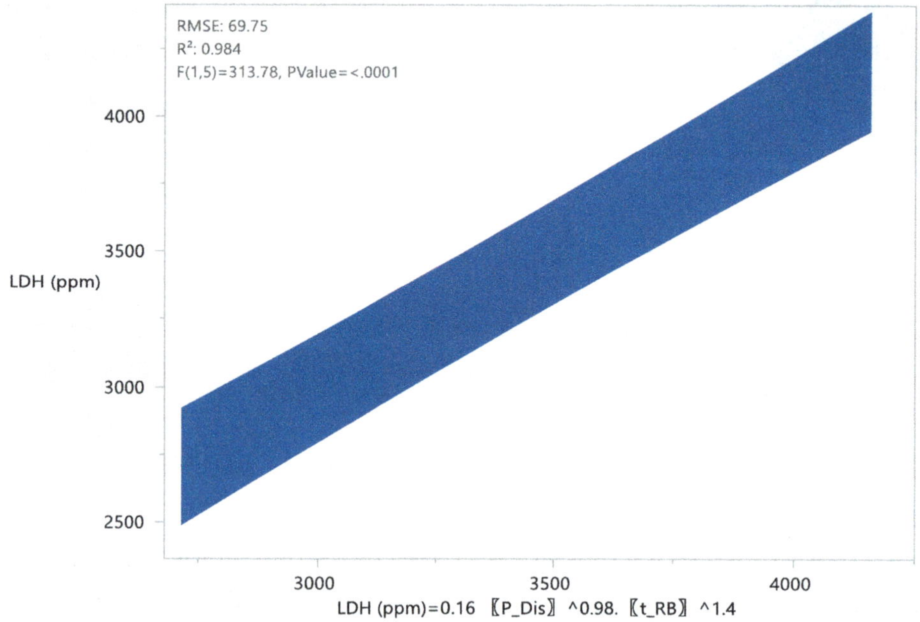


**Figure 5: Predictability of shear produced in a DSC based on the PDM.**

Figure 5 shows the linear relationship between LDH concentration and Equation 19. The $R^2$ value for the prediction expression is a statistical measure of how well the prediction expression can fit the actual data. The $R^2$ value of 0.98 demonstrates that the predictive expression is reliable. Additionally, the p-value of <0.0001 demonstrates that the strength of association between the input variable (Equation 19) and output prediction (LDH concentration) has a high degree of statistical significance. The p-value of <0.0001 also indicates that 99.99% of the LDH variability is explained by Equation 19. Therefore, maintaining a constant value of ($3.9 \times P_{Dis}{}^{1.3} \times t_{RB}{}^{0.49}$) may be an effective method for ensuring a similar shear across different scales of DSC operation.

## Conclusion

DSCs are widely used for cell culture clarification in large-scale biologics manufacturing. Although a well-established Q/Σ method is available for scaling centrifuge operating conditions based on the settling efficiency, our current knowledge of shear assessment in DSC operation is esoteric and not readily available. Therefore, we have presented shear assessment calculations using three different methods and have illustrated the application of these concepts by designing a contour profile that presents a balance between the particle settling capacity and shear as a function of bowl speed and centrifuge feed flow rate.

## References


1. Beckett, P. (2014, September 1). Determining the Best Approach for Carrying Out Clarification Operations. Genetic Engineering & Biotechnology News, 34(15).

2. Richardson, A., & Walker, J. (2018, July 25). Continuous solids are discharging centrifugation to clarify high-cell-density mammalian cell cultures. BioProcess International.

https://bioprocessintl.com/downstream-processing/separation-purification/continuous-solids-discharging-centrifugation-a-solution-to-the-challenges-of-clarifying-high-cell-density-mammalian-cell-cultures/

3. Joseph, A., Kenty, B., Mollet, M., Hwang, K., Rose, S., Goldrick, S., Bender, J., Farid, S. S., & Titchener-Hooker, N. (2016). A scale-down mimic for mapping the process performance of centrifugation, depth, and sterile filtration. Biotechnology and Bioengineering, 113(9), 1934–1941. https://doi.org/10.1002/bit.25967

4. Pham, C. Y. (2010, July 20). Use of depth filtration in series with continuous centrifugation to clarify mammalian cell cultures.

5. Clark, D. S., & Blanch, H. W. (1997). Biochemical engineering (2nd ed.). CRC Press.

6. Mei, R. (1992). An approximate expression for the shear lift force on a spherical particle at finite Reynolds number. International Journal of Multiphase Flow, 18(1), 145-147. https://doi.org/10.1016/0301-9322(92)90012-6

7. Shekhawat, L. K., Sarkar, J., Gupta, R., Hadpe, S., & Rathore, A. S. (2018). Application of CFD in Bioprocessing: Separation of mammalian cells using disc stack centrifuge during production of biotherapeutics. Journal of Biotechnology, 267, 1-11. https://doi.org/10.1016/j.jbiotec.2017.12.016

8. Poon, C. (2020). Measuring the density and viscosity of culture media for optimized computational fluid dynamics analysis of microdevices.

https://doi.org/10.1101/2020.08.25.266221

9. Mannweiler, K. (1989). The recovery of biological particles in high-speed continuous centrifuges with special reference to feed-zone break-up effects [Doctoral dissertation]. https://discovery.ucl.ac.uk/id/eprint/1318045/

10. Nevers, N. D. (2005). Fluid mechanics for chemical engineers. McGraw-Hill Companies.

11. Sylaymon, A. H., & Alwared, A. I. (2016). Prediction of Drag Coefficient for Accelerated Single Sphere in Power Law Fluids. Arab Universities Journal of Engineering Sciences, 23(1), 141-153.

https://jaaru.org/index.php/auisseng/article/view/86/62

12. Muralidharan, N. (2023, February 9). Stirred-tank bioreactor scalability. BioProcess International.

https://bioprocessintl.com/upstream-processing/bioreactors/shear-proof-design-space-scaling-stirred-tank-bioreactors-for-cell-culture-processes/

13. Maybury, J. P., Hoare, M., & Dunnill, P. (2000). The use of laboratory centrifugation studies to predict the performance of industrial machines: Studies of shear-insensitive and shear-sensitive materials. Biotechnology and Bioengineering, 67(3), 265-273. https://doi.org/10.1002/(sic)1097-0290(20000205)67:3<265::aid-bit2>3.0.co;2-j

14. Iammarino, M., Nti-Gyabaah, J., Chandler, M., Roush, D., & K. (2007, November 1). Impact of cell density and viability on primary clarification of mammalian cell broth. BioProcess International.

https://bioprocessintl.com/downstream-processing/filtration/impact-of-cell-density-and-viability-on-primary-clarification-of-mammalian-cell-broth-110120075/

15. Clift, R., Grace, J. R., & Weber, M. E. (2005). Bubbles, drops, and particles. Courier Corporation.

16. Ambler, C. M. (1959). The theory of scaling up laboratory data for the sedimentation type centrifuge. Journal of Biochemical and Microbiological Technology and Engineering, 1(2), 185-205.

https://doi.org/10.1002/jbmte.390010206

17. Parau, M., Johnson, T. F., Pullen, J., & Bracewell, D. G. (2022). Analysis of fouling and breakthrough of process-related impurities during depth filtration using confocal microscopy. Biotechnology Progress.

https://aiche.onlinelibrary.wiley.com/doi/full/10.1002/btpr.3233

18. Maschke, R. W., Seidel, S., Bley, T., Eibl, R., & Eibl, D. (2022). Determination of culture design spaces in shaken disposable cultivation systems for CHO suspension cell cultures. Biochemical Engineering Journal, 177, 108224. https://doi.org/10.1016/j.bej.2021.108224

19. Nienow, A. W. (2020). The impact of fluid dynamic stress in stirred bioreactors – The scale of the biological entity: A personal view. Chemie Ingenieur Technik, 93(1-2), 17-30. https://doi.org/10.1002/cite.202000176

20. Boychyn, M., Yim, S., Ayazi Shamlou, P., Bulmer, M., More, J., & Hoare, M. (2001). Characterization of flow intensity in continuous centrifuges for the development of laboratory mimics. Chemical Engineering Science, 56(16), 4759-4770. https://doi.org/10.1016/s0009-2509(01)00139-7

21. Ludwig, A., Kretzmer, G., & Schügerl, K. (1992). Determination of a "critical shear stress level" applied to adherent mammalian cells. Enzyme and microbial technology, 14(3), 209–213. https://doi.org/10.1016/0141-0229(92)90068-y

22. Doran, P. M. (2013). Bioprocess engineering principles. Academic Press.

23. Bae, Y. B., Jang, H. K., Shin, T. H., Phukan, G., Tran, T. T., Lee, G., Hwang, W. R., & Kim, J. M. (2016). Microfluidic assessment of mechanical cell damage by extensional stress. Lab on a Chip, 16(1), 96-103.

https://doi.org/10.1039/c5lc01006c

24. Pham, O. L., Feher, S. E., Nguyen, Q. T., & Papavassiliou, D. V. (2022). Distribution and history of extensional stresses on vWF surrogate molecules in turbulent flow. Scientific Reports, 12(1). https://doi.org/10.1038/s41598-021-04034-9

25. Aktiengesellschaft, S. (2002, March 1). Concentration and lysis of adenovirus-infected cells in a single unit operation. US Patent, Patent Application and Patent Search - Justia Patents Search. https://patents.justia.com/patent/6773909

# Chapter 5: Process Validation: Pre-Filtration Dirty-Hold Time for Upstream Media and Feed Solutions and its Implications for Establishing In-Process Microbial Control

**Naveenganesh Muralidharan, Emma Bolduc, Thatsinee Johnson, and Mark Davis**

## Introduction

Biopharmaceutical manufacturing processes require that prepared raw materials and product intermediates be held at different stages of the process. However, during the hold time, the process and product intermediates are susceptible to microbial risk due to the presence of bioburden, endotoxins, and exotoxins. Microbial risks arise from a variety of sources, including the facility, equipment, process operations, source of raw materials used, and microbial growth-promoting nature of the prepared intermediate material itself.

The Food and Drug Administration's Guidance for Industry Sterile Drug Products Produced by Aseptic Processing states that "the time limits established for the various production phases should be supported by at-scale data. Bioburden and endotoxin load should be assessed when establishing time limits" [1]. Furthermore, the United States Pharmacopeial USP<1115> states that "manufacturers must properly establish processing hold times considering whether processing steps and hold times could result in changes to bioburden" [2,3]. Therefore, studies on the pre-sterilization filtration hold time must be performed at the manufacturing scale in order to generate microbial data to ensure that the change in microbial load is controlled before the sterilization process.

Preferably, studies on the pre-sterilization microbial hold time should be performed during engineering runs prior to process performance qualification (PPQ) runs or at least during the PPQ runs. Once the maximum pre-filtration hold times are established before or during the PPQ batches, the routine microbial monitoring for pre-filtration upstream media and feed solutions samples may not be required during regular production batches. However, periodic non-routine sampling and monitoring may be performed annually or after a prolonged shutdown period [11]. Furthermore, the unprocessed bulk harvest [UB] samples taken from the production bioreactor are tested for bioburden and endotoxin from all manufacturing batches. The UB sample from the production bioreactor is representative of the entire upstream processes, including raw materials, media, and feed solutions. Hence, the routine monitoring and sampling of pre-filtration media and feed solutions will be a redundant check and may not be value added to the microbial control strategy of the upstream process.

The upstream cell culture media and feed solutions are often sterilized via 0.22-μm filtration. Therefore, pre-sterilization is also referred to as pre-filtration in this article.

Upstream cell culture growth and production media are nutrient-rich, with a neutral pH and a preparation temperature of 25°C – 40°C that supports the growth of most microbes [3]. Therefore, this article emphasizes quantifiable risk assessment methodology for determining the appropriate pre-filtration hold time to ensure that the microbial risk is suitably controlled during the manufacturing process. The risk assessment is based on a conservative calculation that models the change in bioburden load, risk of filtration failure, and impurity safety factor for exotoxins and endotoxins.

**Pre-Filtration Hold Time Challenge for Assessment:** At our company's facility, among all of the batch volumes prepared in upstream operations, the longest preparation time corresponds to the 20,000-L production bioreactor cell culture media. Although medium preparation and filtration are typically performed within a duration $T_p$= 3 hours) from the time of addition of the first component, a four-fold longer preparation time ($4T_p$) is assessed as a challenge for microbial control. The selection of $4T_p$= 12 hours assumes that this four-fold preparation time is a good approximation for addressing any unforeseen issues in manufacturing operations.

**Data-based Microbial Load at Time t=0:** In-house pre-filtration microbial hold samples at time t=0 have been consistently shown to have a bioburden of ≤ 1 colony-forming unit (CFU)/mL for a sample size of 12. However, the cell culture medium preparation is performed in a sanitary, controlled Class-8 clean room rather than a sterile environment. Therefore, there should be some amount of microbial load at the initial time point.

As with any other assay, the bioburden assay is also prone to false-negative results. False negative errors in bioburden analysis might be from non-homogeneous bioburden distribution in the test solution, sample handling error from pipetting during dilutions, and recovery efficiency of bioburden in the assay. In the above-listed errors, both non-homogeneous bioburden distribution and sampling handling errors are inherent to the method itself. However, the error in the recovery of micro-organisms in the bioburden assay is attributed to bioburden density in the test solution and the test volume that is specific to the process. Low bioburden test volume and low microbial load in test solution can both increase the chances of false negative results. In such instances, when bioburden results of the non-sterile sample are reported as below the detectable limit, then the most probable bioburden concentration in the test solution can be calculated for an acceptable chance of false negative results as detailed in step-1 and step-2, as discussed below based on the method detailed by Yang (2013).

**False negative error from bioburden test volume and bioburden density in test solution:**

The European Medicines Agency (EMA) recommends a minimum of 100 mL as the test volume for a bioburden assay, with 10 CFU as an acceptable limit for the pre-sterile filtration bioburden for a sterile drug product. Yang (2013) showed a relationship between the false acceptance probability Vs bioburden test volume and bioburden density in the test solution. Yang (2013) statistically showed that the sensitivity of a bioburden assay in EMA recommended 100-mL test volume to detect 10 CFU is 41.2%; in other words, the probability of falsely accepting a contaminated batch is (100%–41.2%=58.8%). Now, using this information, Field. R (2013) showed the minimum bioburden level in the test solution for different test volumes below 100mL to have a detectability equivalent to 41.2% [36]. Eq.1 is derived from the data provided by Field R (2013) using a non-linear exponential 5-P decay model with JMP14.

**Step-1:** Using Eq.1, one can calculate what is the minimum bioburden limit in a specific test volume to have an assay sensitivity of 41.2%.

$$CFU/100mL_{41.2\%} = 9.87 + 3.6e^{(-0.033v_t)} + 16.4^{(-0.15v_t)} \qquad \text{Eq. (1)}$$

Here, CFU/100mL$_{41.2\%}$ is the minimum bioburden load in test solution at different bioburden test volumes $V_t$ to have a sensitivity of 41.2%, which is equal to detecting 10 CFU in 100-mL test volume.

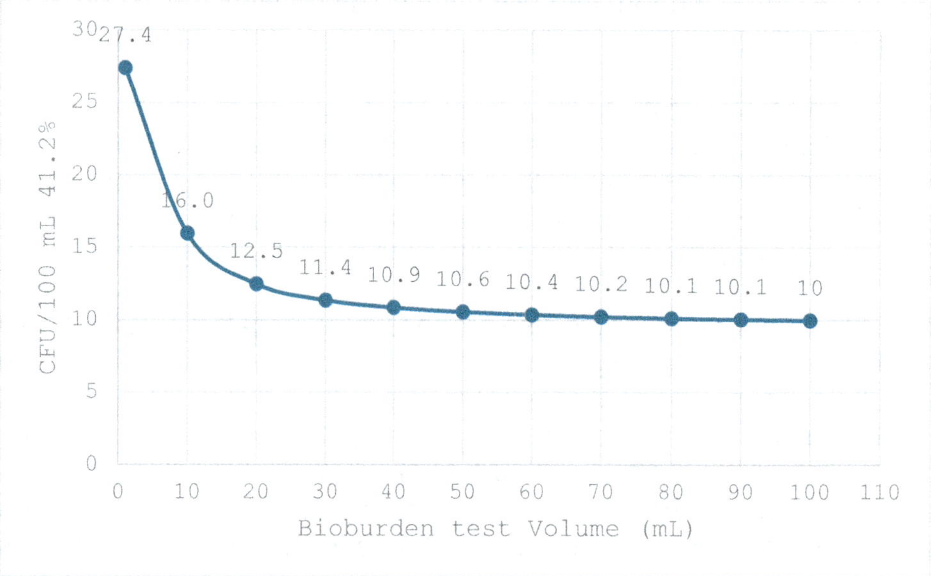


**Figure 1: Minimum microbial load in a bioburden test volume with a sensitivity (41.2%) equal to that of a 100-mL test volume to detect 10 CFU.**

**Step 2:** Using the minimum bioburden concentration calculated for the sensitivity of 41.2% for the respective test volume, as shown in Figure 1, one can also calculate the probability of false negative results at different bioburden concentrations in test solutions at respective test volumes by applying negative binomial distribution model as shown equation-2 [4].

$$P_{false,neg} = 1 - NEGBINOM(F, S, p, True) \qquad \text{Eq. (2)}$$

Where,

$P_{false,\ neg}$ = probability of false negative results of bioburden test.

NEGBINOM: Returns the negative binomial distribution, the probability that there will be "F" failures before the "S" success, with "$P_s$" probability of a success.

F is the bioburden concentration in test solution ranging from 1 CFU/100mL

S is the $CFU/100mL_{41.2\%}$ is the minimum microbial load in a bioburden test volume with a sensitivity of 41.2% for different bioburden test volumes calculated using equation 1.

$P_s$ probability of a success is 41.2%.

Figure 2 shows the false negative probability of the bioburden test at different test volumes and bioburden concentration in test solution using equation 2.

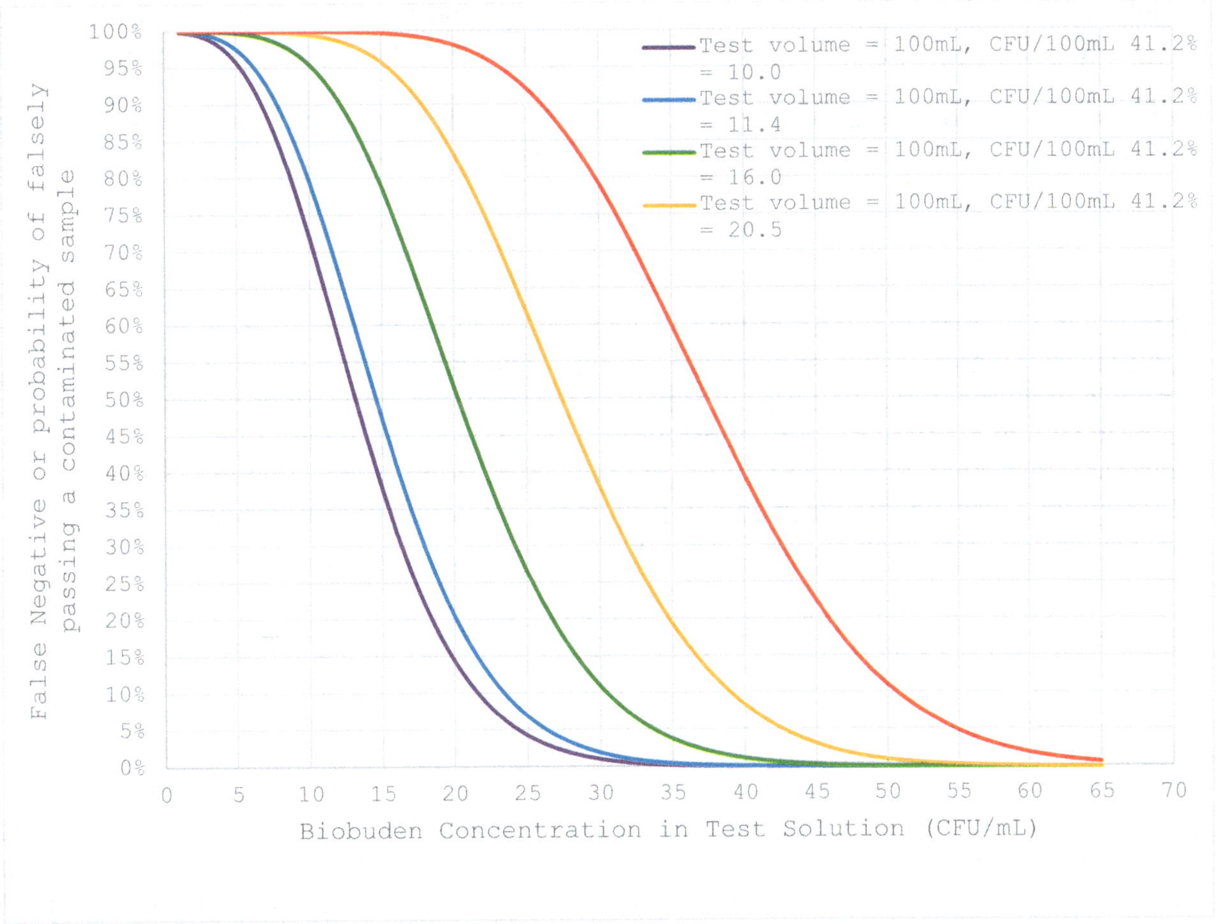


**Figure 2: False negative probability of bioburden test at different test volumes and bioburden concentrations in the test solution.**

From Figure 2, at an acceptable false negative risk of 0.05 on the bioburden test result, for 1mL test volume, the bioburden concentration in the test solution is 55 CFU/100mL. This value is used as the initial bioburden load at the start of the medium preparation, $X_0$ in equation 3, to calculate the change in bioburden load over the hold period.

For any preparation the microbial risks are sourced from starting raw materials and Improperly cleaned or contaminated equipment. Assuming the media preparation is performed in a clean container and in a classified clean room, the major source of bioburden is raw material. For formulation of typical chemically defined (CD) cell culture liquid media, approximately at least 95% of mass constitutes Water for Injection (WFI), and the remaining is constituted using dry powdered cell culture growth supplements [47]. For WFI, the maximum acceptable bioburden limit is 10 CFU/100mL per USP 29 <1231>, and for the dry powdered cell culture supplements, humidity at packing is ≤ 1% to ensure stability [46], which is less than the humidity to promote any microbial growth (USP<1112> reported no microbial growth below water activity of 0.6, which is equivalent to the humidity of 60%). Considering the formulated media constitutes 95% of WFI with a maximum bioburden limit of 10 CFU/mL, and the remaining less than 5% of dry powdered supplement is micro-static in nature over a short period from the time of dispensing to usage. A bioburden load of 55 CFU/100mL is a good conservative estimate for time (t=0).

**Modeling Bioburden Proliferation during the Pre-Filtration Hold Time:** The increase in bioburden load for different hold times is calculated by using Eq. 3 [5].

$$X_i = X_0 \times e^{(\Delta t \times \mu)} \qquad \text{Eq. (3)}$$

Here, $X_0$ is the microbial load at time t=0 as calculated from Eq. 1, $X_i$ is the bioburden load at time t=i, and μ is the specific growth rate. The value of the specific growth rate (μ) is heavily influenced by media preparation temperature. Often, most cell culture media are prepared at ambient room temperature (15°C to 25°C) to avoid nutrient degradation. Therefore, a preparation temperature of 21°C is a good approximation. Rosso et al. (1993) gave a cardinal growth model to predict the Influence of temperature on microbial-specific growth rate, as shown in Eq.4 [16].

$$\mu = \frac{\mu_{max} \times (T - T_{min})^2 \times (T - T_{max})}{(T_{opt} - T_{min}) \times [(T_{opt} - T_{min}) \times (T - T_{opt}) - (T_{opt} - T_{max}) \times (T_{opt} + T_{min} - 2T)]} \qquad \text{Eq. (4)}$$

Where,

$\mu_{max}$ is the maximum specific growth rate. As a conservative approach, the ($\mu_{max}$) is assumed for *Escherichia coli*, one of the fastest-doubling bacterial species with the doubling time $T_d$ of 20 min or 0.3 hr [17] from which the value of $\mu_{max}$ is calculated as 2.1 $hr^{-1}$ using the equation, $\mu_{max}$= Ln(2)/$T_d$, where Ln(2) is the natural logarithm of 2.

$T_{min}$ and $T_{max}$ are minimum and maximum temperatures, respectively, at which microbial growth is no longer observed, and $T_{opt}$ refers to the optimum temperature for microbial growth. Rosson et al.(1993) showed for E.coli, $T_{min}$ = 4.9°C, $T_{opt}$= 41.4°C, and $T_{max}$=45.8°C. [18]. Applying all the above assumptions and media preparation temperature T= 21°C, the calculated value for μ using Eq.3 is 0.5 $hr^{-1,}$ which can be substituted in Eq- 2 to calculate the change in microbial load over hold time.

**Post-filtration Risk:** The post-filtration risk is defined as the probability of having at least 1 CFU pass through the filtration system. This risk can be calculated via Eq. 5 [6]:

$$R_{pf} = 1 - (1 - p_1)^{(V_f \times X_i)} \qquad \text{Eq. (5)}$$

Where $R_{pf}$ is the post-filtration risk for upstream media and feed, any microbial breach is frequently identified by a reduction in pH and/or in the dissolved oxygen trend in the bioreactor early in the process, prior to the purification process, well before the batch is released. Therefore, based on the batch run rate, an $R_{pf}$ value of $10^{-3}$ is well accepted in practice, indicating that only 1 out of 1,000 batches would have a microbial breakthrough during filtration. For a run rate of 10 batches in a 20,000-L production bioreactor per year, one batch per 100 years is an acceptable risk.

The term ($V_f \times X_i$) gives the total microbial load in the solution challenging the 0.22-µm filters (mL/cm$^2$ × CFU/mL= CFU/cm$^2$). $V_f$ is the filtrate throughput in mL/cm$^2$, and $X_i$ is the bioburden load in CFU/mL. $p_1$ is the probability that one bacterium to successfully pass through a filer membrane per cm$^2$, which follows a binomial distribution. $p_1$ can be derived from the binomial confidence interval, calculated as shown in Eq. 6 [6-7].

$$p_1 = \frac{F.DIST(\alpha, S+1, N)}{N + F.DIST(\alpha, S+1, N)} \qquad \text{Eq. (6)}$$

Here, F.Dist calculates the cumulative probability density function for the F Distribution in Microsoft Excel. Statistical confidence (1-α) is assumed to be 0.95 by default. Therefore, α = 0.05 in Eq.6, S is the number of successful events ( Here, the event is defined as be number of bacteria to penetrate through the sterile filter area. Therefore, for one bacterium to go through a sterile filter area, the event (S) is assumed to be =1, and N is the number of trials required for achieving at least one successful event; N is equal to the maximum retention capacity of the filter obtained from filter manufacturers certificate of analysis (COA). In most cases, 0.22-µm sterile filters in the market are rated for a microbial retention capacity of 1E7 CFU per square centimeter based on bacterial species Brevundimonas diminuta.

In the biologics manufacturing process, pre-filtration is often performed using 0.45 µm pore size membrane filters before 0.22 µm sterile filtration. Carter. J (1996) showed a bacterial retention capacity of $10^4$ CFU/cm$^2$ using Pseudomonas diminuta for 0.45 µm pore size membrane filters [27], and PDA technical article No.26 reported the microbial penetration is observed through 0.45 µm pore size membrane filters when challenged with microbial load above $10^{-4}$ to $10^{-6}$ per cm$^2$ [28]. Therefore, conservatively maximum microbial retention capacity (N) for 0.45 µm pore size membrane filters is assumed to be $10^4$ CFU/cm$^2$. In such prefiltration usage instances, the post-filtration risk is calculated independently for 0.45 µm and 0.22 µm pore size membrane filters using Eq-4, and then the risks for both 0.45 µm and 0.22 µm pore size membrane filters are multiplied to get the post-filtration risk on combined set up of prefiltration followed by the post filtration system.

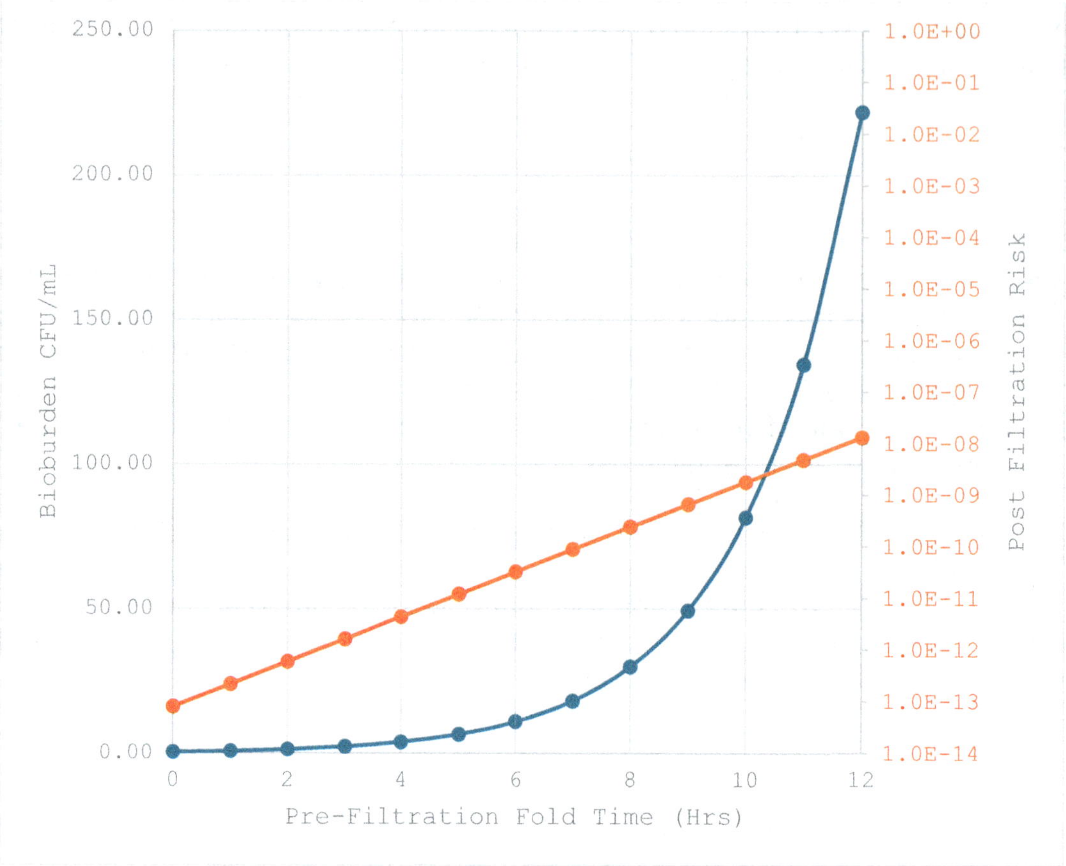


**Figure 3: Change in microbial load and post-filtration risk vs. pre-filtration hold time.**

**Bioburden Acceptance Criteria Vs. Bioburden Load Challenge before Filtration:** Sandle, T. (2022) reported that a maximum pre-sterilization bioburden limit of 1,000 CFU/mL is a suitable limit for the starting material or first stage of a manufacturing process [8]. As shown in Figure 1, the calculated bioburden load after a pre-filtration hold time of $4T_p$= 12 hours is 4.5 folds below the limit of 1,000 CFU/mL = 221 CFU/mL.

**Risk-based Approach for Calculating Pre-Filtration Bioburden Acceptance Criteria:** Yang (2013) presented a risk-based approach for calculating pre-filtration bioburden acceptance criteria, where post-filtration risk is set based on the risk assessment, then pre-filtration bioburden acceptance criteria is calculated as a function of filter area, filtrate volume and maximum retention capacity of the sterile filter that are specific to the process as shown in equation-7. Eq 7 is obtained by re-arranging terms in equation 4.

$$x_{Accp} \leq \left[\frac{\ln(1 - R_{pf})}{\ln(1 - P_1)}\right] \div V_f \qquad \text{Eq. (7)}$$

Box 1 shows the sample Calculation for setting the pre-filtration Bioburden limit.

| **Box-1: Sample Calculation for setting pre-filtration Bioburden limit** |
|---|
| **Step 1:** Calculate the Filtrate throughput in (mL/cm$^2$); for the purpose of illustration, media throughput (**$V_f$**) of 1000 L/m$^2$ equivalent to 100 mL/cm$^2$ is assumed.<br><br>**Step 2:** Setting post-filtration risk (**$R_{pf}$**) based on risk assessment. Acceptable risks are wider in upstream processes and get tighter toward the end of the downstream processes. Using the risk assessment matrix as shown in Table-1, for upstream media and feed pre-filtration, the risk is classified as low, and thereby the post-filtration risk is selected as 1.0E-3.<br><br>**Step 3:** Calculate the **(p1)** the probability that one bacterium will successfully pass through one cm$^2$ filter area.<br><br>$$p_1 = \frac{F.DIST(0.05,(1+1),1E7)}{N + F.DIST(0.05,(1+1),1E7)} = 4.9 \times 10^{-09}$$<br><br>**Step 4:** Calculate the minimum acceptable bioburden limit.<br><br>$$x_{Accp} \leq \left[\frac{\ln(1-1\times10^{-3})}{\ln(1-4.9\times10^{-9})}\right] \div \left[100\,\frac{mL}{cm^2}\right] = 2{,}041\ \text{CFU/mL}$$<br><br>To mitigate any potential risk of a microbial breach during sterile filtration, as a good design practice, sterile filters are often oversized, and therefore, the calculated minimum bioburden acceptance criteria using this procedure is often going to be larger than the recommended 1000 CFU/mL by Sandle T (2022). Therefore, I advocate conservatively using 1000 CFU/mL as acceptance criteria and verify the suitability of using 1000 CFU/mL by risk assessment using calculation as detailed in Box-1. |

**Table 1: Risk Assessment Matrix for Setting Post-Filtration Risk**

| Severity [s] | Occurrence [C] | Detectability [D] | Score | RPN =[S]×[C]×[D] | Risk Category | Post Filtration Risk $R_{pf}$ |
|---|---|---|---|---|---|---|
| No product impact, Potential Impact on the process at an early stage of the process before the start of purification | Effective controls are in place at multiple subsequent unit operations to fully mitigate the risk | Microbial safety is tested as (In-process control) IPC more than once before moving forward into the final DS formulation | 1 | 1 to 25 | Low | 1.0E-03 |

**Table 1: Risk Assessment Matrix for Setting Post-Filtration Risk**

| Severity [s] | Occurrence [C] | Detectability [D] | Score | RPN =[S]×[C]×[D] | Risk Category | Post Filtration Risk $R_{pf}$ |
|---|---|---|---|---|---|---|
| No product Impact or potential impact on the process during purification. | Only limited one stage controls are there before sterile drug formulation. However, not comprehensive enough to fully mitigate the risk at high confidence | Microbial safety is tested as IPC only once before moving forward with the final DS formulation | 3 | 26 to 50 | Medium | 1.0E-04 |
| Potential to impact product safety at the DS/ DP stage | No controls are in place | Microbial safety is tested only on formulated DS/DP | 5 | ≥ 51 | High | 1.0E-06 (1) |

(1) The sterility assurance level (SAL): A SAL of 10-6 means that there is less than or equal to one chance in a million that a single viable microorganism is present on a sterilized item [32].
(2)

The minimum acceptable pre-filtration bioburden limit calculated in (CFU/mL) using Eq.7 is plotted against the filtrate throughput (L/cm$^2$) for different post filtration risk is shown in Figure 4, which can be used as a handy tool.

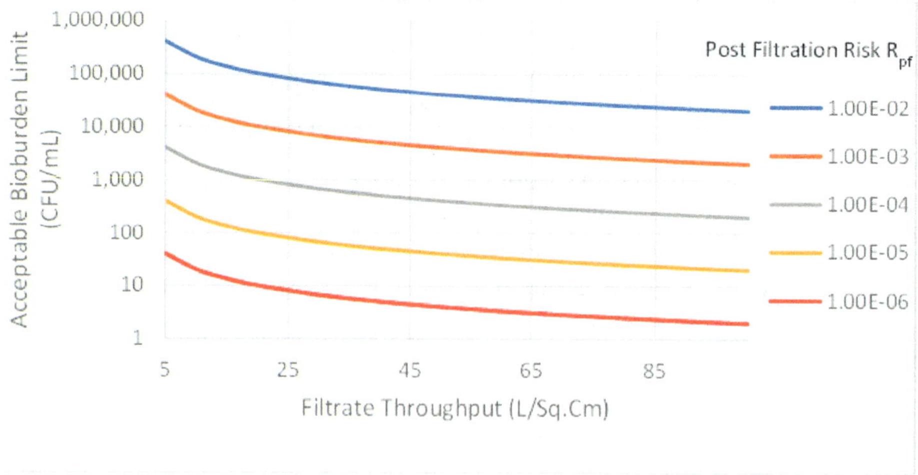


**Figure 4: Minimum acceptable pre-filtration bioburden limit in (CFU/mL) V.s the filtrate throughput (L/cm2) at different post-filtration risk**

**Change in Exotoxin Load and Clearance in Downstream:** Although a bioburden can be easily removed by 0.22-µm filtration, residual microbial by-products may be co-purified with the product and may have detrimental effects on patient safety and product quality. Microbial by-products that can have adverse effects on patient safety primarily include protein exotoxins (e.g., botulinum toxin A), non-protein exotoxins (e.g., aflatoxin, endotoxins, flagellin, microbial DNA, and cell wall polysaccharides). With the exception of endotoxins, there are no available good manufacturing practice (GMP) assays for detecting these microbial by-products. However, levels of exotoxin components can be calculated and compared with safety levels using worst-case assumptions [9].

The in-product impurity dose of produced exotoxin can be conservatively calculated, as shown in Eq. 8. Botulinum toxin-A is an exotoxin that presents safety concerns even at very low doses compared with other exotoxins. Therefore, botulinum A is used as the worst-case representation of all other exotoxins [11, 12].

$$IDP_{Exo} = \Sigma x_i \frac{CFU}{mL} \times Y_{Protein/cell} \frac{pg\ of\ protein}{CFU} \times 0.05\% \times DP \frac{mL}{Kg} \qquad \text{Eq. (8)}$$

Here, $IDP_{Exo}$ is the in-product impurity dose for exotoxin (pg/kg), $\Sigma X_i$ (CFU/mL) is the cumulative amount of microbial load produced until time t=i (Refer Figure:5 for details for calculation), Protein yield per microbial cell $Y_{protein/Cell}$ is assumed to be 0.165 pg of protein/microbial cell [19]. Wintzingerode, F. V. (2017) cited 0.05% of the bacterial protein mass as protein exotoxins. As a conservative approach all the total protein exotoxins calculated is considered as Botulinum-A [12].

The typical range of protein concentration in formulated drug product ranges from 50 and 150 mg/ml for monoclonal antibodies (mAbs) [20], with dosing quantity going as high as 10 mg/kg of patient weight [21]. DP is the drug product dose in mL/kg (for the purpose of illustration DP dose is conservatively calculated as 10 mg/Kg ÷ 50 mg/mL= 0.2 mL/kg of patient body weight.

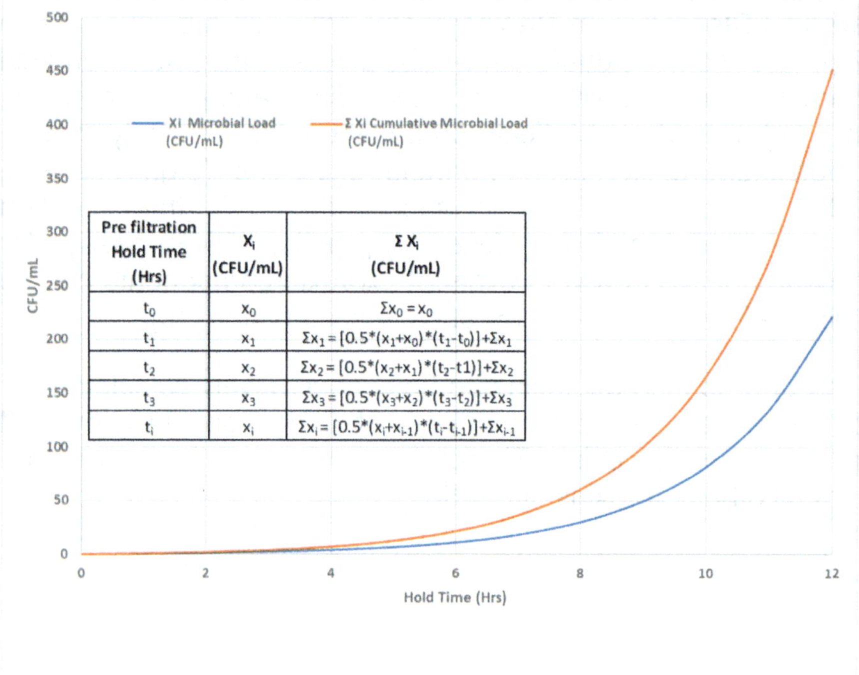


| Pre filtration Hold Time (Hrs) | $X_i$ (CFU/mL) | $\Sigma X_i$ (CFU/mL) |
|---|---|---|
| $t_0$ | $x_0$ | $\Sigma x_0 = x_0$ |
| $t_1$ | $x_1$ | $\Sigma x_1 = [0.5*(x_1+x_0)*(t_1-t_0)]+\Sigma x_1$ |
| $t_2$ | $x_2$ | $\Sigma x_2 = [0.5*(x_2+x_1)*(t_2-t1)]+\Sigma x_2$ |
| $t_3$ | $x_3$ | $\Sigma x_3 = [0.5*(x_3+x_2)*(t_3-t_2)]+\Sigma x_3$ |
| $t_i$ | $x_i$ | $\Sigma x_i = [0.5*(x_i+x_{i-1})*(t_i-t_{i-1})]+\Sigma x_{i-1}$ |

**Figure 5: $\Sigma X_i$ is the cumulative amount of microbial load produced until time t= i (CFU/mL)**

**Exotoxin Clearance Across Protein A Chromatography:** In biologics manufacturing processes, protein A affinity chromatography is typically the first step in purification. The interaction between IgG and protein A has been shown to be highly specific, and this affinity mode of chromatography enables the removal of >99% of process impurities in a single step, starting directly from complex solutions such as cell culture clarified harvest media [23]. Therefore, both exotoxins and endotoxins should be substantially cleared by a protein affinity column process. An exotoxin spike study demonstrated a 1.9 log reduction value (LRV) or 98.7% clearance over MabSelect SuRe [13]. Thus, as a conservative approach, an LRV of 1 may be used for exotoxin clearance calculations.

**Exotoxin Clearance Across Cation Exchange (CEx) Chromatography:** The net protein surface charge changes with the pH of the buffer based on the iso-electric point (PI). At a pH equal to the PI, the protein will carry no net charge. At a pH below the PI, the protein attains a net positive charge; similarly, at a pH above the PI, the protein will attain a net negative charge.

The CEx step is performed in a bind/elute mode. Typically, the buffer has a pH of 4–6, which is below the PI (>7) of most monoclonal antibodies (mAbs). At a buffer pH between 4 and 6, the mAb attains a positive charge, allowing it to bind negatively charged resin. The PI for exotoxins is approximately 2.5. Therefore, exotoxin impurities attain a negative charge and will flow through the chromatography column; thus, the exotoxins should be greatly cleared by the CEx step of the process. An exotoxin spike study showed an LRV of 2.9 in clearance over CEx chromatography [13]. Thus, as a conservative approach, an LRV of 3 may be used for exotoxin clearance calculations across the overall purification process.

**Change in Endotoxin Load:** Endotoxin A is a pyrogenic product present in the bacterial cell wall, which can lead to adverse reactions ranging from fever to death in a patient, even at a trace concentration of 0.1 ng per kg patient body weight. Thus, endotoxins present another risk associated with the microbial load that arises when process intermediates are held. Liposaccharide or endotoxin is produced at $10^{-15}$ g per gram of typical negative bacterium. Endotoxins are reported in endotoxin units (EU), where 0.1 ng is equal to 1 EU [15]. The in-product impurity dose for endotoxins during the pre-filtration medium hold time is calculated as shown in Eq. 9

$$IDP_{endo} = \Sigma X_i \frac{CFU}{mL} \times \frac{10^{-06} ng\ of\ Endotoxin}{CFU} \times DP \frac{mL}{Kg} \qquad \text{Eq. (9)}$$

**Endotoxin Clearance Across anion exchange (AEx) chromatography:** In anion exchange (AEx) chromatography, the protein of interest is recovered in the flow-through mode. In AEx, under neutral or slightly basic pH conditions, endotoxins are negatively charged and bind tightly to positively charged resin and target protein flowing through the column. Additional information on endotoxin clearance is detailed in Box 2.

**Endotoxin Acceptance Criteria:** Acceptable limits for endotoxins can be wider in upstream processes and tighter toward the end of the downstream processes based on an understanding of process risk and endotoxin clearance capabilities. Endotoxin limits for in-process intermediates are determined based on the clearance factor, the total potential for the introduction of endotoxin to the product, and the quantitation limit.

The quantification limits and acceptable endotoxin limit are calculated based on worst-case assay dilution and protein concentration in formulated drug substance (DS), as shown in Box 2.

**Box-2: Sample Calculation for setting pre-filtration Endotoxin limit [14, 25]**

**Step-1:** Maximum Valid Dilution (MVD) is calculated as a function of the sensitivity of the assay technique used, acceptable level of endotoxin in patient dose based on route of administration, maximum product dose, and patient population.

- **λ** is the sensitivity of the assay (EU/mL). However, different techniques like the Gel-Clot Technique, Turbidimetric Technique, or Chromo-clots the lysate are available. The type of endotoxin detection assay used depends on the product and dilution required to overcome inhibition and enhancement as per USP <85>. For the purpose of illustration, sensitivity (λ) =0.005 for Turbidimetric Technique is used.
- **$AL_{Endo}$**: Per USP<85> Acceptable limit of endotoxin is 5 EU/kg of body weight for any route of administration other than intrathecal (for which it is 0.2 EU/kg of body weight). As a conservative approach, we assume $AL_{Endo}$ = 0.2 EU/Kg.
- **$C_{DP}$,** protein concentration in formulated drug product, conservatively assumed to be at 50 mg/mL from a published range of 50 to 100 mg/L [20].

**Box-2: Sample Calculation for setting pre-filtration Endotoxin limit [14, 25]**

- **M** is equal to the maximum recommended bolus dose of product per kg of body weight based on dose, drug type, and population weight as referenced USP <85>. For the purpose of illustration, M is conservatively assumed to be 10 mg/Kg [21].

$$MVD = \frac{\left[AL_{Endo}\,\frac{EU}{kg} \div M\,\frac{mg}{kg}\right] \times C_{DP}\,\frac{mg}{mL}}{\lambda\,\frac{EU}{mL}} = \frac{\left[0.2\,\frac{EU}{kg} \div 10\,\frac{mg}{kg}\right] \times 50\,\frac{mg}{mL}}{0.005\,\frac{EU}{mL}} = 200$$

**Step-2:** Quantification Limit (QL) for worst case Dilution factor and Protein Concentration is calculated as:

$$QL = \lambda \times \frac{MVD}{C_{DP}} = 0.005\frac{EU}{mL} \times \frac{200}{50\frac{mg}{mL}} = 0.02\,\frac{EU}{mg}$$

**Step-3:** Acceptable Endotoxin Limit is calculated based on the QL and clearance factor in purification (CFp) as follows:

$$AL_{Endo} = \left[QL\,\frac{EU}{mg} \times C_{DP}\frac{mg}{mL}\right] \div \left[CF_p \times V_f \times k\right]$$

- Banerjee S (2012) presented Endotoxin clearance from 0.9 LRV to 3.0 LRV across four different AEx resins at different buffer conditions. Additionally, up to 4 LRV clearance has been shown using charged Durapore® 0.22 µm filters, and another 4 LRV reduction using ultrafiltration membrane sizes ranging from 10-1000 KD [26]. However, Magalhães P (2007) indicates in the pharmaceutical industry, diversity among endotoxins based on the source of micro-organisms there is a dilemma in their effective removal from the process stream. As all the above-cited endotoxin clearance is based on spike studies using specific types of endotoxins, as a conservative approach for the purpose of illustration, overall clearance **CFp** = 2.0 LRV or 0.01 factor is selected. Readers should evaluate the selected endotoxin clearance specific to their process.
- The Limulus amebocyte lysate (LAL) endotoxin test is an enzyme-based assay that incurs with expected 2-fold inherent variability as reported by Sandle T (2014) [29,30]. Therefore, $\mathbf{V_f}$ is assumed to be 2.0.
- **K** = 3 is the common statistical tolerance factor used to represent the 99.7% of the population (e.g., ± 3×SD (Standard deviation)); this approach of including 3 × $V_f$ in setting endotoxin limits is used by Wintzingerode, F (2017).

$$AL_{Endo} = \left[0.02\,\frac{EU}{mg} \times 50\frac{mg}{mL}\right] \div [0.01 \times 2 \times 3] = 16\,\frac{EU}{mL}$$

**Note:** Though different cell lines are sensitive to different levels of endotoxin from 0.1 to 10 ng/mL, cell lines like CHO, HeLa, and Murine cells that have been cultured for protein production have been naturally selected for high endotoxin resistance by long-term inadvertent exposure of endotoxin sourced from growth media and sera [33]. The lowest concentration of endotoxin that is shown to affect the recombinant CHO and Murine cell protein production is 10 ng/mL, equivalent to 100 EU/mL [34, 35].
When no historical data is available, for pre-filtration upstream media and feed solution, I advocate conservatively using the lowest reported endotoxin level to impact the cell culture, that is 0.1 ng/mL, equivalent to 10EU/mL as provisional endotoxin limits to start with, which is within the calculated endotoxin safety limits based on extreme worst-case assumptions as shown in this Box-2. Later, as more

| Box-2: Sample Calculation for setting pre-filtration Endotoxin limit [14, 25] |
| --- |
| data is available and knowledge in microbial control with facility set-up is matured, the limits can be narrowed down further. |

**Impurity Safety Factor (ISF) Risk Assessment for Exotoxins and Endotoxins:** Safety risk assessments can be carried out via ISF calculations. The ISF is the ratio of the impurity level in the product to the toxic impurity level. The ISF can be calculated as shown in Eq. 10 [10].

$$ISF = \frac{TD_{Lo}}{Impurity\ Level\ in\ Product\ (IDP)} \quad \text{Eq. (10)}$$

Toxic dose low ($TD_{Lo}$): The lowest dose of a substance introduced by any route, other than inhalation, over any given period of timeand reported to produce any toxic effect in humans or to produce tumorigenic or reproductive effects in animals. A higher ISF indicates a lower safety risk.

Here, we assume the Toxic dose low ($TD_{Lo}$) for botulinum A to be 1.2 pg per kg of patient weight per hour [11]. For Endotoxin, the lowest FDA-recommended dose .2 EU per kg of body weight per hour for intrathecally administered products. Assuming 1 EU = 0.1ng, ($TD_{Lo}$) value for endotoxin is assumed to be 0.02 ng per kg of body weight per hour [22,24]. Figure 6 shows after considering 3LRV clearance of exotoxin and 2 LRV clearance of endotoxin in downstream processes, the calculated exotoxin and endotoxin ISF values are 100,000 and 10,000 times below the toxic dose.

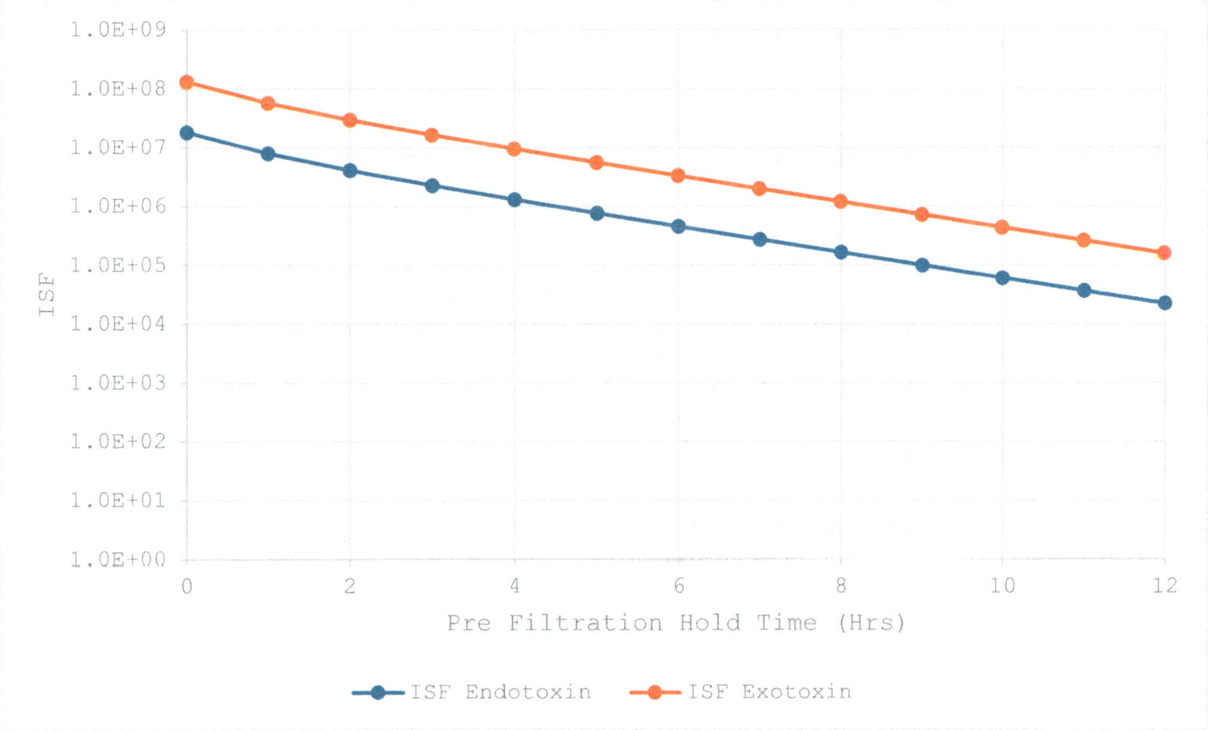


**Figure 6: ISF for endotoxins and exotoxins vs. pre-filtration hold time.**

## Bioburden and Endotoxin Criteria for Routine and Other Process Validation Samples:

The risk assessment for bioburden and endotoxin calculations in Box-1 and Box-2, respectively, may be applied for setting bioburden and endotoxin acceptance criteria for other upstream routine manufacturing and process validation samples. As an extended scope from the pre-filtration microbial control focus, Table, details on guidance and rationale for alert and action limits for routine manufacturing and process validation upstream samples.

| Sample Type | Upstream Unit Operation | Sample Description | Reg. Req. | Bioburden (CFU/mL) | Endotoxin (EU/mL) |
|---|---|---|---|---|---|
| R | Cell Expansion | Testing for bioburden of the final culture vessel from passive control inoculum expansion (Cultibag) to the first active control expansion may be tested or kept as a backup sample (perform a purity check under the microscope in the case of microbial processes). | No [11] | Alert: 1 CFU/10mL (A)<br>Action: 10 CFU/10mL (B) | Not Required |
| R | Seed Bioreactor | Prior to transfer into the next bioreactor, a bioburden sample may be tested or kept as a back-up sample (perform a purity check under microscope in the case of microbial processes). | No [11] | Alert: 1 CFU/10mL (A)<br>Action: 10 CFU/10mL (B) | Not Required |
| RS | Production Bioreactor | In the case of production bioreactors, all batches should be tested for bioburden at the end of production (unprocessed bulk sample). Endotoxin testing is not routinely performed at inoculum expansion stages since these stages are expected to be essentially sterile | Yes [37] | Alert: > 1 CFU/10mL (A)<br>Action:>10 CFU/10mL (B) | Alert: > 5 EU/mL [C]<br>Action: > 10 EU/mL [D] |
| RS | Harvest | Clarified harvest pool (0.22 µm filtered) at the end of harvest operations should be tested for bioburden/endotoxin for all batches just prior to the start of the following process step | Yes [38] | Alert: 1 CFU/10mL (A)<br>Action: 10 CFU/10mL (B) | Alert: > 5 EU/mL [C]<br>Action: > 10 EU/mL [D] |

| Sample Type | Upstream Unit Operation | Sample Description | Reg. Req. | Bioburden (CFU/mL) | Endotoxin (EU/mL) |
|---|---|---|---|---|---|
| PV | Media, Feed Prep / Filtration | Pre filtration sample for upstream growth media and Feeds | Yes: [39] | Alert: >200 CFU/mL [E]<br>Action:>1000 CFU/mL [F] | Alert: > 5 EU/mL [C]<br>Action: > 10 EU/mL [D] |
| PV | Filtered Media Storage in Sterile container | Post filtration media storage for up to 24 hours at 2-8°C or up to 12 hours at room temperature 19 to 25°C in sterile storage tanks/ bags/bioreactors. [40,41] | | Alert: 1 CFU/10mL (A)<br>Action: 10 CFU/10mL (B) | Alert: > 5 EU/mL [C]<br>Action: > 10 EU/mL [D] |
| PV | Production Bioreactor | LIVCA (Limit of Invitro Cell Age) | Yes: [42],[43] | Alert: 1 CFU/10mL (A)<br>Action: 10 CFU/10mL (B) | Not Required |
| PV | Harvest | Equilibration and Chase buffer storage for up to 24 hours at 2-8°C or up to 12 hours at room temperature 19 to 25°C in sterile storage tanks/ bags before use. [40,41] | Yes [39] | Alert: 1 CFU/10mL (A)<br>Action: 10 CFU/10mL (B) | Alert: > 5 EU/mL [C]<br>Action: > 10 EU/mL [D] |

RS: Routine sample
PV: Process validation sample
Reg. Req: Regulatory requirement
[A] No microbial growth is expected in a sterile sample from the bioreactor.
[B] Deutschmann, S., & Thoelken, S. (2022) cited for BDS samples taken aseptically from Class D, C, and B and analyzed in a non-classified microbiological laboratory, a couple of colonies can appear on plates from sampling or handling. This may cause occasional false positive results (Falsely rejecting a batch) [44]. In such instances, setting bioburden an action limit of 10 CFU/10mL in addition to an alert limit of 1CFU/10mL as recommended by Krause S (2015) [14] may be adopted as an acceptable limit to avoid Falsely rejecting a good batch.
[C] As discussed in the endotoxin clearance section, one of the most effective purification steps used downstream for endotoxin removal is anion-exchange chromatography ($A_{EX}$). FDA cited an IPC limit of 5 EU/mL for the Anion exchange product pool downstream for the mAb production process [45]. Therefore, setting 5 EU/mL as provisional alert limits early in the manufacturing process (for upstream media and feed solutions) should be a good, acceptable approach.
[D] Based on the calculation in Box 2.
[E] Based microbial load change data shown in Figure-1.
[F] Based on calculation in Box-1.

## Conclusions

In summary, this report has shown that bioburden and endotoxin test results meet the acceptable criteria for an extended pre-filtration hold time of $4T_p$ = 12 hrs for 20,000L medium preparation. A conservative calculation was applied to model the change in bioburden load, risk of filtration failure, and ISF for exotoxins and endotoxins. The results demonstrated that the risk associated with microbial control during the pre-filtration hold time of 12 hours is well within acceptable risk limits. The risk assessments and calculations for microbial limits shown in this article are only for demonstration of procedures. The readers are highly encouraged to assess the suitability of acceptability of risks in adherence to the company's quality policy. Furthermore, the bioburden and endotoxin limits cited or calculated in this article may be used as provisional limits when no historical data or only limited data is available; I highly recommend that the provisional limits be re-evaluated based on generated data.

## References


1. FDA. (2020, May 4). Sterile drug products produced by aseptic processing — Current good. https://www.fda.gov/regulatory-information/search-fda-guidance-documents/sterile-drug-products-produced-aseptic-processing-current-good-manufacturing-practice

2. General Chapter <1115> Bioburden Control for Non-Sterile Drug Substance and Products. USP 41; U.S. Pharmacopeia 2014

3. Sandle, T. (2015, October). Assessing Process Hold Times for Microbial Risks: Bioburden and Endotoxin. Journal of GXP Compliance, 19(3).

4. Yang, H., Li, N., & Chang, S. (2013). A risk-based approach to setting sterile filtration Bioburden limits. PDA Journal of Pharmaceutical Science and Technology, 67(6), 601-609. https://doi.org/10.5731/pdajpst.2013.00942

5. Doran, P. M. (2013). Bioprocess engineering principles. Academic Press.

6. Coffey, T., & Yang, H. (2018). Statistics for biotechnology process development. CRC Press.

7. Muralidharan, N. (2022, October). Statistical Method for Establishing Control Limits for Nonnormal Data Distribution: Focus on Continued Process Verification Monitoring. Bioprocess International, 20(10), 20-24.

8. Sandle, T. (2022, October 1). What Counts? Establishing a Bioburden Strategy for a New Pharmaceutical Product. American Pharmaceutical Review.

9. Sandle, T. (2014, November 28). The Risk of Bacillus cereus to Pharmaceutical Manufacturing. American Pharmaceutical Review.

https://www.americanpharmaceuticalreview.com/Featured-Articles/169507-The-Risk-of-em-Bacillus-cereus-em-to-Pharmaceutical-Manufacturing/

10. Luo, H., Li, Y., Robbins, D., Wang, S., Xi, G., Cox, M., Nicholson, S. M., Wei, C., Pabst, T. M., & Wang, W. K. (2021). Safety risk management for low molecular weight process-related impurities in monoclonal antibody therapeutics: Categorization, risk assessment, testing strategy, and process development with leveraging clearance potential. Biotechnology Progress, 37(3).

https://doi.org/10.1002/btpr.3119

11. Bain, D., Hardy, D., Bell, B. L., Forng, R., Knight, M., Bawa, A., Ramsey, S., Arbesser-Rastburg, C., Paul, M., Ton, C., Leira, F., Roman, C., McFarland, K., Phillips, D., Stuckey, J., Bauer, C., & Calvo, A. J. (2015). Microbial monitoring for biological drug substance manufacturing: An industry perspective. PDA Journal of Pharmaceutical Science and Technology, 69(3), 451-460.

https://doi.org/10.5731/pdajpst.2015.01070

12.] Wintzingerode, F. V. (2017, April 30). Biologics Production: Impact of Bioburden Contaminations of Non-Sterile Process Intermediates on Patient Safety and Product Quality. American Pharmaceutical Review.

https://www.americanpharmaceuticalreview.com/Featured-Articles/337286-Biologics-Production-Impact-of-Bioburden-Contaminations-of-Non-Sterile-Process-Intermediates-on-Patient-Safety-and-Product-Quality/

13. Cytiva. (2020). Exotoxin clearance from mAb samples in a two-step chromatography process (KA1638100118AN).

https://cdn.cytivalifesciences.com/api/public/content/digi-24162-pdf

14. Krause, S. (2015, March). Alert, Action, and Specification Limits for Bioburden and Endotoxin [Conference session]. PDA Annual Meeting, Las Vegas, NV.

15. Salema, V. F., Saxena, L., & Pattnaik, P. (2009, September 30). Removing endotoxin from biopharmaceutical solutions. Pharmaceutical Technology Europe, 21(10), 16-20.

16. Baka, M., Van Derlinden, E., Boons, K., Mertens, L., & Van Impe, J. F. (2013). Impact of pH on the cardinal temperatures of E. coli K12: Evaluation of the gamma hypothesis. Food Control, 29(2), 328-335.

https://doi.org/10.1016/j.foodcont.2012.04.022

17. Tuttle, A. R., Trahan, N. D., & Son, M. S. (2021). Growth and Maintenance of Escherichia coli Laboratory Strains. Current protocols, 1(1), e20. https://doi.org/10.1002/cpz1.20

18. Membré, J. M., Leporq, B., Vialette, M., Mettler, E., Perrier, L., Thuault, D., & Zwietering, M. (2005). Temperature effect on bacterial growth rate: quantitative microbiology approach including cardinal values and variability estimates to perform growth simulations on/in food. International journal of food microbiology, 100(1-3), 179–186. https://doi.org/10.1016/j.ijfoodmicro.2004.10.015

19.] Milo, R., & Phillips, R. (2015). Cell biology by the numbers. Garland Science.

20. Garidel, P., Kuhn, A. B., Schäfer, L. V., Karow-Zwick, A. R., & Blech, M. (2017). High-concentration protein formulations: How high is high? European Journal of Pharmaceutics and Biopharmaceutics, 119, 353-360.

https://doi.org/10.1016/j.ejpb.2017.06.029

21. Sachs, J. R., Mayawala, K., Gadamsetty, S., Kang, S. P., & de Alwis, D. P. (2016). Optimal Dosing for Targeted Therapies in Oncology: Drug Development Cases Leading by Example. Clinical cancer research: an official journal of the American Association for Cancer Research, 22(6), 1318–1324. https://doi.org/10.1158/1078-0432.CCR-15-1295

22. EMD Millipore. (n.d.). Endotoxin Removal The Solution With Membrane Separation Technology Application Note. White Paper.

https://www.sigmaaldrich.com/deepweb/assets/sigmaaldrich/product/documents/219/983/tb2999en-ms.pdf

23. Mehta, K., Soderquist, R., Shah, P., Marchand, N., & Bolton, G. (2018, February 16). Comparing Performance of New Protein A Resins for Monoclonal Antibody Purification. American Pharmaceutical Review.

https://www.americanpharmaceuticalreview.com/Featured-Articles/347357-Comparing-Performance-of-New-Protein-A-Resins-for-Monoclonal-Antibody-Purification/

24. Food and Drug Administration (FDA). (2020). Setting Endotoxin Limits During Development of Investigational Oncology Drugs and Biological Products. Center for Drug Evaluation and Research. https://www.fda.gov/media/140410/download

25. General Chapter <85> Bacterial Endotoxins Test.; U.S. Pharmacopeia 2012.

26. Banerjee, S., & Somasundaram, G. (2012). Endotoxin Control and Clearance in Biomanufacturing. Millipore Sigma.

https://www.sigmaaldrich.com/US/en/collections/webinars/endotoxin-control-and-clearance-in-biomanufacturing

27. Carter J. (1996). Evaluation of recovery filters for use in bacterial retention testing of sterilizing-grade filters. PDA journal of pharmaceutical science and technology, 50(3), 147–153.

28. PDA Technical Report No.26, (TR 26) Revised 2008. Sterilizing Filtration of Liquids. (2008). PDA journal of pharmaceutical science and technology.

29. Sandle, T. (2014, August 28). Variability and Test Error with the LAL Assay. American Pharmaceutical Review.

https://www.americanpharmaceuticalreview.com/Featured-Articles/167404-Variability-and-Test-Error-with-the-LAL-Assay/

30. Wintzingerode, F. (2017). Setting Endotoxin In-Process Controls for Recombinant Therapeutic Proteins. American Pharmaceutical Review, 20-23.

31. https://www.acciusa.com/pdfs/supplements/Endotoxin%20Detection%20Part%20V/Setting_Endotoxin_In_Process.pdf

32. Magalhães, P. O., Lopes, A. M., Mazzola, P. G., Rangel-Yagui, C., Penna, T. C., & Pessoa, A., Jr (2007). Methods of endotoxin removal from biological preparations: a review. Journal of Pharmacy & Pharmaceutical Sciences: a publication of the Canadian Society for Pharmaceutical Sciences, Societe canadienne des sciences pharmaceutiques, 10(3), 388–404.

33. ANSI/AAMI ST79:2017/(R)2022; COMPREHENSIVE GUIDE TO STEAM STERILIZATION AND STERILITY ASSURANCE IN HEALTH CARE FACILITIES. (2017). AAMI.

34. Corning. (2020, June). Endotoxins and Cell Culture.

www.corning.com/lifesciences .

https://www.corning.com/catalog/cls/documents/application-notes/TC-305.pdf

35. Epstein, J., Kelly, C. E., Lee, M. M., & Donahoe, P. K. (1990). Effect of E. Coli endotoxin on mammalian cell growth and recombinant protein production. In Vitro Cellular & Developmental Biology, 26(12), 1121-1122.

https://doi.org/10.1007/bf02623686

36. Sibley, C. H., Terry, A., & Raetz, C. R. (1988). Induction of kappa light chain synthesis in 70Z/3 B lymphoma cells by chemically defined lipid precursors. Journal of Biological Chemistry, 263(11), 5098-5103.

https://doi.org/10.1016/s0021-9258(18)60684-2

37. Field, R. (2013, May). Bioburden Control at the Sterile Filtration Step: A risk-based approach [Conference session]. European Biopharmaceutical Enterprises. https://docplayer.net/49110306-Bioburden-control-at-the-sterile-filtration-step-a-risk-based-approach.html

38. ICH. (1997). ICH Topic Q 5 A (R1) Quality of Biotechnological Products: Viral Safety Evaluation of Biotechnology Products Derived from Cell Lines of Human or Animal Origin (CPMP/ICH/295/95).

https://www.ema.europa.eu/en/documents/scientific-guideline/ich-q-5-r1-viral-safety-evaluation-biotechnology-products-derived-cell-lines-human-animal-origin_en.pdf

39. FDA. (2021). CHAPTER 56—DRUG QUALITY ASSURANCE.

https://www.fda.gov/media/75208/download

40. FDA. (2004). Guidance for Industry Sterile Drug Products Produced by Aseptic Processing — Current Good Manufacturing Practice.

https://www.fda.gov/media/71026/download

41. EMA. (2017). Guideline on the manufacture of the finished dosage form (EMA/CHMP/QWP/245074/2015). https://www.ema.europa.eu/en/documents/scientific-guideline/guideline-manufacture-finished-dosage-form-revision-1_en.pdf

42. Broughton. (n.d.). Aseptic Processing of Biological Products: Current Regulatory Issues "Facing the Challenges of Drug Product Manufacturing." FDA.

https://www.fda.gov/files/drugs/published/Aseptic-Processing-of-Biological-Products--Current-Regulatory-Issues--Candace-Gomez-Broughton--PhD.pdf

43. European Medicines Agency. (1996). ICH Topic Q 5 B Quality of Biotechnological Products: Analysis of the Expression Construct in Cell Lines Used for Production of r-DNA Derived Protein Products.

https://www.ema.europa.eu/en/documents/scientific-guideline/ich-q-5-b-analysis-expression-construct-cell-lines-used-production-r-dna-derived-protein-products_en.pdf

44. Agalloco, J., DeSantis, P., Grilli, A., & Pavell, A. (2021). Handbook of validation in pharmaceutical processes (4th ed.). CRC Press.

45. Deutschmann, S., & Thoelken, S. (2022, July 29). Bioburden - Regulatory Expectations and Practical Experiences. GMP Journal. https://www.gmp-journal.com/current-articles/details/q-a-from-european-gmp-conference-bioburden-regulatory-expectations-and-practical-experiences.html

46. FDA. (2021). Q12 Technical and Regulatory Considerations for Pharmaceutical Product Lifecycle Management Annexes Guidance for Industry.

https://www.fda.gov/media/148477/download

47. BioPlan Associates, Inc. (2014). Powder Culture Media Packaging, Preparation, and Market Trends. www.thermofisher.com. https://assets.thermofisher.com/TFS-Assets/LSG/brochures/PowderMediaWhitePaper_LifeTech_Jan2014.pdf

48. Gibco. (2018, June). CD CHO Medium User Guide. thermofisher.com.

https://assets.thermofisher.com/TFS-Assets/LSG/manuals/MAN0007311_CD_CHO_Medium_UG.pdf

# Chapter 6: Statistical methods to calculate the number of PPQ runs using MS Excel with illustrative examples.

**Naveenganesh Muralidharan**

## Introduction

The 2011 process validation (PV) guidance document from the Food and Drug Administration (FDA) states, "*The number of samples should be adequate to provide sufficient statistical confidence of quality both within a batch and between batches. The confidence level selected can be based on risk analysis as it relates to the particular attribute under examination.*" [1]

In alignment with the FDA's expectations, this article details two statistical methodologies for calculating the number of process performance qualification (PPQ) runs, namely, the tolerance interval (TI) method and the process capability (PpK) method. Both methods are performed by applying the following steps in sequence to demonstrate that the PPQ results obtained have an acceptable statistical confidence:

1. Assess the risk of the attribute/parameter to be monitored.
2. Statistically assess the reliability for the sample size of data used to gain process knowledge.
3. Define the target statistical confidence and reliability based on a risk assessment matrix.
4. Compensate for the uncertainty of the limited sample size by replacing the sample mean and sample standard deviation using appropriate confidence intervals to model the data distribution at the desired confidence.
5. Estimate the risk of failure to meet predefined acceptable ranges based on the modeled data distribution.
6. Calculate the adequate number of PPQ runs based on the minimum sample size required to control the uncertainty on the estimated risk of failure.

This article also details how to consider both inter- and intra-batch variability when calculating the number of PPQ runs. Although other statistical approaches, such as methods based on expected coverage, probability of batch success have been reported for calculating the number of PPQ runs, these methods have limitations in either arbitrarily assigning risk ratings or not being driven by historical process knowledge gained.[2]

Furthermore, this article provides a step-by-step procedure for calculating the number of PPQ runs using MS Excel as a tool with illustrative examples for both methods (PpK and TI) for easy adaptation and implementation by the reader.

### Risk assessment for setting statistical confidence

A risk assessment matrix can be built according to recommendations from "Standard Guide for Risk Assessment and Risk Control for Pharmaceutical Manufacture" (ASTM E2476-09). ASTM E2479-06 states that the "risk estimation will incorporate the following factors:

- Severity of the consequences.
- Likelihood of occurrence.
- Likelihood of detection (of a problem or of a detection failure) once the problem/failure has occurred before harm has been incurred. This should include a recognition that detection may not be possible." [3]

In alignment with ASTM standard recommendations, a risk assessment matrix can be designed by scoring the attributes/parameters to be monitored in PPQ runs based on the three above-mentioned criteria, as shown in Table 1.

- The severity score is based on the impact on product quality or process productivity and consistency.
- The occurrence score is based on controls in place. The highest score is assigned when occurrence is unknown.
- The detectability score is based on the availability of the testing methodologies and monitoring systems in place. Some testing methods, such as bioburden methods, that carry some level of uncertainty based on sample volume are rated with a medium risk score, whereas other attributes with well-defined testing methods with high precision and repeatability are rated with a low risk score.

**Table 1. Risk assessment scoring matrix.**

| Severity (S) | Occurrence (O) | Detectability (D) | Score |
|---|---|---|---|
| • Critical process parameter: Directly/indirectly impacts the quality attributes of the product with predefined proven acceptable ranges.<br>• Critical quality attributes: Used as the release criteria for the product with predefined specification values. | Most likely to occur | Poor chance of detecting failure | 5 |
| • Key process parameter (KPP): Parameters that impact the productivity or batch yield with predefined normal operating ranges.<br>• In-process controls: Parameters that are monitored at any intermediate stage of the manufacturing process before continuing to the next step with predefined acceptable limits. | Could occur | May detect failure | 3 |

| Severity (S) | Occurrence (O) | Detectability (D) | Score |
|---|---|---|---|
| • Non-KPP: Typically well controlled and unlikely to impact the quality or productivity. | Not likely to occur | Will detect failure every time | 1 |

The risk priority number (RPN) is generated from the product of the three scores (RPN = (S) x (O) x (D)), and the risk for each parameter is classified as high, medium, or low, as identified in the RPN scoring matrix shown in Table 2. Table 2 also shows recommendations for setting statistical confidence (1-α) and residual risk (1-p) by defining the proportion (p) of population to cover based on risk classification.

**Table 2. Guidance for selecting the statistical confidence and population proportion.**

| RPN score | Risk classification | Confidence (1-α)/proportion to cover (p) determined by ISPE method |
|---|---|---|
| 1–25 | Low | 0.90/0.50 |
| 26–50 | Medium | 0.95/0.70 |
| ≥51 | High | 0.97/0.80 |

The confidence level (1-α) and proportion of population to cover (p) for the different risk categories shown in Table 3 were adopted from a guidance document from the International Society for Pharmaceutical Engineering (ISPE) [14]. Different (1-α) and (p) values can be adapted based on other published articles, regulatory documents, or company quality risk management policies that are more appropriate for a given manufacturing process.

## Reliability for a sample size of historic data used to gain process knowledge

Often, only limited data are available from stage 1 (process development and characterization phase) before the stage-2 PPQ phase is entered. Therefore, the first step in calculating the number of PPQ runs is to ensure the reliability of the sample size used to gain process knowledge. One such method is to assess the power of estimation as a function of sample size used at an acceptable statistical confidence.

The required sample size for a t-test at the desired confidence, power, and detectability is given in Equations 1 and 2.[5]

$$n_s = \frac{\left(t_{1-\alpha/2,df} + t_{1-\beta,df}\right)^2}{\left(\frac{\Delta}{\sigma}\right)^2} \quad for\ a\ two-sided\ test \qquad \text{Eq. (1)}$$

$$n_s = \frac{\left(t_{1-\alpha,df} + t_{1-\beta,df}\right)^2}{\left(\frac{\Delta}{\sigma}\right)^2} \quad for\ a\ one-sided\ test \qquad \text{Eq. (2)}$$

Where $n_s$ is the sample size, $df=n_s-1$, which represents degrees of freedom, and $t_{(1-\alpha,\ df)}$ represents the inverse of the cumulative t distribution at 1-α and df.

Here, the significance (α) value or type I error is often set at an acceptable value of 0.05,[4] indicating a 5% chance of false rejection of an actually true null hypothesis or, in other words, the statistical confidence (1–α) is 100%–5%=95%.

For the β value or type II error, the widely acceptable minimum (β) value is 0.20, [4] indicating a 20% chance of failure to reject a null hypothesis that is actually false or, in other words, the statistical reliability (1-β) is 100%-20%=80%.

The detectability/effect (Δ/σ) is the acceptable distance from the mean, expressed as the number of standard deviations, to support the null hypothesis H0 that there is no difference between the sample and the population. Therefore, relaxing the criteria for H0 by increasing the value of δ will decrease the required sample size. A (Δ/σ) value of 1.0–1.5 has been reported as acceptable for calculating the required sample size.[11] The FDA guidance document on “statistical review and evaluation” states that a (Δ/σ) value of 1.5 at 90% confidence (1-α) is adequate to conclude equivalence between two groups. In reference to this article, this value is the size of a sample that can represent the population.[15]

Equations 1 and 2 for the sample size are rearranged to solve for the power of estimation, as shown in Equations 3 and 4.

For a two-sided interval, we have

$$Power\ (1-\beta) = t.dist\left(\left(\frac{\left(\frac{\Delta}{\sigma}\right)}{\sqrt{\frac{1}{n_s}}} - t_{(1-\alpha/2,\ df)}\right), (df)\right) \qquad \text{Eq. (3)}$$

For a one-sided interval, we have

$$Power\ (1-\beta) = t.dist\left(\left(\frac{\left(\frac{\Delta}{\sigma}\right)}{\sqrt{\frac{1}{n_s}}} - t_{(1-\alpha,\ df)}\right), (df)\right) \qquad \text{Eq. (4)}$$

Where t.dist is the cumulative distribution function of the t distribution, according to Cohen (1988), the generally accepted minimum power (1-β) is 80% for a confidence (1-α) of 95%.[4, 16]

As an example of a two-sided interval, the power was calculated for a randomly selected sample size of 10 using MS Excel, as shown in Table 3.

**Table 3. Power calculation for a sample size of 10 using MS Excel.**

| | C | D | E | F |
|---|---|---|---|---|
| 3 | **Symbol** | **Description** | **Value** | **Formula/Comments** |
| 4 | $n_s$ | Number of samples | 10 | User-entered |
| 5 | Δ/σ | Detectable difference | 1.0 | User-defined, default=1.0 to 1.5 |
| 6 | 1-α | Percent confidence | 0.95 | User-defined, default=0.95 |
| 7 | A | Type I error, | 0.05 | =1-E6 |
| 8 | Df | Degrees of freedom | 9 | =E4-1 |
| 9 | N/A | $[(\Delta/\sigma)/\sqrt{(1/n_s)}]- t_{1-\alpha/2,\ df}$ | 0.90 | =E5/SQRT((1/E4))-T.INV((1-E7/2),E8) |
| 10 | 1-β | Power | 0.80 | =T.DIST(E9,E8,TRUE) |

## Tolerance Interval (TI) Method

The TI is the range that gives a fixed proportion (p) of the population at a stated statistical confidence (1-α) based on the assumption that the sample data are taken from a normally distributed population.[5, 11]

### Two-sided TI

A two-sided TI is expressed as shown in Equation 5:

$$TI = X_{avg} \pm k.s \qquad \text{Eq. (5)}$$

Where TI represents the tolerance interval, $X_{avg,}$ and s represent the sample mean and sample standard deviation, respectively, and k is the tolerance interval estimator, which is the number of standard deviations away from the mean that covers a certain fixed proportion of the population at the desired statistical confidence.

Equation 5 can be rearranged as follows:

$$k = \frac{TI \pm x_{avg}}{s} \qquad \text{Eq. (6)}$$

In Equation 6, replacing the TI with the specification limit (SL) will yield the maximum acceptable tolerance estimator $k_{max,\ accep}$ that can ensure that the process remains within the predefined specifications. This estimator can be written as follows:

$$k_{\max accep} = \frac{SL \pm x_{avg}}{s} \qquad \text{Eq. (7)}$$

In other words, $k_{max,\ accept}$ is the maximum acceptable distance in terms of the number of standard deviations from the mean for an acceptable specification.[12] $k_{max,\ accep}$ can be elaborated as shown in Equation 8 for attributes with two-sided acceptable limits or specification limits.

$$k_{\max accep} = maximum\left\{\frac{USL - X_{avg}}{s}, \frac{X_{avg} - LSL}{s}\right\} \qquad \text{Eq. (8)}$$

**Uncertainty with sample mean and sample standard deviation**

Because of the limited sample size available before the stage-2 process qualification, the uncertainty involved in using the sample mean and sample standard deviation can be compensated for by replacing the sample mean and sample standard deviation with their respective confidence intervals. The confidence interval is a range that gives a single-valued parameter, such as the mean or standard deviation, of a population at a stated confidence.

The confidence intervals around the mean and standard deviation are shown in Equations 9 and 10.[5]

$$x_{UCI} = x_{avg} + t_{\left(1-\frac{\alpha}{2}, n_s-1\right)} \frac{s}{\sqrt{n_s}} \text{ , } x_{LCI} = x_{avg} - t_{\left(1-\frac{\alpha}{2}, n_s-1\right)} \frac{s}{\sqrt{n_s}} \qquad \text{Eq. (9)}$$

$$s_{UCI} = s. \sqrt{\frac{n_s - 1}{\chi^2_{(n_s-1),(\alpha)}}} \qquad \text{Eq. (10)}$$

Here, $x_{UCI}$ and $x_{LCI}$ represent the upper and lower confidence interval values for the mean and

$S_{UCL}$ represents the upper confidence interval value for the standard deviation.

Substituting Equations 9 and 10 in Equation 8 yields the maximum acceptable tolerance estimator $k_{max,\ accep}$ with compensation for the uncertainty associated with the small sample size:

$$k_{\max accep} = maximum \left\{ \frac{USL - \left(x_{avg} + t_{\left(1-\frac{\alpha}{2}, n_s-1\right)} \frac{s}{\sqrt{n_s}}\right)}{s. \sqrt{\frac{n_s - 1}{\chi^2_{(n_s-1),(\alpha)}}}}, \frac{\left(x_{avg} - t_{\left(1-\frac{\alpha}{2}, n_s-1\right)} \frac{s}{\sqrt{n_s}}\right) - LSL}{s. \sqrt{\frac{n_s - 1}{\chi^2_{(n_s-1),(\alpha)}}}} \right\} \qquad \text{Eq. (11)}$$

Howe (1969) gave an estimate of the TI estimator k value as a function of sample size (n), confidence (1-α), and proportion (p), as shown in Equation 12.[5]

$$k = z_{\left(\frac{p+1}{2}\right)} \sqrt{\frac{(n-1)(1+\frac{1}{n})}{\chi^2_{\alpha,n-1}}} \qquad \text{Eq. (12)}$$

Where z and $\chi^2$ are the inverse of the cumulative normal distribution and chi-square distribution, respectively.

Later, Guenther corrected Howe's approximation by using k' instead of k for smaller samples, as shown in Equation 13.[5]

$$k' = z_{\left(\frac{p+1}{2}\right)} \sqrt{\frac{(n-1)(1+\frac{1}{n})}{\chi^2_{\alpha,n-1}}} \cdot \sqrt{1+\frac{n-3-\chi^2_{\alpha,n-1}}{2(n+1)^2}} \quad \text{Eq. (13)}$$

The confidence estimator (k') should be less than the maximum confidence limit estimator ($k_{max,accep}$) to ensure that the process remains within the predefined specification limits. Now, the number of PPQ runs (n) can be calculated by using the MS Excel solver function or by iteratively changing the value of n starting from n=3 until the k' value is approximately ≤($k_{max,\ accep}$),[11] as shown in Equation 14:

$$k' = z_{\left(\frac{p+1}{2}\right)} \sqrt{\frac{(n-1)(1+\frac{1}{n})}{\chi^2_{\alpha,n-1}}} \cdot \sqrt{1+\frac{n-3-\chi^2_{\alpha,n-1}}{2(n+1)^2}} \leq k_{max\,accep} \quad \text{Eq. (14)}$$

## Example for sample data and risk assessment

As an example of the TI method, 12 samples were randomly generated to follow a normal distribution, with a mean of 100 and a standard deviation of 2, in Excel using the function "=NORM.INV(RAND(),100,2)."

The upper and lower specification limit values were set to 95 and 105, respectively.

We assume a case in which this random variable is a critical quality attribute, there is not a clear understanding of the control strategy, and the testing method has a high inherent variability. According to the risk assessment matrix in Table 2, the **PRN** score is = **5** (S) x **5** (O) x **3** (D) = **75**; therefore, the risk is considered **High**. Hence, the target confidence is set at 0.97, and the proportion is set at 0.80, as determined by Table 3.

**Table 4. Twelve randomly generated data values for illustrating the TI method.**

| | | |
|---|---|---|
| 96.94 | 97.63 | 97.72 |
| 94.80 | 100.99 | 98.35 |
| 99.77 | 98.56 | 95.52 |
| 99.52 | 95.13 | 98.28 |

**Table 5. Illustration of calculating the number of PPQ runs via the TI method in Excel for two-sided specifications.**

| 1 | E | F | G | H |
|---|---|---|---|---|
| 2 | Symbol | Description | Value | Formula |
| 3 | $X_{avg}$ | Sample Average | 97.77 | =AVERAGE(A2:C5) |
| 4 | S | Sample Standard Deviation | 1.91 | =STDEV.S(A2:C5) |
| 5 | LSL | Lower Specification Limit | 95 | User-defined |
| 6 | USL | Upper Specification Limit | 105 | User-defined |
| 7 | Ns | Sample Size | 12.00 | User-defined |
| 8 | 1-α | Confidence | 0.97 | User-defined based on risk assessment |
| 9 | 1-β | Proportion | 0.80 | User-defined based on risk assessment |
| 10 | A | Acceptable Risk | 0.03 | =1-G8 |
| 11 | $\mu_{UCB}$ | Estimated Upper Confidence Value for the Mean | 97.79 | =G3+(T.INV(1-G8/2,G7-1))*(G4/SQRT(G7)) |
| 12 | $\mu_{LCB}$ | Estimated Lower Confidence Value for the Mean | 97.75 | =G3-(T.INV(1-G8/2,G7-1))*(G4/SQRT(G7)) |
| 13 | $\sigma_{UCB}$ | Estimated Upper Confidence Bound for the Standard Deviation | 1.99 | =(SQRT((G7-1)/CHISQ.INV(G8/2,G7-1)))*G4 |
| 14 | ATL | Acceptable Tolerance Limit | 3.629947 | =MAX((G6-G11)/G13,(G12-G5)/G13) |
| 15 | **n** | **Number of PPQ Runs** | **6** | **User-entered; start with 3 and iteratively increase n by 1 for each iteration until the k' value is approximately ≤ATL** |
| 16 | df | Degrees of Freedom | 5 | =G15-1 |
| 17 | $Z_{(p+1)/2}$ | The inverse of Normal Distribution at (p+1)/2 | 1.282 | =NORM.S.INV((G9+1)/2) |
| 18 | $\chi^2_{\alpha, df}$ | The inverse of $\chi^2$ Distribution at α and df | 0.903 | =CHISQ.INV(G10,G16) |
| 19 | k | k via Howe's Method | 3.257 | =G17*SQRT(G16*(1+1/G15)/G18) |

| 1 | E | F | G | H |
|---|---|---|---|---|
| 2 | Symbol | Description | Value | Formula |
| 20 | k' | Corrected k Value via Guenther's Method | 3.25 | =G19*SQRT((1+(G15-3-G19)/(2*G15+1)^2)) |

## One-sided TI

For a one-sided TI, an approximate value for the k factor has been given by Natreilla as follows:[5]

$$k1 = \frac{z_p + \sqrt{z_p^2 - a.b}}{a} \qquad \text{Eq. (15)}$$

where

$$a = 1 - \frac{z_\alpha^2}{2(n-1)} \qquad \text{Eq. (16)}$$

$$b = z_p^2 - \frac{z_\alpha^2}{n} \qquad \text{Eq. (17)}$$

To illustrate the use of the TI method for a one-sided TI, we apply the same example used for the two-sided TI method with only the upper specification limit.

**Table 6. Example of calculating the number of PPQ runs via the TI method for a one-sided specification.**

| 1 | E | F | G | H |
|---|---|---|---|---|
| 2 | Symbol | Description | Value | Formula |
| 3 | $X_{avg}$ | Sample Average | 97.77 | =AVERAGE(A2:C5) |
| 4 | s | Sample Standard Deviation | 1.91 | =STDEV.S(A2:C5) |
| 5 | LSL | Lower Specification Limit | 95 | User-defined |
| 6 | USL | Upper Specification Limit | 105 | User-defined |
| 7 | ns | Sample Size | 12.00 | User-defined |
| 8 | 1-α | Confidence | 0.97 | User-defined based on risk assessment |

| 1 | E | F | G | H |
|---|---|---|---|---|
| 2 | Symbol | Description | Value | Formula |
| 9 | $1\text{-}\beta$ | Proportion | 0.80 | User-defined based on risk assessment |
| 10 | $\alpha$ | Acceptable Risk | 0.03 | =1-G8 |
| 11 | $\mu_{UCB}$ | Estimated Upper Confidence Value for the Mean | 97.79 | =G3+(T.INV(1-G8/2,G7-1))*(G4/SQRT(G7)) |
| 12 | $\mu_{LCB}$ | Estimated Lower Confidence Value for the Mean | 97.75 | =G3-(T.INV(1-G8/2,G7-1))*(G4/SQRT(G7)) |
| 13 | $\sigma_{UCB}$ | Estimated Upper Confidence Bound for the Standard Deviation | 1.99 | =(SQRT((G7-1)/CHISQ.INV(G8/2,G7-1)))*G4 |
| 14 | ATL | Acceptable Tolerance Limit | 3.629947 | =MAX((G6-G11)/G13,(G12-G5)/G13) |
| 8 | n | **Number of PPQ Runs** | 5 | User-entered; start with 3 and iteratively increase n until the k1 value is approximately ≤ATI |
| 12 | $z_p$ | The inverse of Normal Distribution at p | 0.842 | =NORM.S.INV(G9) |
| 13 | $z_\alpha$ | The inverse of Normal Distribution at 1-α | 1.881 | =NORM.S.INV(G8) |
| 14 | a | N/A | 0.558 | =1-G17^2/(2*(G15-1)) |
| 15 | b | N/A | 0.001 | =G16^2-G17^2/G15 |
| 16 | k1 | k1 Factor for One-sided TI | 3.017 | =(G16+SQRT(G16^2-G18*G19))/G18 |

## Process Capability Method

### Process performance index (PpK)

The ability of a process to meet predefined specifications is determined by PpK, which is defined as the ratio of the distance from the process mean and nearest specification to the one-sided spread of the process ($3\sigma$ variation) based on the overall standard deviation for a normally distributed population.[6] PpK is calculated as shown in Equations 18 and 19:[7]

$$P_{pK} = minimum\{PpL\ , PpU\} \qquad \text{Eq. (18)}$$

$$P_{pK} = minimum\left\{\frac{USL - \mu}{3\sigma}, \frac{X_{avg} - \mu}{3\sigma}\right\} \qquad \text{Eq. (19)}$$

Where $P_{pK}$ is the process performance index, PpL is the lower process performance index, PpU is the upper process performance index, USL and LSL represent the upper and lower specification limits, respectively, and μ and σ represent the underlying true population mean and overall true population standard deviation, respectively.

## Uncertainty with the sample mean, sample standard deviation, and sigma factor

The above equation (19) for PpK is typically employed when the sample size is at least 25. However, the sample size generated before the stage-2 process qualification phase is often less than 25, and the underlying true population mean and population standard deviation are unknown. As discussed for the TI method, the uncertainty of using the sample mean, and sample standard deviation due to a small sample size can be compensated for by replacing the sample mean and sample standard deviation with confidence intervals around the mean and standard deviation.

The sigma factor of ±3 in the 3σ term in Equation 19 represents the number of standard deviations from the mean that covers 99.7% of the true population. However, because the proportion of the population to cover is based on the risk assessment and in order to accommodate the uncertainty involved in a limited available sample size, the term ±3 is replaced in Equation 19 with r, which is the number of sigma factors from the mean covering the desired proportion of the population.

Now, by substituting Equations 9 and 10 in Equation 19, PpK can be rewritten as follows:

$$P_{pK} = min\left\{\frac{USL-\left(x_{avg}+t_{\left(1-\frac{\alpha}{2},n_s-1\right)}\frac{s}{\sqrt{n_s}}\right)}{r.s.\sqrt{\frac{n_s-1}{\chi^2_{(n_s-1),(\alpha)}}}}, \frac{\left(x_{avg}-t_{\left(1-\frac{\alpha}{2},n_s-1\right)}\frac{s}{\sqrt{n_s}}\right)-LSL}{r.s.\sqrt{\frac{n_s-1}{\chi^2_{(n_s-1),(\alpha)}}}}\right\} \quad \text{Eq. (20)}$$

The r value can be calculated iteratively by increasing the value of k from k=0 in Equation 10 to achieve the desired population proportion based on the risk assessment.

$$p = \left(NORM.S.DIST\left(\frac{1}{\sqrt{n_s}}+r\right),TRUE\right)-\left(NORM.S.DIST\left(\frac{1}{\sqrt{n_s}}-r\right),TRUE\right) \quad \text{Eq. (21)}$$

**Uncertainty with PpK estimation**

Bissell's approximated confidence interval for a capability index that accommodates uncertainty for the PpK calculation is shown in Equation 22.[8, 9, 10]

$$P_{pK}-Z_{1-\alpha}\sqrt{\frac{1}{k^2n}+\frac{P^2_{pK}}{2(n-1)}} \leq Ppk \leq P_{pK}-Z_{1-\alpha}\sqrt{\frac{1}{k^2n}+\frac{P^2_{pK}}{2(n-1)}} \quad \text{Eq (22)}$$

FDA's 2011 PV guidelines state, "The CGMP regulations require that manufacturing processes be designed and controlled to assure that in-process materials and the finished product meet predetermined quality requirements and do so consistently and reliably." A capability index value of 1.0–1.3 indicates that the process is capable and most likely to routinely meet the specifications,[7] which is in alignment with the expectation from the FDA's 2011 PV guidance. Therefore, the number of process validation batches (n) can be calculated by iteratively increasing the value of n from 3 to achieve a lower capability confidence interval (LCCI) of 1.0–1.3.

$$LCCI = P_{pK}-Z_{1-\alpha}\sqrt{\frac{1}{k^2n}+\frac{P^2_{pK}}{2(n-1)}} \geq 1.0 \quad \text{Eq. (23)}$$

**Wu and Kuo's method for approximating the number of PPQ runs for a sample size of ≥30**

When the available sample size is ≥30, the LCCI equation can be simplified by replacing k with 3 and rearranging as follows:[9]

$$LCCI = C_{pK} - Z_{1-\alpha}\sqrt{\frac{1}{3^2 n} + \frac{C_{pK}^2}{2(n-1)}} \qquad \text{Eq. (24)}$$

Wu and Kuo rearranged the above equation and solved for the number of PPQ runs needed to meet the predefined specification at a specified confidence level (α), as shown in Equation 25 when the available sample size is ≥30:[8]

$$n = \frac{z_{\alpha}^2\left(\left(\frac{1}{9C_{pK}}\right) + 0.5\right)}{\left(1 - \frac{LCCI}{C_{pK}}\right)^2} \qquad \text{Eq. (25)}$$

The same randomly generated data used for the TI method were applied to illustrate the use of the PpK method.

**Table 7. Illustration of the PpK method for calculating the number of PPQ runs using Excel for a sample size of <25.**

| 1 | E | F | E | F |
|---|---|---|---|---|
| 2 | Symbol | Description | Value | Formula |
| 3 | $X_{avg}$ | Sample Average | 97.77 | =AVERAGE(sample data) |
| 4 | s | Sample Standard Deviation | 1.91 | =STDEV.S(sample data) |
| 5 | LSL | Lower Specification Limit | 95 | User-defined |
| 6 | USL | Upper Specification Limit | 105 | User-defined |
| 7 | $n_s$ | Sample Size | 12.00 | User-defined |

| 1 | E | F | E | F |
|---|---|---|---|---|
| 2 | Symbol | Description | Value | Formula |
| 8 | α | Target Confidence | 0.97 | User-defined based on risk assessment |
| 9 | p | Target Proportion | 0.80 | User-defined based on risk assessment |
| 10 | $\mu_{UCB}$ | Estimated Upper Confidence Value for the Population Mean | 97.79 | =G3+(T.INV(1-G8/2,G7-1))*(G4/SQRT(G7)) |
| 11 | $\mu_{LCB}$ | Estimated Lower Confidence Value for the Population Mean | 97.75 | =G3-(T.INV(1-G8/2,G7-1))*(G4/SQRT(G7)) |
| 12 | $\sigma_{UCB}$ | Estimated Upper Confidence Bound for the Population Standard Deviation | 1.99 | =(SQRT((G7-1)/CHISQ.INV(G8/2,G7-1)))*G4 |
| 13 | r | Interval Covering the Desired Proportion of the Population | 1.33 | User-entered; start with 0 and iteratively increase r until the p' value is approximately less than the target p |
| 14 | p' | Proportion Calculated by Changing r | 0.80 | =(NORM.S.DIST(1/SQRT(G7)+G13,TRUE))-(NORM.S.DIST(1/SQRT(G7)-G13,TRUE)) |
| 15 | k | Number of Sigma Factors | 2.206339 | =G13*(SQRT((G7-1)/CHISQ.INV(1-G8,G7-1))) |
| 16 | PpK | Capability Index | 2.511 | =MIN((G10-G5)/G15*G12,(G6-G11)/G15*G12) |

| 1 | E | F | E | F |
|---|---|---|---|---|
| 2 | Symbo l | Description | Value | Formula |
| 17 | n | **Number of PPQ Runs** | 6 | User-entered: start with 3 and iteratively increase n until the LCCI value is approximately 1.0 to 1.33 |
| 18 | LCCB | Lower Capability Confidence Bound | 1.0 | =G16-(NORM.S.INV(G8)*(SQRT((1/(G17*(G15^2)))+(G16^2/(2*(G17-1)))))) |

**Table 8 Illustration of calculating the number of PPQ runs via the PpK method using Excel when the sample size is >25**

| 1 | E | F | E | F |
|---|---|---|---|---|
| 3 | Symbo l | Description | Value | Formula |
| 4 | $X_{avg}$ | Sample Average | 97.77 | =AVERAGE(sample data) |
| 5 | s | Sample Standard Deviation | 1.91 | =STDEV.S(sample data) |
| 6 | LSL | Lower Specification Limit | 95 | User-defined |
| 7 | USL | Upper Specification Limit | 105 | User-defined |
| 8 | PpK | Estimated Process Capability | 1.762496 | =MIN((G7-G4)/3*G5,(G4-G6)/3*G5) |
| 9 | LCCI | Target, Lower Bound Process Capability | 1 | Default set to 1 |
| 10 | 1-α | Confidence | 0.97 | User-defined based on risk assessment |
| 11 | α | Acceptable Risk | 0.03 | =1-G10 |
| 12 | n | **Number of PPQ Runs** | 11 | =((NORM.S.INV(G11))^2)*((1/(9*G8))+0.5)/((1-(G9/G8))^2) |

## Intra-batch and Inter-batch variation

Intra-batch variability: Data gained during the stage-1 product life cycle through process development runs, process characterization runs at the bench scale, and scale-up runs at the pilot and manufacturing scale often incorporate sources of variation to the process introduced from differences in lot numbers of raw materials, differences in scales of operation, differences in controllers, and operation across a range of conditions and personnel. Therefore, data from stage-1 pre-PPQ studies will provide a reliable measure of within- or intra-batch variability.[13]

Inter-batch variability: Large datasets are required to reliably assess inter-batch, otherwise known as batch–batch variability. However, because sample data are typically limited before and after PPQ runs, it is difficult to make reliable assessments of inter-batch variation. Therefore, compensating the risk of uncertainty with a limited sample size by using the confidence and tolerance intervals when calculating the number of PPQ runs will incorporate the inter-batch variability. The TI and PpK methods for calculating the number of PPQ runs consider both inter- and intra-batch variation.

## Conclusion

Process and product understanding is established using the data from the early process development phase, previous experience from a similar process, scale-up activities, scale down model verification runs, and process characterization studies [10]. Unlike biologics and small molecules, the in-depth product knowledge in defining the Critical Quality Attributes (CQA) and characterization of Critical Process Parameters (CPPs) in manufacturing processes with a detailed understanding of variability introduced from raw materials and processes are yet to be established for new therapeutic technologies like gene-modified ex-vivo cell-based therapies and in-vitro gene therapies [17]. Therefore, though traditionally, three batches might be considered sufficient for process qualification to address the risk associated with product knowledge in new technologies to robustly meet the acceptable ranges, a risk-based approach based on historical product knowledge to meet predefined specifications at predefined statistical confidence should be used to calculate the number of PPQ runs as recommended in 2011 FDA validation guidance document. This article has provided detailed, step-by-step guidance on two such methods based on process capability and process tolerance, along with illustrative examples using MS Excel for easy adaptation and implementation by the reader. A single statistical method does not fit all manufacturing processes or even all attributes assessed in a single manufacturing process. Therefore, when selecting a statistical method and performing risk assessment to set confidence values, one should carefully evaluate not only the nature of the data and the reliability of historical knowledge but also the cost associated with manufacturing, testing, and releasing the product.

## References


1. U.S. Department of Health and Human Services Food and Drug Administration. (2011, January). Guidance for Industry Process Validation: General Principles and Practices.

http://www.fda.gov/downloads/Drugs/Guidances/UCM070336.pdf

2. James, D., Nesta, D. P., Desai, K. D., & Lewis, R. A. (2017, June 30). Stage 2 Process Validation: Regulatory Expectations and Approaches to Determine and Justify the Number of PPQ Batches. Biopharma International, 30(7).

3. ASTM E2476-09 Standard Guide for Risk Assessment and Risk Control as it Impacts the Design, Development, and Operation of PAT Processes for Pharmaceutical Manufacture.

4. Lakens, D. (2013). Calculating and reporting effect sizes to facilitate cumulative science: A practical primer for T-TesTs and ANOVAs. Frontiers in Psychology, 4. https://doi.org/10.3389/fpsyg.2013.00863

5. NIST/SEMATECH. (2012). Handbook of Statistical Methods. NIST. https://doi.org/10.18434/M32189

6. Cohen, J. (1988). Statistical Power Analysis for the Behavioral Sciences (2nd ed.). LAWRENCE ERLBAUM ASSOCIATES.

7. *Utilization of statistical methods for production monitoring*. (2012). Parenteral Drug Association. https://www.pda.org/bookstore/product-detail/1842-tr-59-utilization-of-statistical-methods

8. Charoo, N. A. (2018). Estimating number of PPQ batches: Various approaches. Journal of Pharmaceutical Innovation, 13(2), 188-196.

https://doi.org/10.1007/s12247-018-9316-2

9. Wu, C. C., & Kuo, H. L. (2004). Sample Size Determination for the Estimate of Process Capability Indices. Information and Management Sciences, 15(1), 1-12.

10. Yang, H. (2016). Emerging non-clinical biostatistics in Biopharmaceutical development and manufacturing. CRC Press.

11. Durivage, M. (2016, October 27). How To Establish Sample Sizes For Process Validation Using Statistical Tolerance Intervals. Bioprocess Online.

12. Vasta, A. (2021). Determining sample size for specification limits verification with tolerance intervals. Quality and Reliability Engineering International, 37(5), 1718-1739. https://doi.org/10.1002/qre.2821

13. Pazhayattil, A., Alsmeyer, D., Chen, S., Hye, M., Ingram, M., & Sanghvi, P. (2015). Stage 2 process performance qualification (PPQ): A scientific approach to determine the number of PPQ batches. AAPS PharmSciTech, 17(4), 829-833. https://doi.org/10.1208/s12249-015-0409-7

14. Bryder, M., Etling, H., Fleming, J., Hu, Y., & Levy, P. (2014, February 1). Topic 1 – Stage 2 Process Validation: Determining and Justifying the Number of Process Performance Qualification Batches (version 2). ISPE | International Society for Pharmaceutical Engineering.

https://ispe.org/publications/papers/stage-2-process-validation-process-performance-qualification-batches

15. Weng, Y. (2016). STATISTICAL REVIEW AND EVALUATION (Reference ID: 4026576). FDA. https://www.fda.gov/media/105013/download

16. Schuirmann, D. J. (1987). A comparison of the two one-sided test procedures and the power approach for assessing the equivalence of average bioavailability. Journal of Pharmacokinetics and Biopharmaceutics, 15(6), 657-680. https://doi.org/10.1007/bf01068419

17. Heidaran M. (2019, April 25). Manufacturing Controls at Commercial Scale: A Major Hurdle for the Cell and Gene Therapy Industry. Regulatory Focus. https://www.raps.org/news-and-articles/news-articles/2019/4/establishing-manufacturing-controls-a-hurdle-for

# Chapter 7: Comparison of Tolerance Interval and Process Capability Methods to Set Specifications Limits using MS Excel with Illustrative Examples

Naveenganesh Muralidharan

## Introduction

The critical quality attributes of biopharmaceutical products, such as safety, efficacy, purity, and identity, are effectively monitored and controlled to meet the predefined specification limits. Setting specifications is not only critical but also challenging for control strategy because setting narrow specification limits will lead to the risk of falsely rejecting the good batch, and setting broad specification limits will lead to the risk of falsely accepting the bad batch. [1]. Limited sample size, homogenous results obtained from limited variability from raw materials, and inherent variability associated with testing methodology can all sum up and lead to setting tighter specification limits and potentially cause challenges in meeting the specification limits in the long term during commercial production. Therefore, in this article two most commonly used statistical approaches for setting specification limits are discussed and compared. One is based on the historical performance of the process, namely the Tolerance Interval (TI) approach, and the other is based on predicting the capability of the process to consistently meet the specification by understanding the uncertainty in historic process data, namely Process Capability Index (PpK) approach. For setting specifications, one should use statistical methods only as a supporting tool and always consider the regulatory agencies' expectations, experience from similar products, and clinical & non-clinical study results. [1]

Furthermore, this article provides a step-by-step procedure for above mentioned statistical approaches using MS Excel as a tool with illustrative examples for easy adaptation and implementation by the reader.

## Tolerance Interval (TI) Method

The TI is the range that gives a fixed proportion (p) of the population at a stated statistical confidence (1-α) based on the assumption that the sample data are taken from a normally distributed population.[2, 3]

## Two-sided TI

A two-sided TI is expressed as shown in Equation 1:

$$TI_{UL} = (\mu) + k.(\sigma), \qquad TI_{LL} = (\mu) - k.(\sigma) \qquad \text{Eq. (1)}$$

Where TI represents the tolerance interval, μ and σ represent the population mean and population standard deviation, respectively, and k is the tolerance interval estimator, which is the number of standard deviations away from the mean that covers a certain fixed proportion of the population at the desired statistical confidence.

## Uncertainty with sample mean and sample standard deviation

Because of the limited sample size available during the process understanding phase, the underlying true population mean and population standard deviation are unknown. This uncertainty involved in using the limited sample size can be compensated by replacing the population mean and population standard deviation using confidence intervals of sample mean and sample standard deviation, respectively. The confidence interval is a range that gives a single-valued parameter, such as the mean or standard deviation, of a population at a stated confidence.

The confidence intervals around the mean and standard deviation are shown in Equations 2 and 3.[2]

$$x_{UCI} = x_{avg} + t_{\left(1-\frac{\alpha}{2}, n_s-1\right)} \frac{s}{\sqrt{n_s}}, x_{LCI} = x_{avg} - t_{\left(1-\frac{\alpha}{2}, n_s-1\right)} \frac{s}{\sqrt{n_s}} \qquad \text{Eq. (2)}$$

$$s_{UCI} = s.\sqrt{\frac{n_s - 1}{\chi^2_{(n_s-1),(\alpha)}}} \qquad \text{Eq. (3)}$$

Here, $x_{UCI}$ and $x_{LCI}$ represent the upper and lower confidence interval values for the mean, $S_{UCL}$ represents the upper confidence interval value for the standard deviation, $n_s$ is the sample size, $t_{(1-\alpha/2,\ df)}$ represents the inverse of the cumulative t distribution, $\chi^2$ represents the inverse of the cumulative chi-square distribution, The significance (α) value or type I error is often set at an acceptable value of 0.05,[4] indicating a 5% chance of false rejection of an actually true null hypothesis or in other words, the statistical confidence (1–α) is 100%–5%=95%.

Substituting Equations 2 and 3 in Equation 1 yields two-sided TI as:

$$TI_{UL} = (x_{UCI}) + k.(s_{UCI}) \ , TI_{LL} = (x_{LCI}) - k.(s_{UCI}) \qquad \text{Eq. (4)}$$

Howe (1969) gave an estimate of the TI estimator k value as a function of sample size (n), confidence (1-α), and proportion (p) of population to cover, as shown in Equation 12.[2]

$$k = z_{\left(\frac{p+1}{2}\right)} \sqrt{\frac{(n-1)(1+\frac{1}{n})}{\chi^2_{\alpha,n-1}}} \qquad \text{Eq. (5)}$$

Where z is the inverse of the cumulative normal distribution.

Later, Guenther corrected Howe's approximation by using k' instead of k for smaller samples, as shown in Equation 13.[2]

$$k' = z_{\left(\frac{p+1}{2}\right)} \sqrt{\frac{(n-1)(1+\frac{1}{n})}{\chi^2_{\alpha,n-1}}} . \sqrt{1 + \frac{n-3-\chi^2_{\alpha,n-1}}{2(n+1)^2}} \qquad \text{Eq. (6)}$$

## Sample data for illustration

For the purpose of illustration, Drug product potency data was adopted from Coffey, T., & Yang, H. (2018) with average and sample Standard deviation at 99.2% and 5.29%, respectively, at sample size (n)= 10. The calculation of two-sided specification limits using MS Excel is illustrated in Table 1. [10]

**Table 1. Illustration of calculating the specification limits via the TI method in Excel for two-sided specifications.**

| | A | B | C | D |
|---|---|---|---|---|
| 1 | Symbol | Description | Values | Formula |
| 2 | $X_{avg}$ | Sample Average | 99.20 | =AVERAGE(Sample Date) |

| | A | B | C | D |
|---|---|---|---|---|
| 1 | Symbol | Description | Values | Formula |
| 3 | s | Sample Standard Deviation | 5.29 | = STDEV.S(Sample Date) |
| 4 | ns | sample size | 10.00 | User Defined |
| 5 | 1-α | Confidence | 0.95 | User Defined |
| 6 | p | Proportion | 0.99 | User Defined |
| 7 | α | Acceptable Risk | 0.05 | =1-C5 |
| 8 | $\mu_{UCB}$ | Estimated Upper confidence on Mean | 99.31 | =C2+(T.INV(1-C5/2,C4-1))*(C3/SQRT(C4)) |
| 9 | $\mu_{LCB}$ | Estimated Lower confidence on Mean | 99.09 | =C2-(T.INV(1-C5/2,C4-1))*(C3/SQRT(C4)) |
| 10 | $\sigma_{UCB}$ | Estimated Upper confidence bound on Std | 5.58 | =(SQRT((C4-1)/CHISQ.INV(C5/2,C4-1)))*C3 |
| 11 | df | Degrees of freedom | 9 | =C4-1 |
| 12 | $z_{(p+1)/2}$ | Inverse Normal distribution at (p+1)/2 | 2.576 | =NORM.S.INV((C6+1)/2) |
| 13 | $\chi^2_{\alpha,\, df}$ | The inverse of $\chi^2$ distribution at α with df | 3.325 | =CHISQ.INV(C7,C11) |
| 14 | k | k using Howe's Method | 4.445 | =C12*SQRT(C11*(1+1/C4)/C13) |
| 15 | k' | corrected k value using Guenther's Method | 4.46 | =C14*SQRT((1+(C4-3-C14)/(2*C4+1)^2)) |
| 16 | USL | Upper Specification Limit | 124.18 | =C8+C15*C10 |
| 17 | LSL | Lower Specification Limit | 74.22 | =C9-C15*C10 |

## One-sided TI

For a one-sided TI, an approximate value for the k factor has been given by Natreilla as follows:[2]

$$k1 = \frac{z_p + \sqrt{z_p^2 - a.b}}{a} \qquad \text{Eq. (7)}$$

Where,

$$a = 1 - \frac{z_\alpha^2}{2(n-1)} \quad \text{Eq. (8)}$$

$$b = z_p^2 - \frac{z_\alpha^2}{n} \quad \text{Eq. (9)}$$

To illustrate the use of the TI method for a one-sided TI, we apply the same example used for the two-sided TI method. The calculation performed using MS Excel is detailed in Table 2.

**Table 2. Example of calculating the specification limits via the TI method for a one-sided specification.**

| | E | F | G | H |
|---|---|---|---|---|
| 1 | Symbol | Description | Values | Formula |
| 2 | $X_{avg}$ | Sample Average | 99.20 | =AVERAGE(Sample Data) |
| 3 | s | Sample Standard Deviation | 5.29 | =STDEV.S(Sample Data) |
| 4 | ns | sample size | 10.00 | User-defined |
| 5 | 1-α | Confidence | 0.95 | =1-C5 |
| 6 | p | Proportion | 0.99 | =C2+(T.INV(1-C5/2,C4-1))*(C3/SQRT(C4)) |
| 7 | α | Acceptable Risk | 0.05 | =C2-(T.INV(1-C5/2,C4-1))*(C3/SQRT(C4)) |
| 8 | $\mu_{UCB}$ | Estimated Upper confidence on Mean | 99.31 | =(SQRT((C4-1)/CHISQ.INV(C5/2,C4-1)))*C3 |
| 9 | $\mu_{LCB}$ | Estimated Lower confidence on Mean | 99.09 | =NORM.S.INV(C6) |
| 10 | $\sigma_{UCB}$ | Estimated Upper confidence bound on Std | 5.58 | =NORM.S.INV(C5) |
| 11 | $z_p$ | Inverse Normal distribution at p | 2.326 | =1-C12^2/(2*(C4-1)) |
| 12 | $z_\alpha$ | Inverse Normal distribution at 1-α | 1.645 | =C11^2-C12^2/C4 |
| 13 | a | N/A | 0.850 | =(C11+SQRT(C11^2-C13*C14))/C13 |

| | E | F | G | H |
|---|---|---|---|---|
| 1 | Symbol | Description | Values | Formula |
| 14 | b | N/A | 5.141 | =C8+C15*C10 |
| 8 | k1 | k1 factor for One Side TI | 3.940 | =1-C5 |
| 12 | USL | Upper Specification Limit | 121.3 | =C2+(T.INV(1-C5/2,C4-1))*(C3/SQRT(C4)) |

## Process Capability Method

### Process performance index (PpK)

The ability of a process to meet predefined specifications is determined by PpK, which is defined as the ratio of the distance from the process mean and nearest specification to the one-sided spread of the process (3σ variation) based on the overall standard deviation for a normally distributed population.[6] PpK is calculated as shown in Equations 10:[5]

$$PpU = \frac{USL - \mu}{3\sigma}, \qquad PpL = \frac{LSL - \mu}{3\sigma} \qquad \text{Eq. (10)}$$

Where PpL is the lower process performance index, PpU is the upper process performance index, and USL and LSL represent the upper and lower specification limits, respectively.

### Uncertainty with the sample mean, sample standard deviation, and sigma factor

The above equation (10) for PpK is typically employed when the sample size is at least 25. However, the sample size generated stage-1 process understanding phase is often less than 25, and the underlying true population mean and population standard deviation are unknown. As discussed for the TI method, the uncertainty of using the sample mean, and sample standard deviation due to a small sample size can be compensated for by replacing the sample mean and sample standard deviation with confidence intervals around the mean and standard deviation.

The sigma factor of ±3 in the 3σ term in Equation 10 represents the number of standard deviations from the mean that covers 99.7% of the true population. However, in order to accommodate the uncertainty involved in a limited available sample size, the term ±3 in

Equation 10 is replaced with r, which is the number of sigma factors from the mean covering the desired proportion of the population.

Now, by substituting Equations 2 and 3 in Equation 10, PpU and PpL can be rewritten as follows:

$$PpU = \frac{USL - (x_{UCI})}{r.s.\sqrt{\frac{n_s - 1}{\chi^2_{(n_s-1),(\alpha)}}}} \quad \text{Eq. (11)}$$

$$PpL = \frac{(x_{LCI}) - LSL}{r.s.\sqrt{\frac{n_s - 1}{\chi^2_{(n_s-1),(\alpha)}}}} \quad \text{Eq. (12)}$$

The r value can be calculated iteratively by increasing the value of r from r=0.1 in Equation 13 to achieve the desired population proportion (p).

$$p = \left(NORM.S.DIST\left(\frac{1}{\sqrt{n_s}} + r\right), TRUE\right) - \left(NORM.S.DIST\left(\frac{1}{\sqrt{n_s}} - r\right), TRUE\right) \quad \text{Eq. (13)}$$

**Uncertainty with PpK estimation**

Bissell's approximated confidence interval for a capability index that accommodates uncertainty for the PpK calculation is shown in Equation 22.[6, 7, 8]

$$P_{pK} - Z_{1-\alpha}\sqrt{\frac{1}{k^2 n} + \frac{P_{pK}^2}{2(n-1)}} \le Ppk \le P_{pK} + Z_{1-\alpha}\sqrt{\frac{1}{k^2 n} + \frac{P_{pK}^2}{2(n-1)}} \quad \text{Eq (14)}$$

Where,

$$k = r.\sqrt{\frac{n_s - 1}{\chi^2_{(n_s-1),(\alpha)}}} \quad \text{Eq. (15)}$$

A capability index value of 1.0–1.3 indicates that the process is capable and most likely to routinely meet the specifications [5]. Therefore, the specification can be calculated by iteratively changing the value of the observed mean to achieve a lower capability confidence interval (LCCI) of 1.0.

$$LCCI = P_{pK} - Z_{1-\alpha}\sqrt{\frac{1}{k^2 n} + \frac{P_{pK}^2}{2(n-1)}} \geq 1.0 \quad \text{Eq. (16)}$$

Upper and Lower Specification limits to meet the minimum process capability can be calculated by solving the below in-equalities in equations 17 and 18.

$$\frac{USL-(x_{UCI})}{k.s} - Z_{1-\alpha}\sqrt{\frac{1}{k^2 n} + \frac{\left(\frac{USL-(x_{UCI})}{k.s}\right)^2}{2(n-1)}} \geq 1.0 \quad \text{Eq. (17)}$$

$$\frac{(x_{LCI})-LSL}{k.s} - Z_{1-\alpha}\sqrt{\frac{1}{k^2 n} + \frac{\left(\frac{(x_{LCI})-LSL}{k.s}\right)^2}{2(n-1)}} \geq 1.0 \quad \text{Eq. (18)}$$

**Table 7. Illustration of the PpK method for calculating the number of PPQ runs using Excel**

| | A | B | C | D |
|---|---|---|---|---|
| 1 | Symbol | Description | Values | Formula |
| 2 | $X_{avg}$ | Sample Average | 99.20 | =AVERAGE(Sample Date) |
| 3 | s | Sample Standard Deviation | 5.29 | = STDEV.S(Sample Date) |
| 4 | ns | sample size | 10.00 | User Defined |
| 5 | 1-α | Confidence | 0.95 | User Defined, default = 0.95 |
| 6 | p | Proportion | 0.99 | User Defined, default = 0.99 |
| 7 | α | Acceptable Risk | 0.05 | =1-C5 |

| | A | B | C | D |
|---|---|---|---|---|
| 1 | Symbol | Description | Values | Formula |
| 8 | $\mu_{UCB}$ | Estimated Upper confidence on Mean | 99.31 | =C2+(T.INV(1-C5/2,C4-1))*(C3/SQRT(C4)) |
| 9 | $\mu_{LCB}$ | Estimated Lower confidence on Mean | 99.09 | =C2-(T.INV(1-C5/2,C4-1))*(C3/SQRT(C4)) |
| 10 | r | Interval Covering the Desired Proportion of the Population | 2.6 | User-entered; start with r value =0.1 and iteratively increase the r by 0.1 value until p' is approximately equal to p |
| 11 | p' | Proportion Calculated by Changing r | 0.99 | =NORM.S.DIST(((1/SQRT(C4))+C10),TRUE)-(NORM.S.DIST(((1/SQRT(C4))-C10),TRUE)) |
| 12 | k | Number of Sigma Factors | 4.277 | =C10*(SQRT((C4-1)/CHISQ.INV(1-C5,C4-1))) |
| 13 | PpK | Minimum Desired PPK | 1 | 1 |
| 14 | LSL | Lower Specification Limit | 137 | User-entered; start with mean value and iteratively increase until the $LCCI_{USL}$ value is approximately ≥ 1.0 |
| 15 | USL | Upper Specification Limit | 61 | User-entered; start with mean value and iteratively decrease until the $LCCI_{USL}$ value is approximately ≥ 1.0 |
| 16 | $LCCI_{USL}$ | Calculated LCCI for USL | 1.01 | =((C14-C8)/(C12*C3))-NORM.S.INV(C5)*SQRT((1/((C12^2)*C4))+(((C14-C8)/(C12*C3))^2/(2*(C4-1)))) |
| 17 | $LCCI_{LSL}$ | Calculated LCCI for LSL | 1.02 | =((C9-C15)/(C12*C3))-NORM.S.INV(C5)*SQRT((1/((C12^2)*C4))+(((C9-C15)/(C12*C3))^2/(2*(C4-1)))) |

## Conclusion

In this article, it has been shown that for the same data set, the calculated specification limits using the process capability method are wider than the tolerance interval method. Though traditionally, tolerance interval is the most widely used approach, the process capability method is recommended when detailed product knowledge is yet to be established, and there is a risk in robustly meeting the acceptable specification ranges at the commercial production phase. Alternatively, the PpK method can also be adapted to justify the wider product specification in Biological License Application (BLA) preparation under the post-approval section.

## References

1. EMA. (2019). Report on the expert workshop on setting specifications for biotech products (EMA/CHMP/BWP/30584/2012).

https://www.ema.europa.eu/en/documents/report/report-expert-workshop-setting-specifications-biotech-products_en.pdf

2. NIST/SEMATECH. (2012). Handbook of Statistical Methods. NIST. https://doi.org/10.18434/M32189
3. Durivage, M. (2016, October 27). How To Establish Sample Sizes For Process Validation Using Statistical Tolerance Intervals. Bioprocess Online.
4. Lakens, D. (2013). Calculating and reporting effect sizes to facilitate cumulative science: A practical primer for T-TesTs and ANOVAs. Frontiers in Psychology, 4. https://doi.org/10.3389/fpsyg.2013.00863
5. Utilization of statistical methods for production monitoring. (2012). Parenteral Drug Association. https://www.pda.org/bookstore/product-detail/1842-tr-59-utilization-of-statistical-methods
6. Charoo, N. A. (2018). Estimating number of PPQ batches: Various approaches. Journal of Pharmaceutical Innovation, 13(2), 188-196.

https://doi.org/10.1007/s12247-018-9316-2

7. Wu, C. C., & Kuo, H. L. (2004). Sample Size Determination for the Estimate of Process Capability Indices. Information and Management Sciences, 15(1), 1-12.
8. Yang, H. (2016). Emerging non-clinical biostatistics in Biopharmaceutical development and manufacturing. CRC Press.
9. Krause, S. O. (2015). PCMO I01--setting specifications for biological Investigational medicinal products. PDA Journal of Pharmaceutical Science and Technology, 69(5), 569-589. https://doi.org/10.5731/pdajpst.2015.01065
10. Coffey, T., & Yang, H. (2018). Statistics for biotechnology process development. CRC Press.

# Chapter 8: Sample Size for CAPA effectiveness check to demonstrate Zero failures.

Naveenganesh Muralidharan

## Introduction

Biopharmaceutical manufacturers often implement corrective and preventive actions (CAPA) as a mitigation strategy to address deviations based on the identified root cause from investigations. CAPA implementation is frequently followed by effectiveness checks. The CAPA effectiveness is demonstrated by ensuring a specific parameter can meet the acceptable requirement.

If the monitored parameter to ensure CAPA effectiveness does not follow any specific data distribution or results reports as pass/ fail, then the statistical approach for the selection of sample size to ensure the reliability of the effectiveness check is not necessarily straightforward. Therefore, this article details one such appropriate statistical approach to calculate the sample size named "Reliability Demonstration Tests" (RDT) to verify whether a product/process has met a certain reliability requirement at a stated statistical confidence level when the underlying data distribution is unknown.

Though different RTD methods (Cumulative Binomial, Non-Parametric Binomial, Exponential Chi-Squared, and Non-Parametric Bayesian) are available, this article focuses on two of the simplest and easy to adopt methods, named Non-Parametric Binomial and Exponential Chi-Squared methods as the rest of the methods have limitations such as feeding prior information based on assumptions, and there is no one "correct way of calculating prior information" and different approaches give different results. Furthermore, this article also recommends risk assessment methodology for the selection of acceptable reliability and statistical confidence that may be used in the above discussed two RDT methods.

## Non-Parametric Binomial Method:

This method is also called the Classical Reliability Demonstration Test. When "x" is the number of observed failures out of "n" trials. And the probability of each trial "p" is an independent Bernoulli trial. Then, the probability of at least "c" failure can be calculated using binomial distribution.

$$Prob\,\{obataining\ \text{"c" or}\ less\ failures\} = \sum_{x=0}^{c} C_x^n \times p^x(1-p)^{n-x}$$

Eq-1

For zero failures, assuming "c" = 0, the above equation-1 reduces to equation 2:

$$Prob\,\{zero\ occorence, \text{"}c = 0\text{"}\} = (1-p)^n$$

Eq-2

(1-p) is also termed as reliability (R).

Equation 2 can be re-written as:

$$(1-p)^n = R^n \qquad \text{Eq-3}$$

Now, the number sample size can be determined by equating equation-3 to significance value (α) type-1 error, in other words probability of falsely rejecting a true null hypothesis.

$$(1-p)^n = R^n \geq \alpha \qquad \text{Eq-4}$$

Taking Logarithms on both sides in the above equation 4 and solving for sample size (n), we obtain:

$$n \geq \frac{ln(\alpha)}{ln(R)} = \frac{ln(1-C)}{ln\,(R)}$$
Eq-5

In the above equation 5, the term "C" is confidence. Equation 5 tells us to have C % confidence, and the CAPA is R % reliable; a minimum of n samples needs to be tested to ensure zero failure as acceptance criteria.

**Exponential Chi-Squared Method:**

In the exponential chi-squared method, the sample size for zero failure is again calculated as a function of reliability and confidence, as shown in equation 6.

$$n \geq \frac{\chi^2_{(1-C,2)}}{2 \times (1-R)}$$

Were,

$\chi^2_{(1\text{-}C,\,2)}$ represents the inverse of the right-tailed probability of the chi-squared distribution at 1-C probability and "2" degrees of freedom. In Microsoft Excel, this value can be calculated using =CHISQ.INV.RT(probability, degrees of freedom) function.

**Risk Assessment:** The American Society for Testing and Materials (ASTM) outlines three criteria that are used to create a risk assessment matrix for the attributes/parameters to be monitored: the **severity of the consequences** if a problem or failure occurs, the **likelihood of occurrence**, and the **likelihood of detection** (of a problem or of a detection failure).[3] Each of these criteria can then be scored on a scale from 1 to 5, as shown in **Table 1**. [2]

**Table 1. Risk assessment scoring matrix based on ASTM recommendations.**

| Severity (S) | Occurrence (O) | Detectability (D) | Score |
|---|---|---|---|
| • Critical process parameter: Directly/indirectly impacts the quality attributes of the product with predefined proven acceptable ranges.<br>• Critical quality attributes: Used as the release criteria for the product with | • The root cause is not clearly identified.<br>• Only potential root causes or contributing factors are identified. | Poor chance of detecting failure before impacting patient health | 5 |

| Severity (S) | Occurrence (O) | Detectability (D) | Score |
|---|---|---|---|
| predefined specification values. | • A potential control strategy for failure modes is in place.<br>• The chance for re-occurrence is uncertain. | | |
| • Key process parameter (KPP): Parameters that impact the productivity or batch yield with predefined normal operating ranges.<br>• In-process controls: Parameters that are monitored at any intermediate stage of the manufacturing process before continuing to the next step with predefined acceptable limits. | • The root cause is identified,<br>• Only a potential control strategy for failure mode is in place.<br>• It may occur again. | May detect failure | 3 |
| • Non-KPP: Typically well-controlled and unlikely to impact the quality or productivity. | • Root cause and Control strategy for failure mode is well established.<br>• Unlikely to occur gain. | Will detect failure every time | 1 |

The product of the three scores ((S) x (O) x (D)) gives a "risk priority number (RPN)." Based on the RPN of a given attribute/parameter, the risk associated with the attribute/parameter is classified as high, medium, or low, as shown in **Table 2**. For each risk classification, Table 2 also shows the recommendations for Confidence (C) and Reliability. The selection of reliability is based on Rules of thumb on Cronbach`s Alpha coefficient that measures the measures' reliability, or internal consistency [3].

**Table 2. Guidance for selecting statistical confidence and population proportion.**

| RPN score | Risk classification | Confidence (1-C) | Reliability (R) | The number of samples required is based on the Non-Parametric Binomial Method. | The number of samples required is based on the Exponential chi-square method. |
|---|---|---|---|---|---|
| **1–25** | Low | 0.90 | 0.60* | 5 | 6 |
| **26–50** | Medium | 0.90 | 0.70 * | 6 | 8 |
| **≥ 51** | High | 0.95 | 0.80 | 13 | 15 |
| (A) 0.6 And 0.7 reliability scores are acceptable based on the assumption that investigation has led to precisely identifying the root cause and control strategy for failure mode is well reliable and only the statistical confidence on the corrective action implemented needs to be demonstrated. | | | | | |

## Conclusion:

It is highly recommended to document the statistical methods and rationality for selecting the sample size to ensure that the CAPA is effective. Determining sample sizes using both methods (Non-Parametric Binomial and Exponential Chi-Squared) is are widely accepted practice in FDA-regulated industries. As shown in Table 2, there is no significant difference in the calculated sample size with either of the approaches. Therefore, any of the above methods can be used.

The confidence and reliability discussed in this article are for illustration purposes only. However, based on the nature of the process, batch run rate, and cost associated with the batch, it is highly recommended to use more suitable confidence and reliability values by drug manufacturers in adherence to their quality policy.

### References


1. The Quality, Reliability and Continuous Improvement Institute (QR&CII). (n.d.). Determining the Experimental Sample Size.

https://web.cortland.edu/romeu/ExperSampSizeQR&CII.pdf.

2. Muralidharan, N. (2023, May). Process Validation: Calculating the Necessary Number of Process Performance Qualification Runs. Bioprocess International, 21(5), 37-43.

3. Salkind, N. J. (2007). Encyclopedia of measurement and statistics. SAGE.

4. Gorski, A. (1985). CHI-square probabilities are Poisson probabilities in disguise. IEEE Transactions on Reliability, R-34(3), 209-211.

https://doi.org/10.1109/tr.1985.5222117

# Chapter 9: CPV Monitoring - Optimization of Control Chart Design by reducing the False Alarm Rate and Nuisance signal.

**Naveenganesh Muralidharan*, Thatsinee Johnson, Mark Davis**

## 1. Introduction

The Food and Drug Administration (FDA) 2011 Process Validation Guidance recommends continued process verification (CPV) during stage-3 process monitoring for drug manufacturers. In CPV, Shewhart control charts are employed as a statistical tool for monitoring process parameters and attributes (critical process parameters (CPPs), Key process parameters (KPPs), In-process controls (IPCs), and release specifications). In control charts, the calculated process average is utilized as the center line, and control limits are placed at a distance k = ±3 short-term standard deviations ($\sigma_R$) away from the process average. The control chart, along with Nelson rules, serves as a tool for detecting out-of-control (OOC) data, defined as data that falls beyond the set control limits, and out-of-trend (OOT) data, defined as a group of data that forms a non-random pattern (shift in mean or increasing/decreasing pattern) [1-3]. Although control charts are commonly applied across the industry to assess the statistical stability of a process, this approach introduces two types of risk: 1) false alarms, i.e., signals that are incorrectly identified as OOC or OOT when the data actually belong to normal variability of the process itself, and 2) nuisance alarms, i.e., signals that are too small to have any impact on the process or lack sufficient statistical reliability [4, 5]. In practice, small process variations and shifts are anticipated in many processes; therefore, control charts should detect moderate to large shifts that have more practical application rather than small or practically insignificant shift signals. Both high false alarm rates (FARs) and frequent nuisance alarms will reduce the reliability of control chart signals. Therefore, in this article, we provide a review of the current state of understanding of FARs associated with different Nelson rules, properties of data distributions (skewness and kurtosis) and their impact on control chart FAR, and methods for reducing FARs by optimizing the usage of Nelson rules and adjusting the value of k (the number of standard deviations from the mean) to accommodate variability and asymmetricity in data distribution.

## 2. Functional Modules of CPV.

CPV program is driven by four functional models, as identified in Figure 1. CPV standard operating procedure (SOP): Drug manufacturers define the standard operating procedure for CPV as a guidance document that minimum should discuss 1) the criteria for selection parameters to be monitored and trended, 2) the Frequency of cross-functional team to perform data review meetings to monitor and analyze the trends of parameters and attributes, 3) Participants in the cross-functional CPV data review meeting, 4) Discuss different statistical methods to assess the process capability and stability based on the type of data distribution, 5) Method of the controlled way of documenting the meeting minutes of CPV data review meeting, 6) Guidance on the frequency of CPV report generation based on batch run rate, and 7) Guidance on reaction and response to signals from CPV data monitoring system.

CPV Plan: As per the recommendations in CPV SOP, the CPV plan is generation for each drug substance intermediate stage, which lists out all the parameters to be monitored and trended, type of data distribution, and statistical method that may be applied to assess the stability and capability.

CPV data review meeting: As recommended in the CPV SOP, the parameters listed in CPV plans are charted and analyzed for signals of unexpected variation from historical performance as a cross-functional team that includes minimum participation from manufacturing, quality assurance (QA), manufacturing science and technology (MSAT) and quality control (QC). During the data review, the identified statistical process control signals for OOT or OOC are discussed on: 1. Magnitude of signal, 2. Statistical reliability of signal 3. Risk and severity on product quality and/or process performance and decision on how to respond to the signal is warranted. If the signal is identified as a nascence signal or not practically significant enough or not statistically significant enough, then no response or action is required. If the signal is identified to be real and has both practical and statistical strength but is still not significant enough to impact product quality, then a technical evaluation may be warranted to understand the cause of variation. Details of evaluation and results should be followed up in subsequent CPV meetings, and findings should be documented in CPV meeting minutes. If the signal is identified to be real, has both practical and statistical significance, and the magnitude is significant enough to potentially impact the product quality, then an investigation under a quality management system may be required.

CPV reports: CPV reports are generated either annually, semiannually, or quarterly basis based on batch run rate. Here all parameters and attributes listed in CPV pans are monitored and trended along with summary stability and capability discussions along with all the CPV data review meeting minutes. Recommendations from the CPV reports on changes in the frequency of monitoring or retiring parameters from CPV monitoring may be implemented in CPV plans.

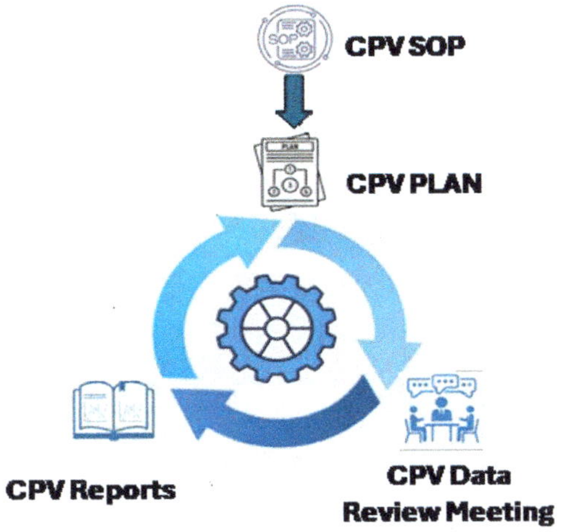


**Figure 1. Functional modules of CPV**

## 2. FARs in control charts

In 1924, Walter Andrew Shewhart introduced the concept of data analysis using control charts, which was later adopted by the pharmaceutical and biopharmaceutical industries when regulatory agencies requested that drug manufacturers perform CPV [6]. In control charts or XBar charts, the center line is placed at the average, and control limits are typically placed at k standard deviations from the average. Typically, k = 3 is utilized, for which there is a 0.135% probability that any data point belonging to a normally distributed population will fall outside ±3 standard deviations (σ). This approach gives an interval of expected future observations if the process does not change. If observations are within these limits, it can be assumed that the validated state is maintained; if observations are outside these limits, the mean and/or standard deviation has probably changed, potentially requiring attention. σ is often calculated as a short-term $\sigma_R$, which causes the limits to be more sensitive to drift, as expressed in (1).

$$CL = \mu \pm 3(\sigma_R) \qquad (1)$$

The control chart is divided into six zones based on distance from the center line, as shown in Figure 2. Each zone is one standard deviation ($\sigma_R$) wide. The 3-$\sigma_R$ limits on both sides of the center line show the upper control limit and lower control limit. The 2-$\sigma_R$ limits indicate the upper and lower warning limits, and the 1-$\sigma_R$ limits on each side of the center line are the upper and lower one-sigma limits. Control charts, along with Nelson rules 1–8 (summarized in Table 1), are used to monitor process control and process stability based on the location of data in different zones, the frequency of occurrence of any patterns, and the distance from the mean [6]. To correctly apply the Nelson test rule signals in a control chart, it is imperative to understand the normal, acceptable probability for a data point to fall within or outside of the control chart zones. For instance, for a hypothetical mean μ=0 and standard deviation σ=1, the probability that normally distributed data will fall between -3 SD and +3 SD is given by (2).

$$p = 1 - [\Phi(x = 3) - \Phi(x = -3)] \quad (2)$$

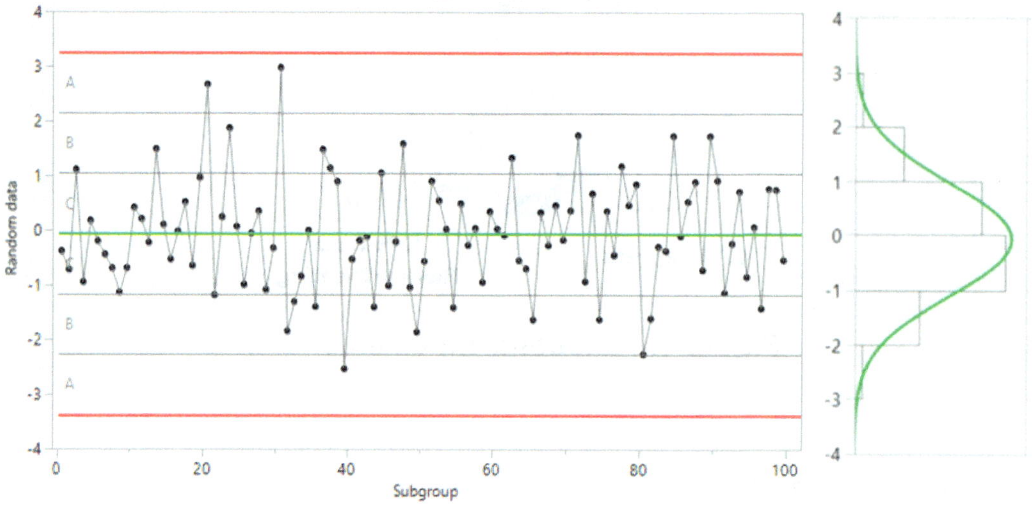


**Figure 2. Sample X control chart constructed from randomly generated data.**

### *2.1 Optimizing the number of Nelson test rules used in a control chart*

In statistical process control, the FAR or rate of type I errors, often identified by the symbol α, indicates the likelihood that data will be falsely identified as an abnormal signal when the data actually correspond to the normal variability of the process. Table 1 summarizes the different Nelson rules and their purposes, along with the probability of a false alarm for each Nelson rule [7].

The FARs from all eight Nelson rules identified in Table 1 sum up to 2.65%. Although it might be intriguing to use all eight Nelson test rules, Nelson (1984) suggested keeping the FAR below 1% [6]. Nelson also stated that tests 5 and 6 should be included only when there is an economical desire to have an early warning, as these test rules increase the FAR by 2%. Tests 7 and 8 are used to diagnose stratifications and both test 7 and 8, react only when each reported results in control charts are from an average of 2 or more samples (i.e. subgroup size "m" ≥ 2). However, in the biopharmaceutical industry, the results reported for a batch is typically from a test performed on single sample; therefore, unless multiple samples are tested and averaged to report a single value in the control chart, rules 7 and 8 do not add value for data monitoring and trending. Adhibhatta et al. (2017) showed that Nelson tests 1, 2, and 3 are adequate for monitoring OOC and OOT data, with a combined false alarm probability of 0.94 [8]. Thus, considering the practical application of test rules for biopharmaceuticals and to limit the FAR below 1.0%. It is recommended that only Nelson test rules 1 to 3 be utilized in a control chart for biopharmaceutical application.

**Table 1. FARs for different Nelson test rules.**

| Test number | Purpose | Probability of false alarm |
|---|---|---|
| **Rule 1**: One data point outside the control limit | Detect OOC data | p fal-Nel(1) = 0.00270 |
| **Rule 2**: Nine consecutive data points on one side of the center line | Detect a process shift | p fal-Nel(2) = 0.00391 |
| **Rule 3**: Six consecutive data points either increasing or decreasing | Detect a process drift | p fal-Nel(3) = 0.00278 |
| **Rule 4:** Fourteen consecutive data points alternating up and down | Detect a process alternating between two states | p fal-Nel(4) = 0.00457 |
| **Rule 5:** Two out of three data points falling outside two sigma from the center line | Detect an intermediate shift | p fal-Nel(5) = 0.00306 |
| **Rule 6**: Four out of five data points falling outside two sigma from the center line | Detect a small shift | p fal-Nel(6) = 0.00553 |
| **Rule 7:** Fifteen data points falling within one sigma from the center line | Detect a reduction in process variability | p fal-Nel(7) = 0.00326 |
| **Rule 8:** Eight consecutive data points falling outside one sigma from the center line | Detect mixed process behavior | p fal-Nel(8) = 0.00010 |

## 3. FAR in an OOC signal from a limited sample size

OOC data are detected via Nelson rule 1 when a single data point falls outside 3 SD from the mean, with the assumptions that the data are normally distributed, the underlying true population means (μ) and population standard deviation (σ) are known, and there is no error due to sampling variability. However, for new products, based on the batch run rate, there is a high likelihood of having a very limited sample size during the first couple of years. For small sample sizes, the estimation of the population mean with the sample mean ($\bar{x}$) and of the population standard deviation with the sample standard deviation (SD) and the establishment of control limits will lead to an increased FAR [9, 14]. The risk of an increased FAR due to limited sample size in control limits has been calculated by Bischak et al. (2007) as a function of the number of standard deviations from the mean (k), the number of observations (n), and the size of the subgroup in each observation (m). As discussed above, biopharmaceutical companies typically perform testing on a single sample taken from a batch; therefore, two subsequent lots are used to calculate the short-term standard deviation, and hence, m is assumed to be 2. The FAR for a limited number of observations or sample size (n) is expressed in (3). Here, ($C_4$) is an unbiased estimator of standard deviation. The uncertainty that arises from using the sample standard deviation (SD) instead of the underlying true population standard deviation is compensated for by using an unbiased standard deviation estimator ($C_4$) calculated as a function of subgroup size, as expressed in (4) [10, 13]. Here, Φ is the cumulative normal probability density function.

$$FAR_{(n)} = 2 \times \Phi\left(\frac{-k}{\sqrt{1+\frac{1}{n}\left(1+\frac{k^2(1-c_4^2)}{c_4^2}\right)}}\right) \quad (3)$$

$$C_4 = \left[\frac{\Gamma(\frac{m}{2})}{\Gamma(\frac{m-1}{2})}\right] \times \sqrt{\frac{2}{m-1}} \quad (4)$$

The probability of a false alarm caused by utilizing a limited sample size when setting the control limit at k = 3 (i.e., 3 standard deviations from the mean) is calculated by applying

(3) and (4), as shown in Figure 3. Figure 3 shows that the reduction in FAR follows an exponential decay curve; we observe a sharp drop below 5% for a sample size of n = 10, followed by a plateau after approximately n = 30 and a further decrease below 1% at n = 100. Therefore, we recommend using a run chart when the sample size is ≤10, using the calculated control limits as tentative control limits for monitoring and updating control limits for sample sizes of 30–100, and using fixed long-term control limits when the sample size is ≥100. Another alternative solution for mitigating the uncertainty in the calculation of control limits for a small sample size (n < 30) is the use of prediction limits. Prediction limits account for the estimation uncertainty that arises from using the sample standard deviation (SD) by replacing the normal quantile with the t quantile at (n–1) degrees of freedom and also accommodates the uncertainty due to the sample mean by including the standard error of the mean, as expressed in (5).

$$CL = \bar{X} \pm t_{(1-\frac{\alpha}{2},\ n-1)} . SD . \sqrt{1 + 1/n} \qquad (5)$$

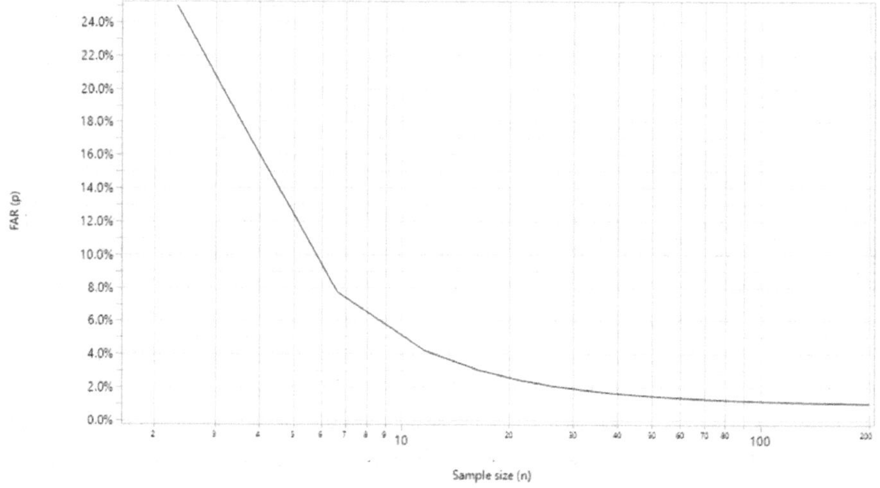


**Figure 3. FAR in an OOC signal from a limited sample size.**

## 4. FAR in an OOC signal from a skewed or heavy-tailed distribution

The application of Nelson test rules in a control chart is based on a normality assumption. However, if the data are severely skewed or if the variance in the data is excessively broad with a heavy-tailed distribution, this can lead to an increase in the FAR. The asymmetry and tail length in data with reference to a normal distribution are measured as skewness ($K_3$) and kurtosis ($K_4$), respectively [14].

### 4.1. Modeling FAR for an asymmetric data distribution

Control charts are based on the assumption that a data distribution is symmetric on either side of the center average line. However, in practice, the data distribution may be off-centered or asymmetric. Skewness ($K_3$) is a measure of the degree of asymmetry observed in a data distribution. A distribution can have either right-skewed or left-skewed data or no skew at all. A right-skewed distribution is longer on the right side of its peak, and a left-skewed distribution is longer on the left side of its peak. Skewness in a distribution can be calculated from (6) [11]. A highly skewed distribution can lead to a high FAR in control chart signals. The probability distribution function of a skewed data spread can be modeled by a log-normal distribution [12], which is delineated by two parameters, namely, the shape (Sh) or mean (μ) and the scale parameter (Sc) or standard deviation (σ). The FAR caused by skewness in data distribution with control limits placed at ± 3 ($\sigma_R$) from the mean can be determined by knowing the relationship between the skewness value and shape parameter (Sh). A correlation expression between skewness and shape parameter (Sh) was developed from the data reported by Derya et al. (2012), as shown in Figure 4A [12]. Assuming a scale parameter of Sc = 0 with the shape parameter (Sh) calculated via the correlation shown in Figure 4A, the FAR for various degrees of skewness can be calculated via Equation (7), as shown in Figure 4B. Here, k is the number of standard deviations from the mean; for control limits placed at 3 SDs from the mean, k = 3. Figure 4B shows that a skewness below 1.5 keeps the control limit signal at an acceptable FAR of <1.0%.

$$K_3 = \frac{\sum_1^n (X_i - \bar{X})^3}{(n) \times \sigma^3} \quad (6)$$

$$FAR_{K3} = 1 - \Phi\left(\frac{ln(k) - Sc}{Sh}\right) \quad (7)$$

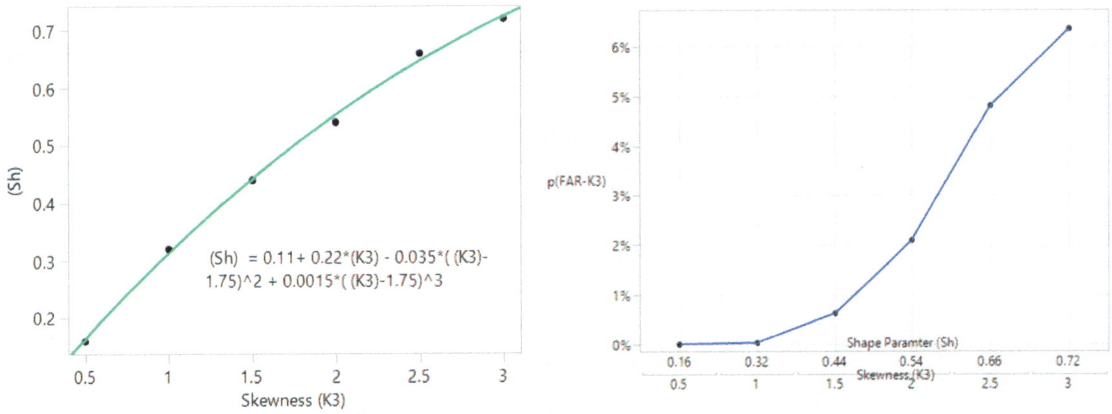


**Figure 4. (A) Correlation between skewness and log-normal shape factor. (B) FAR for an OOC signal from an asymmetric data distribution.**

### 4.2. Modeling FAR for a heavy-tailed distribution

Kurtosis is a measure of whether data are heavy-tailed or light-tailed relative to a normal distribution. A data distribution with high kurtosis tends to have heavy tails or outliers. In contrast, a data distribution with low kurtosis tends to have light tails or a lack of outliers. A standard normal distribution has a kurtosis of zero. The kurtosis ($K_4$) can be calculated from expression (8) [11, 14]. A positive kurtosis indicates a "heavy-tailed" distribution. A t-distribution has fatter tails than a normal distribution. Therefore, a t-distribution can be used as a model to represent kurtosis, which will allow for a more realistic calculation of the FAR from excess kurtosis [11]. The FAR caused by kurtosis can be modeled via a t-distribution, as expressed in (9) and as shown in Figure 5, by knowing the relationship between kurtosis ($K_4$) and degrees of freedom (df) for the t-distribution. Here, k is the number of standard deviations from the mean; for control chart limits placed at 3 SDs from the mean, k = 3. df is the number of degrees of freedom for the t-distribution, and $df_{t.\,Dist}$ can be calculated from the kurtosis ($K_4$) in the data distribution, as expressed in (10) [15].

$$K_4 = \frac{\sum_1^n (X_i - \bar{X})^4}{(n) \times \sigma^4} - 3 \qquad (8)$$

$$FAR_{K4} = 2 \times \left[1 - t.dist\left((k), (df_{t.dist})\right)\right] \qquad (9)$$

$$df_{t.dist} = 4 + \left(\frac{6}{K4-1}\right) \qquad (10)$$

### 4.3 Adjustment to k to accommodate skewed and heavy-tailed distributions.

Braden et al. (2022) showed that the FAR for a severely skewed or heavy-tailed distribution can be reduced by replacing the control limits at k = 3 ($\sigma_R$) from the mean with limits based on adjusted k values (k'), as expressed in (11) and (12), to accommodate skewness or heavy tails in the data distribution. Branden also stated that Equations (11) and (12) are valid only when the skewness or kurtosis of the distribution meets the criteria expressed in (13) [14]. The factor adjustment for skewness and kurtosis is shown in Figure 6.

$$k' = 3 + \frac{4}{3}\left(\frac{K_3}{\sqrt{n}}\right) \qquad (11)$$

$$k' = 3 + \left(\frac{K_4}{n + 0.33\,K_4}\right) \qquad (12)$$

$$-2.489 \le \frac{K_3}{\sqrt{n}} \le 2.489 \; and \; 0 \le \frac{K_4}{n} \le 11.549 \qquad (13)$$

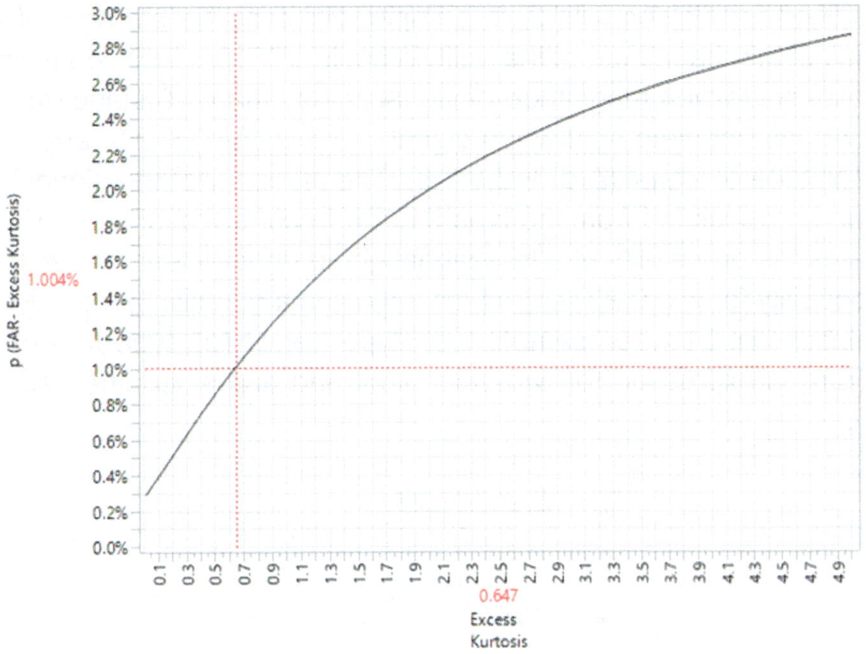


**Figure 5. FAR in an OOC signal due to kurtosis.**

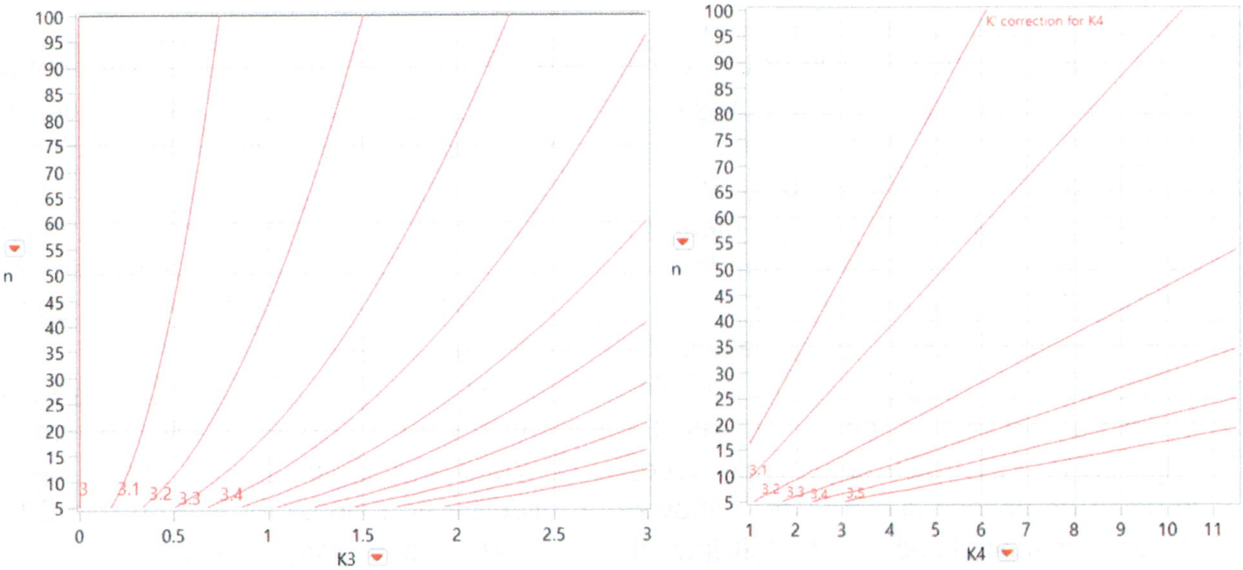


**Figure 6. (Left) Adjustment of k for skewness. (Right). Adjustment of k for kurtosis.**

## 5. Nuisance signal from Nelson rule 2 and its reliability

According to Nelson rule 2, nine consecutive data points on one side of the center line can be used to detect a shift in the mean, which can result in a nuisance signal, as the magnitude of this shift in the mean can be potentially insignificant. Therefore, when a signal is identified for Nelson rule 2, it is imperative that the strength of the signal be assessed against the magnitude of the shift. Wheeler (2010) classified Nelson test rule 2 signals as small shift when magnitude of signal is less than 1.5 standard deviation from mean ($\Delta/\sigma$). An intermediate shift when signal is $1.5 \geq (\Delta/\sigma) \leq 2.5$, and as a large shift when the magnitude of signal $(\Delta/\sigma) > 2.5$ [16]. The reliability of the signal for the desired shift effect can be calculated from the type II error. In control charts, the ($\beta$) value or type II error indicates the probability of a true signal going undetected. The widely acceptable minimum probability for $\beta$ is 0.20 [17], which indicates a reliability ($1-\beta$) of 100% – 20% = 80%. The relationship between sample size, type I error ($\alpha$), type II error ($\beta$), and shift from mean ($\Delta/\sigma$) is expressed for two-sided limit and one-sided limit, as shown in (14) and (15) [21].

$$n_T = \frac{\left(t_{1-\alpha/2,df} + t_{1-\beta,df}\right)^2}{\left(\frac{\Delta}{\sigma}\right)^2} \quad (14)$$

$$n_T = \frac{\left(t_{1-\alpha,df} + t_{1-\beta,df}\right)^2}{\left(\frac{\Delta}{\sigma}\right)^2} \quad (15)$$

Here, $n_T$ is the total sample size in the analysis, where $n_T = n_{his} + n_{sis}$. $n_{his}$ is the number of historic samples, and $n_{Sis}$ is the number of data points on one side of the center line showing a positive signal for Nelson test rule 2: therefore, $n_{Sis} = 9$. $df = n_{sig} + n_{his} - 2$, which represents the degrees of freedom, and $t_{(1-\alpha,\ df)}$ represents the inverse of the cumulative t-distribution at $1 - \alpha$ and df.

Here, an acceptable value of the significance ($\alpha$) value or type I error is often set at 0.05 [18], indicating a 5% probability of falsely identifying a signal as positive when the data corresponds to normal variability within the process. In this case, the statistical confidence ($1 - \alpha$) is 100% – 5% = 95%.

The detectability/shift from the mean ($\Delta/\sigma$) is the acceptable distance from the mean, expressed as a number of standard deviations. The FDA guidance document on "statistical review and evaluation" states that a ($\Delta/\sigma$) value of 1.5 at 95% confidence ($1 - \alpha$) is adequate to conclude equivalence between two groups [19-20].

Equations (14) and (15) for the sample size are rearranged to solve for reliability ($1-\beta$) as expressed in (16) and (17), respectively. According to Cohen (1988), minimum reliability $(1 - \beta) \geq 80\%$ is generally accepted to statistically conclude that no true signal is going un-noticed [17]. Figure 7 shows the reliability of a signal for Nelson rule 2 for different combinations of the shift from the mean ($\Delta/\sigma$) and historic sample size ($n_{his}$). Assuming signal sample size ($n_{sig} = 9$; i.e. nine data points on one side of the center line for the Nelson test rule 2), the reliability is calculated via Equation (16) for different values of the shift from the mean ($\Delta/\sigma$) as shown in Figure 7. Figure 7 demonstrates that if the observed shift in the mean is ≤1 SD, then the signal can be considered as a nuisance signal as the minimum reliability criteria of $(1-\beta) \geq 0.80$ is not met even when the historical sample size $n_{his}$ is as large as 100.

$$Power\ (1-\beta) = t.dist\left(\left(\frac{\left(\frac{\Delta}{\sigma}\right)}{\sqrt{\frac{1}{n_{sig}}+\frac{1}{n_{his}}}} - t_{\left(1-\alpha/_{2},\ df\right)}\right), (df)\right) \tag{16}$$

$$Power\ (1-\beta) = t.dist\left(\left(\frac{\left(\frac{\Delta}{\sigma}\right)}{\sqrt{\frac{1}{n_{sig}}+\frac{1}{n_{his}}}} - t_{(1-\alpha,\ df)}\right), (df)\right) \tag{17}$$

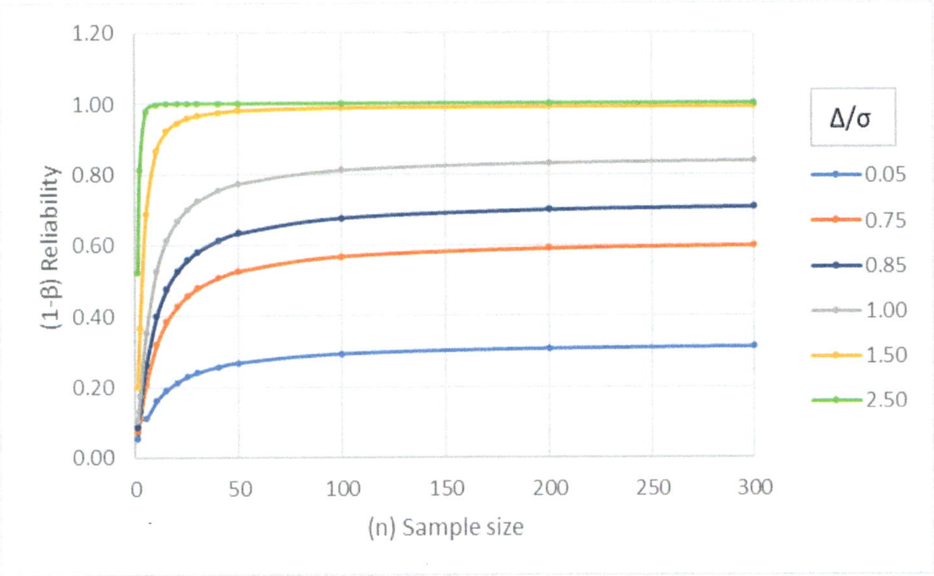


**Figure 7. Reliability vs. sample size for different values of Δ/σ.**

## 6. Conclusions

Challenges in CPV review sessions include assessing a control chart signal for reliability and deciding whether to initiate an investigation followed by action for corrective or preventive action. However, control charts are susceptible to false alarms and nuisance alarms. Trusting incorrect signals from the control chart and initiating quality control actions can lead to a waste of resources and time. Therefore, it is imperative to understand false alarm probabilities in control charts in association with different Nelson test rules. In this article, we reviewed the current state of understanding of FARs inherent to control charts and the impact on FARs of data distributions that deviate from normal distribution assumptions. We also discussed methods for optimizing the use of control charts by selecting the Nelson test rules to be applied and correcting the number of sigma factors (k) used for calculating control limits to accommodate skewness and kurtosis in a data distribution to reduce the FAR and nuisance signals and to improve the reliability of data trending and monitoring.

## Abbreviations

df: Degrees of freedom
FAR: False alarm rate
SD: Standard deviation
OOC: Out-Of-Control
Xbar: Sample mean
p: Probability
$n_{sig} = 9$: Number samples on one side of the control chart
$n_{his}$: Number of samples used for historic samples
$K_3$: Kurtosis
$K_4$: Skewness
k: Number of standard deviations from the mean for the placement of control limits
$\Delta/\sigma$: Number of standard deviations from the mean for considering the reliability of a shift in the mean
$\beta$: Type II error
$\alpha$: Type I error
$\mu$: Population mean
$\sigma$: Population standard deviation
$\Phi$: Cumulative normal density function

## References

1. Guidance for Industry: Process Validation — General Principles and Practices. US Food and Drug Administration: Silver Spring, MD, 2011;

https://www.fda.gov/files/drugs/published/Process-Validation–General-Principles-and-Practices.pdf.

2. PDA Technical Report 59: Utilization of Statistical Methods for Production Monitoring. (2012). Parenteral Drug Association, Bethesda, MD.

https://www.pda.org/bookstore/product-detail/1842-tr-59-utilization-of-statistical-methods.

3. Heigl, N., Schmelzer, B., Innerbichler, F., & Shivhare, M. (2021). Statistical quality and process control in Biopharmaceutical manufacturing—Practical issues and remedies. PDA Journal of Pharmaceutical Science and Technology, 75(5), 425-444. https://doi.org/10.5731/pdajpst.2020.011676

4. Adams, B. M., Woodall, W. H., & Lowry, C. A. (1992). The use (and misuse) of false alarm probabilities in control chart design. Frontiers in Statistical Quality Control 4, 155-168. https://doi.org/10.1007/978-3-662-11789-7_11

5. Walker, E., Philpot, J. W., & Clement, J. (1991). False signal rates for the Shewhart control chart with supplementary runs tests. Journal of Quality Technology, 23(3), 247-252. https://doi.org/10.1080/00224065.1991.11979330

6. Nelson, L. S. (1984). The Shewhart control chart—Tests for special causes. Journal of Quality Technology, 16(4), 237-239.

https://doi.org/10.1080/00224065.1984.11978921

7. Griffiths, D., Bunder, M., Gulati, C., & Onizawa, T. (2010). The probability of an out-of-control signal from Nelson's supplementary zig-zag test. Journal of Statistical Theory and Practice, 4(4), 609-615.

https://doi.org/10.1080/15598608.2010.10412007

8. Adhibhatta, S., DiMartino, M., Falcon, R., Haman, E., Legg, K., Payne, R., Pipkins, K., & Zamamiri, A. (2017, February). Continued process verification (CPV) signal responses in Biopharma. ISPE | International Society for Pharmaceutical Engineering.

https://ispe.org/pharmaceutical-engineering/january-february-2017/continued-process-verification-cpv-signal

9. Trietsch, D., & Bishak, D. (2007). The Rate of False Signals for Control Charts with Limits Estimated from Small Samples. Journal of Quality Technology, 39(1), 52-63.

https://prism.ucalgary.ca/server/api/core/bitstreams/dae8e651-1a93-4337-a3a1-1c2dbe3ae66c/content

10. Bischak, D. P., & Trietsch, D. (2007). The rate of false signals in u control charts with estimated limits. Journal of Quality Technology, 39(1), 54-65.

https://doi.org/10.1080/00224065.2007.11917673

11. Richard A. Groeneveld, Glen Meeden, (1984). Measuring Skewness and Kurtosis, Journal of the Royal Statistical Society, 33(4),391–399,

https://doi.org/10.2307/2987742

12. Karagöz, D., & Hamurkaroğlu, C. (2012). Control charts for skewed distributions : Weibull, gamma, and lognormal. Metodološki Zvezki, 9(2), 95–106.

http://www.stat-d.si/mz/mz9.1/karagoz.pdf

13. Munoz, J., Moya Fernandez, P., Alvarez, E., & Blanco-Encomienda, F. (2020). An alternative expression for the constant c4[n] with desirable properties. Scientia Iranica, 0(0), 3388-3393. https://doi.org/10.24200/sci.2020.52702.2846

14. Braden, P., & Matis, T. (2022). Cornish–fisher-based control charts inclusive of skewness and kurtosis measures for monitoring the mean of a process. Symmetry, 14(6), 1176. https://doi.org/10.3390/sym14061176

15. Kenneth L. Lange, Roderick J. A. Little & Jeremy M. G. Taylor (1989) Robust Statistical Modeling Using the t Distribution, Journal of the American Statistical Association, 84(408), 881-896. https://www.jstor.org/stable/2290063

16. D J. Wheeler and R Stauffer. (2017). When Should We Use Extra Detection Rules? Using process behavior charts effectively. Quality Digest, 322, 1-14. https://www.spcpress.com/pdf/DJW322.Oct.17.Using%20Extra%20Detection%20Rules.pdf

17. Muralidharan, N. (2023). Process Validation: Calculating the Necessary Number of Process Performance Qualification Runs. Bioprocess International, 21(5), 37-43. https://bioprocessintl.com/analytical/upstream-validation/process-validation-calculating-the-necessary-number-of-process-performance-qualification-runs/

18. Kim H. Y. (2015). Statistical notes for clinical researchers: Type I and type II errors in statistical decision. Restorative dentistry & endodontics, 40(3), 249–252. https://doi.org/10.5395/rde.2015.40.3.249

19. Durivage M. (2016). How To Establish Sample Sizes for Process Validation Using Statistical Tolerance Intervals. Bioprocess Online

https://www.bioprocessonline.com/doc/how-to-establish-sample-sizes-for-process-validation-using-statistical-tolerance-intervals-0001.

20. Weng Y. Statistical Review and Evaluation. US Food and Drug Administration: Rockville, MD, 21 March 2016; https://www.fda.gov/media/105013/download.

21. NIST/SEMATECH. Engineering Statistics Handbook. National Institute of Standards and Technology: Gaithersburg, MD, 2012;

https://doi.org/10.18434/M32189

# Chapter 10: Statistical Methodologies to establish Control or Alert limits for Nonparametric distributed numeric variables with a focus on Bio-Pharmaceutical.

Naveenganesh Muralidharan

## Introduction

According to the FDA's 2011 Process Validation Guidance, critical quality attributes and critical process parameters are trended to assess the statistical stability and ability to meet acceptable criteria as a part of a continuous process verification program using control charts. In the control charts, control limits (CL) are used to assess the statistical stability of the process parameters and attributes. When the data are normally distributed, control limits are established in a straightforward manner by placing the control limits three standard deviations away from the process average [1]. However, biological industry data are often not normally distributed, and therefore, a regular I-chart with control limits placed three standard deviations from the process mean cannot be used. These data include censored data, which are often reported as being below the limit of quantification (LOQ); trending mutually exclusive events (e.g., a fraction of defective items), whose data follow a binomial distribution; or zero-inflated data, which are often reported as zeros that follow a negative binomial distribution. Herein, we describe a detailed step-by-step procedure using Excel formulas for easy establishment of alert limits or statistical control limits for non-normally distributed censored data, binomially distributed data, and negative binomially distributed data. For the below discussed statistical alert limit setting methods for non-normally distributed data, it has been shown that a minimum of 25 to 30 samples are required to estimate the mean and standard deviation at acceptable levels of confidence. Furthermore, the data set should have a minimum of 4 to 5 discrete values; if not un-rounded data can be used for the parameter estimation in the below discussed methods [2].

## Censored Data

In bio-pharmaceutical industries, safety-related contaminants, such as endotoxin or product/process-related trace contaminants, are often reported as being below the LOQ because of the limitations of analytical methods. Restricted maximum likelihood methods (RML), originally proposed by Persson and Rootzen in 1977, have been suggested to be a more appropriate method for estimating unbiased process averages and standard deviations for censored data [2]. The alert limits can be placed three unbiased standard deviations away from the unbiased process average. This RML method is used when the number of samples reported as LOQ is up to 50% of the total sample size; if the number of LOQ samples is greater than 50%, it is recommended to trend the data using a run chart or frequency table [2]. The unbiased mean and unbiased standard deviation for censored data can be estimated as shown below [2,3]:

| **Table 1: Unbiased mean and unbiased standard deviation for censored data** |
|---|
| A value below which the results are reported as below the LOQ, $X_0$ |
| Total number of samples, n |
| The number of samples reported as below the LOQ, blog |
| Number samples reported as above in the LOQ:<br>$K = n\text{-}n_{LOQ}$ |
| $\lambda$ = NORM.S.INV($n_{LOQ}$ /n) |
| Calculate A (only for the samples reported as above the LOQ) = $\Sigma(x_i\text{-}x_0)$ |
| Calculate B (only for the samples reported as above the LOQ) = $\Sigma(x_i\text{-}x_0)^2$ |
| Calculate biased sigma:<br>$$\sigma *= \frac{1}{2}\left(\frac{\lambda.A}{k}\right) + \left[\left(\left(\frac{\lambda.A}{k}\right)^2\right) + 4\left(\frac{B}{k}\right)\right]^{1/2}$$ |
| Calculate biased mean:<br>$$\mu^* = 1 - (\lambda.\sigma^*)$$ |
| Calculate unbiased mean estimators:<br>$$B_\mu = -EXP(1)^{\left[2.692 - \frac{(5.439\,(n-k))}{(n+1)}\right]}$$ |
| Calculate unbiased sigma estimators:<br>$$B_\sigma = -\left[0.312 + \frac{(0.859\,(n-k))}{(n+1)}\right]^2$$ |
| Calculate unbiased mean:<br>$$\mu = \mu^* - \left(\frac{\sigma^*.B_\mu}{n+1}\right)$$ |
| Calculate unbiased overall sigma:<br>$$\sigma = \sigma^* - \left(\frac{\sigma^*.B_\sigma}{n+1}\right)$$ |

## Binomially Distributed Data

The proportion or fraction of defective items in a population is often trended in the pharmaceutical industry at the drug product stage. Typically, vials filled with drug products are inspected for one or more quality attributes (e.g., fill volume, particles in the vial filled with solution, proper screwing of vial caps shut, or proper labeling of vials) are inspected simultaneously. If only one attribute does not meet the predefined acceptable standard, the item is classified as defective. The fraction or proportion of defective items is often expressed as a percentage for trending the batch performance because the sample size typically differs among batches. Furthermore, the proportion of defective items in successive batches is independent of the previous defective rate; therefore, the probability of the proportion of nonconforming events follows a binomial distribution. The calculation of alert limits for binomially distributed data is a two-step process: first, the confidence interval is calculated with the Clopper-Pearson exact binomial method, and then the tolerance bound at a tolerance interval of 99% is calculated with the method of Hahn and Chandra [4–7].

| |
|---|
| **Step 1: Calculation of the upper confidence bound or confidence interval for the proportion defective in the process** |
| Total sample number, n |
| Number of defects, x |
| Calculate the proportion defective in the current process, $p_0 = x/n$ |
| Acceptable risk (default 0.05), α |
| Calculate confidence, (1-α) |
| Calculate the upper confidence bound for the estimate of the population mean proportion defective:<br>$CL_u$= Beta.Inv(1-α,x+1,n-x) |
| **Step 2: Calculation of the upper tolerance bound for the number of defects in an average batch size** |
| Proportion for tolerance interval, ($P_r$) default value = 0.99 |
| Average sample size per batch, $n_A$ |
| Upper tolerance bound per n samples per batch:<br>$N_u$ = Binom.Inv ($n_A$, $CL_u$, $P_r$) |
| **Calculation of tolerance bound as a percentage** |
| % Upper tolerance bound, % $N_u$ = 100 x $N_u$/n |

## Negative Binomially Distributed Data

Data for environmental monitoring in biopharmaceutical manufacturing clean rooms (e.g., particle counts or bioburden) are often reported as zeros. These data follow a negative binomial distribution, and the data distribution is modeled on the basis of both the chance of occurrence of an event and the intensity of the event.

The negative binomial distribution is characterized by two parameters: μ and k, where k is typically termed the negative binomial dispersion parameter, and μ is the mean. Various methods are available for estimating the μ and k. Here in, both parameters are estimated with the simplest method, called the method of moments. Furthermore, because a reactions. However, immune responses in GT are caused by a combination of effects depending on the vector capsid type, vector load, and other encapsidated residual cellular impurity components, such as host cell proteins and plasmid DNA in the product [7, 15]. Therefore, the immunogenicity of a product is often evaluated by controlled studies; consequently, the immunogenicity of residual hcDNA is beyond the scope of the risk assessment in this article.

### Acceptable safety margin for identified risks

For genotoxic impurities with no identified threshold mechanisms, such as oncogenic and infectivity risks, the FDA Vaccines and Related Biological Products Advisory Committee (VRBPAC) considers frequency of occurrence at one in 10-million or ($10^{-7}$) as acceptable risk. [7]

### Estimation of frequency of risk for inducing an oncogenic event by activation of POG or inactivation of TSG.

**Step1: Calculate the probability of activation of POG or inactivation of TSG:** Non-enveloped virus infection starts when the virus reaches the surface of the cells and enters the endocytic pathway using specific receptors on the cell surface. Endocytosis is the internal cargo mechanism by which many viruses enter and reach the nucleus of the cell and transfer their genic material into the host. In parallel, the recipient host cells have developed many molecular mechanisms to limit the transduction of virus genetic material in the cytoplasm of the cell before it reaches the nucleus. Even after viral capsids release the DNA to the nucleus, not all DNA molecules can integrate into the chromosome. It has been reported that after DNA molecules enter the cells, they will undergo ligations, mutations and especially deletions. Furthermore, the hcDNA fragments packaged in the AAV capsid are predicted to be single-stranded, making it unstable and likely to be degraded once released into the nuclei of the transduced cells of the recipient patient. Therefore, DNA molecules carried by AAV capsids entering the cells must pass through multiple steps before activating a proto-oncogene or inactivating a tumor suppression gene as summarized in Table 1: [1, 21- 22] negative binomial distribution is not a symmetric distribution, using a quantile limit is more appropriate than using limits three standard deviations above and below the mean. [8].

Let $X_i$ denote the count of the particles or bioburden, where (i = 1, 2, 3......n)

| **Calculation of alert limit for negatively distributed data** |
| --- |
| Calculate the average, $\mu$ = Average (X) |
| Calculate the sample variance, $\sigma^2$ = VAR.S (X) |
| Calculate the dispersion coefficient: $$K = \frac{\sigma^2 - \mu}{\mu^2}$$ |
| Calculate the probability density function (PDF) for each $X_i$ value: $$PDF_{X=i} = ((K * \mu)^\wedge X_i)/(1 + K * \mu)^\wedge(X_i + (1/K)) * ((GAMMA(X_i + (1/K)))/((FACT(X_i)) * GAMMA(1/K)))$$ |
| Calculate the cumulative probability density function (CPDF) at each $X_i$ value: $$CPDF_{X=i} = PDF_i + \sum_{X=0}^{X=i-1} PDF_{X=i}$$ |
| The alert limit can be placed at 0.99 quantiles; therefore, the alert limit can be identified by placing it at an X value corresponding to $CPDF_{x=i}$ = 0.99 |

## References:

1. Utilization of statistical methods for production monitoring. (2012). Parenteral Drug Association. https://www.pda.org/bookstore/product-detail/1842-tr-59-utilization-of-statistical-methods

2. Heigl, N., Schmelzer, B., Innerbichler, F., & Shivhare, M. (2021). Statistical Quality and Process Control in Biopharmaceutical Manufacturing-Practical Issues and Remedies. *PDA journal of pharmaceutical science and technology*, *75*(5), 425–444. https://doi.org/10.5731/pdajpst.2020.011676

3. Gibbons, R. D. (1994). Statistical methods for groundwater monitoring. John Wiley & Sons.

4. Hahn, G. J., & Chandra, R. (1981). Tolerance intervals for Poisson and binomial variables. Journal of Quality Technology, 13(2), 100-110. https://doi.org/10.1080/00224065.1981.11980998

5. Agresti, A., & Coull, B. A. (1998). Approximate is better than "Exact" for interval estimation of binomial proportions. The American Statistician, 52(2), 119. https://doi.org/10.2307/2685469

6. Binomial parameter, Clopper-Pearson interval estimation. (2014). Wiley StatsRef: Statistics Reference Online.

https://doi.org/10.1002/9781118445112.stat01453

7. Meeker, W. Q., Hahn, G. J., & Escobar, L. A. (2017). Statistical intervals: A guide for practitioners and researchers. John Wiley & Sons.

8. Hoffman, D. (2003). Negative binomial control limits for count data with extra-Poisson variation. Pharmaceutical Statistics, 2(2), 127-132.

https://doi.org/10.1002/pst.51

# Chapter 11: Effective Usage of Multivariate Hotelling's $T^2$ Statistic to Identify False Metabolite Measurements in Upstream Cell Culture Bioreactor Monitoring

Naveenganesh Muralidharan*, Thatsinee Johnson, and Emma Bolduc

## Introduction

Cell culture bioreactor operations are actively monitored for metabolites through offline analyzers such as Nova Flex or BGA blood gas analyzers. However, these offline analyzers introduce inherent variability in metabolite measurements. The magnitude of the measurement variability depends on the measurement range. Mammalian cells are sensitive to the concentration of one such metabolite: dissolved $CO_2$. In cell cultures, the $CO_2$ level is often reported as the partial pressure ($pCO_2$) in mmHg.

It has been repeatedly reported that elevated $pCO_2$ concentrations have adverse impacts on cell health, causing a change in the metabolic state, a decrease in cell productivity, and an altered glycosylation profile of the therapeutic protein.[1, 2, 3] Therefore, in biologics production, the $CO_2$ concentration in a cell culture bioreactor is often designated as a critical process parameter or an in-process control parameter, with action limits of approximately 50–150 mmHg to avoid the above-mentioned issues.

Multiple factors affect the dissolved $CO_2$ concentration in cell culture bioreactors, including the pH set point, bicarbonate concentration, cell density, and cell lactate production rate. Although various methodologies for controlling $pCO_2$ are used across the industry, the simplest and most frequently used methodology is manual feedback control. In this method, dissolved $CO_2$ is measured in the cell culture, and if the $CO_2$ level exceeds a threshold value (i.e., the action limit), then the overall gas flow rate is increased by a certain amount.

To use manual feedback $CO_2$ control, the measured $pCO_2$ value must be reliable, and any false measurements must be detected before process changes are made to keep the $pCO_2$ level within the desired limits.

This article provides a detailed, step-by-step description of an easy-to-adopt procedure to develop a tool for identifying false $pCO_2$ measurements using Hotelling's $T^2$ statistic in MS Excel.

In 1947, Harold Hotelling introduced the concept of the $T^2$ statistic for multivariate analysis. Here, the relationship between two or more interrelated variables is established by blending information from the mean and the dispersion across variables from a large sample, and the reliability of suspicious data is assessed based on the difference from the historic relationship.

## Selection of Inter-related Variables

**Medium Chemistry:** Based on the Henderson–Hasselbalch equation, in typical cell culture conditions near a neutral pH, the culture pH is related to conjugate acids (dissolved $CO_2$ and lactate), conjugate bases (bicarbonate ions), and pKa, an acid ionization constant for bicarbonate, as shown in Equation 1.[4]

$$pH = p_{Ka} \times \frac{[Conjugate\ Base]}{[Conjugate\ Acid]}$$ Equation 1

Therefore, the parameters related to $pCO_2$ measurements are pH, lactate concentration, and bicarbonate ion concentration. However, as the process under investigation does not consume a variable amount of base titrant across multiple batches and the Nova Flex2 analyzer does not measure bicarbonate ions, the selection of related measured variables is reduced to three variables (pH, lactate concentration, and $pCO_2$).

**Filtering Outliers:** All of the available sample points for pH, lactate concentration, and $pCO_2$ are screened for outliers, and outliers with a known cause are removed, such as those attributed to a replacement in sensor cards or reagents in the measuring instrument.

**Calculation of the Upper Control limit (UCL):** For the case of three interrelated variables (k=3) with sample size (n), the UCL is calculated from Equation 2:[5]

$$UCL = \frac{k(n+1)(n-1)}{(n^2 - n.k)} \times F.INV.RT(\alpha, n-k)$$ Equation 2

Where F. INV. RT can be used to return critical values from the F distribution. α is the probability of an acceptable error in prediction; a default value of 0.01 is widely accepted.

**Calculation of the Mean Vector:** The mean vector ($A_{vg}$) of three selected variables is calculated as ($pH_{Avg}$, $pCO2_{Avg}$, and $Lac_{Avg}$), as shown in Figure 1.

**Calculation of $T^2$:** In statistics, when a single variable is under analysis, the “t ratio” is used to detect any shifts outside the historic trend. The t ratio is the ratio of the signal to noise, as shown in Equation 3:[5,6]

$$t = \frac{x - \mu}{s}$$ Equation 3

Where x is the suspicious data point being analyzed to detect a shift from the historic performance, µ is the historical mean, (x-µ) is the signal or distance between the sample and historic mean, and s is the sample standard deviation. In univariable analysis, the standard deviation (s) measures the dispersion of the dataset.

As a counterpart of the t ratio in univariate analysis, In Multivariate analysis, the $T^2$ value also measures the ratio of signal to noise. Here, the signal is measured as the difference between the mean vectors of two or more datasets, and the noise of the data is measured as the covariance.

$T^2$ is obtained by squaring the t ratio, as shown in Equation 4:[5,6]

$$T^2 = \frac{(x-\mu)^2}{[s^2]} \qquad \text{Equation 4}$$

Where $[s^2]$ is the variance and $(x\text{-}\mu)^2$ is the squared distance from the mean, corresponding to the signal.

For multivariable analysis, the variance $s^2$ is replaced by a covariance matrix [S]. The covariance measures the direction of dispersion of one variable with respect to another in a two-dimensional matrix space, as shown in Equation 5. In other words, the covariance measures the signal noise.

$$T^2 = \frac{(x-\mu)^2}{s^2} = \frac{(x-\mu)^2}{[S]} = (x-\mu)^2.[S]^{-1} \qquad \text{Equation 5}$$

By replacing the population mean (µ) with the sample mean ($x_{avg}$) and applying matrix algebra ($(x\text{-}\mu)^2 = (x\text{-}\mu) \cdot (x\text{-}\mu)^T$), one can rewrite Equation 3 as Equation 6:[5,6]

$$T^2 = [x_i - x_{avg}].[S]^{-1}.[x_i - x_{avg}]^T \qquad \text{Equation 6}$$

Where $[X_1\text{-}X_{avg}]$ represents the distance from the mean matrix and $[X_1\text{-}X_{avg}]^T$ represents the transpose of the distance from the mean matrix. $X_i$ is the group of variables from individual observations ($pH_i$, $pCO2_i$, and $Lac_i$) that are being tested for any shift from the historic performance.

The distance from the mean vector in matrix format is calculated as shown in Equation 7:

$$[x_i - x_{avg}] = [pH_i - pH_{Avg} \quad pCO2_i - pCO2_{avg} \quad Lac_i - Lac_{Avg}] \qquad \text{Equation 7}$$

The covariance matrix is calculated via the Excel function "Covariance.S" for each combination of variables. The inverse of this matrix can be calculated by applying the MINVERSE function and selecting the covariance matrix in Excel. Finally, the $T^2$ value is calculated in Excel via the matrix function formula. The steps for these calculations are displayed in Figure 1.

**Determination of False Results:** The calculated $T^2$ value for the variables encompasses the suspected variable compared to the calculated UCL value. If the $T^2$ value is less than the UCL, then the group of related variables encompassing the suspected variable is declared to be within the historic dispersion, and the measured data are confirmed as correct. If the $T^2$ value is greater than the UCL, then the group of variables that encompasses the suspected variable is declared to be outside the expected historic dispersion; thus, the measured data may be false, and re-sampling and/or re-testing is recommended. [5,6]

## Conclusions

Biologics manufacturing is complex and sometimes demands simultaneous monitoring of two or more related variables for improved understanding and process control to ensure product quality. In such instances, multivariate statistics based on the Hotelling $T^2$ method are frequently used. One such instance is presented as a case study in this article, where $pCO_2$ is monitored as an in-process control parameter and a pCO2 value exceeding a predefined action limit will call for a change in the bioreactor gassing strategy. However, the risk of frequent false $pCO_2$ measurements from the metabolite analyzer demands that a detection system be established to identify any false $pCO_2$ measurements. This article demonstrates how we have successfully built and verified a system for detecting false $pCO_2$ in-process measurements using Hotelling's $T^2$ statistic. Additionally, the same concepts can be used to confirm any false out-of-expectation (OOE) or out-of-specification (OOS) results when inter-related parameters are identified in order to justify the re-testing of OOE or OOS results.

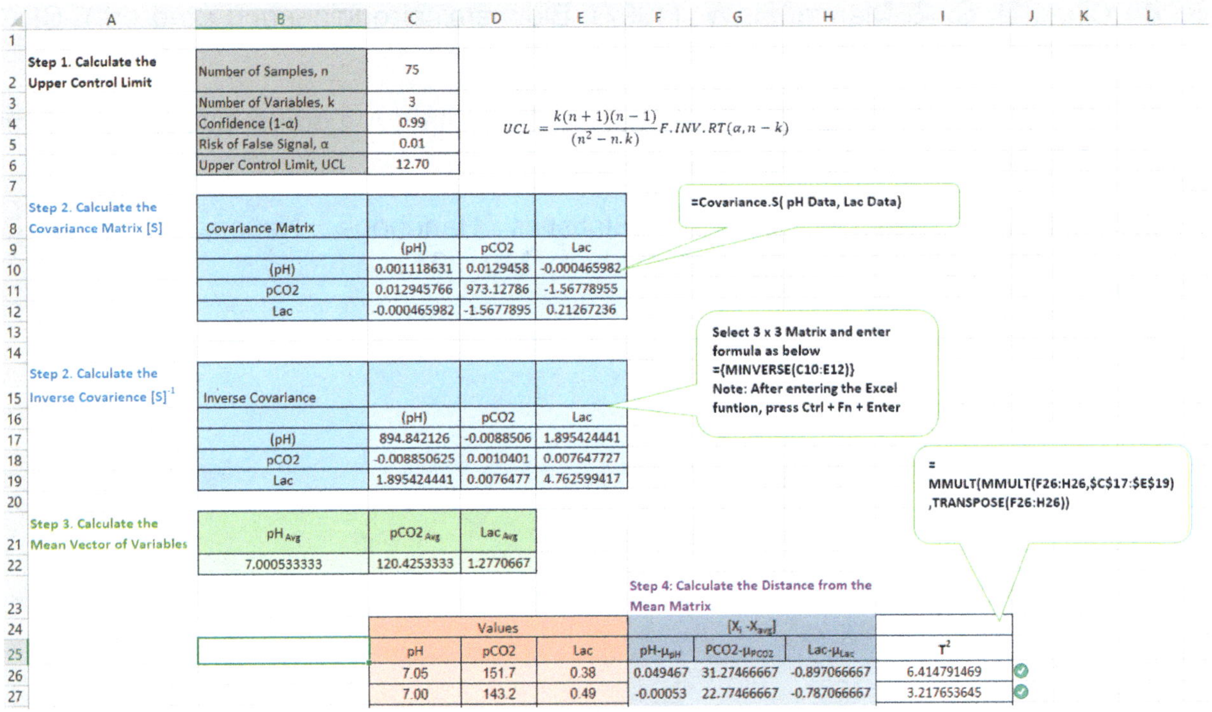


**Figure 1: Sample Excel sheet illustrating the use of Hotelling's $T^2$ statistic as a false measurement identification tool for $pCO_2$ monitoring in cell culture bioreactors.**

## References

1. Schmelzer, A., & Miller, W. (2002). Hyperosmotic stress and elevated pCO2 alter monoclonal antibody charge distribution and monosaccharide content. Biotechnology Progress, 18(2), 346-353. https://doi.org/10.1021/bp010187d

2. Brunner, M., Doppler, P., Klein, T., Herwig, C., & Fricke, J. (2017). Elevated pCO<sub>2</sub> affects the lactate metabolic shift in CHO cell culture processes. Engineering in Life Sciences, 18(3), 204-214.

https://doi.org/10.1002/elsc.201700131

3. DeZengotita, V. M., Kimura, R., & Miller, W. M. (1998). Effects of CO2 and osmolality on hybridoma cells: Growth, metabolism and monoclonal antibody production. Current Applications of Cell Culture Engineering, 213-227. https://doi.org/10.1007/978-94-011-4786-6_22

4. Clark, D. S., & Blanch, H. W. (1997). Biochemical engineering (2nd ed.). CRC Press.

5. Montgomery, D. C. (2013). Statistical quality control: A modern introduction. John Wiley & Sons.

6. NIST/SEMATECH. Engineering Statistics Handbook. National Institute of Standards and Technology: Gaithersburg, MD, 2012;

https://doi.org/10.18434/M32189

# Chapter 12: Quantitative Risk Assessment of Residual Host Cell DNA Limits to Ensure Patient Safety for In Vitro Gene Therapies Produced Using Human-Derived Cell Lines

**Naveenganesh Muralidharan**

## Introduction

Viral vectors expressing therapeutic genes manufactured from cell-substrate production systems can contain residual amounts of host cell DNA (hcDNA). hcDNA in a final purified product presents a safety risk to the recipient patients. Therefore, the levels of residual hcDNA in purified products are monitored and controlled by drug manufacturers [1, 2]. The United States Food and Drug Administration (FDA) and other regulatory agencies recommend tight quantifiable limits for hcDNA levels, at 10 ng/dose, with the DNA fragment size being less than the functional gene size of 200 base pairs (bp) for biological products [3]. However, for gene therapy (GT), because of the inherent nature of hcDNA encapsidation in viral capsids, the FDA has recommended to minimize the level and size of hcDNA based on risk assessment, rather than recommending quantifiable limits for hcDNA levels. Thus, manufacturers define their own hcDNA specification limits in a final product based on risk assessments to ensure patient safety [4].

Risk assessments of hcDNA levels in a final product for ensuring patient safety are not necessarily straightforward and may not be easily available. Therefore, in this article, the risk assessment methodology for evaluating hcDNA levels with respect to patient safety is described in the following sequence:

- Identify a possible risk event for residual hcDNA based on the nature of the cell line used and the manufacturing process.
- Determine the safety margin for the identified risk.
- Determine the frequency of risk occurrence in nature or from controlled studies
- Conservatively estimate the frequency of the risk event per dose under the worst-case assumption.

This article details the process for calculating the frequency of risk events identified for residual hcDNA impurities in GT products, with an illustrative example for easy adaptation and implementation by the reader. The risk assessment in this article is confined to viral vector GT products produced only using human-derived cell lines.

## Risk event for residual hcDNA based on the nature of the cell line and manufacturing process

The properties and risks associated with hcDNA depend on the manufacturing platform for adeno-associated virus (AAV) production using either human-derived cells or insect cells. Compared with DNA from insect cells, human-derived hcDNA encapsidated within viral capsids has a higher risk of genotoxicity. Oncogenicity and infectivity are two types of genotoxic risk that have been identified for human-derived cell lines [5, 6].

The different mechanisms of oncogenicity and infectivity risks to patients from residual hcDNA impurities are as follows: [7, 21-22]

- **Inactivation of Tumor suppression gene (TSG):** The residual hcDNA could integrate into the specific genes responsible for cell cycle control or into tumor suppressor genes, such as the p53 gene or retino blastoma susceptibility gene. Loss of tumor suppression genes has been shown to cause certain human tumors.

- **Activation of proto-oncogene (POG):** The integration of residual cell-substrate DNA could result in the activation of cellular regulatory genes by promoter/enhancer insertion, which could lead to the development of a neoplastic phenotype.

- **Introduction of dominant oncogene:** Residual DNA may have dominant activated oncogenes that could integrate and express in recipient patient cells. In viral vector production, HEK293 and HeLa cells are the most widely used human-derived cell lines. The Ad5 E1 gene in HEK293 cells and human papillomavirus E6 and E7 genes in HeLa are examples of dominant oncogenes.

- **Introduction of Infectious agent**: If the genome of a DNA virus or the provirus of a retrovirus is present in the cell substrate, then the residual DNA has the potential, upon inoculation into the recipient patient, to produce infectious virus and thus establish a productive infection.

The immunomodulatory activity of DNA is another risk associated with extracellular DNA in a GT product and does not require gene expression. Vertebrates, including humans, have evolved with the ability to recognize the microbial components of bacterial and viral infection by the presence of unmethylated cytosine–guanine dinucleotide (CpG) motifs in microbial DNA, which stimulate an immune response. Residual DNA impurities in a GT product could contain immunostimulatory unmethylated CpG motifs. The extent of CpG motifs in residual DNA impurities depends on the source of residual DNA; these motifs are not normally present in human-derived cells. Therefore, residual hcDNA in viral vectors produced via human-derived cell lines has less potential to cause immunogenic

**Table 1: Steps and probability for activation of POG or inactivation of TSG.**

| Steps | Probability | | Reference |
|---|---|---|---|
| | Activation of POG | Inactivation of TSG | |
| Probability of integration of cellular DNA into chromosome | $1 \times 10^{-3}$ | $1 \times 10^{-3}$ | Kurth (1995) |
| Probability of integration into a functional coding sequence (only a fraction of the genome codes for functional genes, and coding sequences are randomly scattered among non-coding DNA sequences called exons. Human genes are spaced between 3,000 to 30,000 genes over a genome size of $3 \times 10^9$ bp) | $1 \times 10^{-5}$ | $1 \times 10^{-5}$ | Kurth (1995) |
| Probability of integration into a gene enhancing sequence. Temin (1990) reported that there should be a minimum of 100 POG per cell. | $1 \times 10^{-2}$ | | Temin (1990) |
| Probability of integration into a tumor suppressor gene. Temin (1990) reported that the gene enhancers, promotor and genes responsible for chromosomal re-arrangements are clustered in chromosomes and represent only approximately 1% of the genome. | | $1 \times 10^{-2}$ | Temin (1990) |
| Probability of activation of the proto-oncogene after the DNA molecule integrates into the proto-oncogene or inactivation of tumor suppression gene. | $1 \times 10^{-2}$ | $1 \times 10^{-2}$ | Kurth (1995) |
| **Probability (pf) of a single intracellular DNA molecule to activate a single POG or to inactivate a single TSG = $[3 \times 10^{-3}] \times [10^{-5}] \times [10^{-2}] \times [10^{-2}]$** | **$3 \times 10^{-12}$** | **$3 \times 10^{-12}$** | |

Tumor formation is a multistep process. Activating one gene affects the phenotype of the cells, and inactivating just one copy of a TSG represents only one event in a multistep oncogenesis process, which is not sufficient to turn the cell cancerous. It is certainly not sufficient for tumor formation. Therefore, both copies of a relevant TSG must be inactivated, two different TSG must be destroyed, or more than two proto oncogenes must be activated for a cancer event in a cell. Hence, the probability of the risk event must be calculated for the activation of POG or the inactivation TSG for two independent events, i.e., **$(p_f)^2 \approx 1 \times 10^{-23}$ per DNA molecule**. This is in alignment with a previously reported probability value of $10^{-19} \times 10^{-23}$ by Peden (2005) for inducing an oncogenic event by integrating a DNA molecule. [21, 22 and 23].

**Step 2: Calculate the number of molecules in Residual DNA impurity in the product.**

$[A_{hcDNA}]$ is the amount of hcDNA in the product per dose (ng). This value can be calculated as:

$$[A_{hcDNA}] = D_{vg} \times Wt_p \times C_{hcDNA} \qquad \text{Equation-1}$$

Where $D_{vg}$ is the dosage of vector genome per patient weight (vg/kg), $Wt_p$ is the patient's weight (kg), and $C_{hcDNA}$ is the normalized concentration of hcDNA (pg per $10^{13}$ vg).

For a wide variety of AAV serotypes, vector genome doses ranging from $2\text{x}10^{11}$ to $2\text{x}10^{14}$ (vg per kg) and residual hcDNA limit values ranging from 0.8 to 5 ($10^5$ pg per $10^{13}$ vg) have been reported [8,9]. For the purpose of illustration, the residual hcDNA limit and vector dose were randomly selected within the above reported ranges, with the hcDNA level at < $5\text{x}10^5$ pg per $10^{13}$ vg and the vector dose at $2\text{x}10^{13}$ vg/kg.

The amount of residual hcDNA in a GT product for an average patient weighing 70 kg can be calculated from Equation-1 as follows:

$$[A_{hcDNA}] = 2E13\,\frac{vg}{kg} \times 70\,kg \times 5E05\,\frac{pg}{E13\,vg} \times \frac{0.001\,ng}{1\,pg} = 70{,}000\,ng$$

$M_{hcDNA,p}$- Number of molecules of hcDNA impurity per dose.

$$M_{hcDNA} = \frac{[A_{hcDNA}] \times 6.02 \times 10^{23}\,\frac{molecules}{mol}}{hcDNA\,fragment\,size \times Mol\,wt\,of\,DNA\,\frac{g}{mol.bp}}$$

Where,

**hcDNA fragment size :** In viral vector manufacturing based on human-derived cell lines via transfection with a plasmid or transduction with a helper virus or stable expression systems, two types of hcDNA contaminants have been reported. The first type is process-related free-floating non-encapsidated hcDNA, and the second is product-related hcDNA encapsidated in viral capsids. Process-related non-encapsidated free-floating DNA can be effectively digested by nuclease enzymes such as Benzonase and can be removed via well-characterized purification techniques. However, clearing product-related encapsidated hcDNA from the purified product is challenging, due to their resistance to nuclease treatment and their close proximity to the desired product (vector capsids) [12, 14]. The FDA has reported that contamination levels of 1%–3% are typically observed for non-vector DNA impurities in purified AAV products [13]. Furthermore, it has been reported that encapsulated non-target hcDNA impurity fragment sizes can range from 600 bp to 4500 bp, with an average size of 1500 bp [14]. Therefore, as a conservative approach, it is assumed that all of the hcDNA in the purified product comes only from product-related encapsidated hcDNA.

**Molecular Weight of DNA:** 660 g/ (mole. bp)

**Avogadro number:** 6.02 x10 [23] molecules / mole

Using the above assumptions, the number of molecules in residual hcDNA can be calculated as:

$$M_{hcDNA} = \frac{7 \times 10^{-5} g \times 6.02 \times 10^{23} \frac{molecules}{mol}}{1500\ bp \times 660 \frac{g}{mol.bp}} = 4.3 \times 10^{13}\ molecules$$

Now, the frequency of risk for inactivation of TSG or by activation of POG by the residual hcDNA impurity in the product per dose can be calculated as:

$$\mathrm{FR_1} = \mathrm{p_f^2} \times \mathrm{M_{hcDNA}} = \frac{1\times10^{-23}}{\mathrm{molecules}} \times 4.3 \times\ 10^{13}\mathrm{molecules} = 4.3 \times 10^{10}$$

**Estimation of frequency of risk for the integration of dominant oncogene and infectious gene**

Frequency of a risk event (FR) is calculated from the ratio of the amount of impurity in the product to the amount of impurity that can cause a risk event.

$$FR_2 = \frac{eAm_{PRe,Prd}}{Am_{RE}} \times f_1 \times f_2 \qquad \text{Equation-2}$$

Here,

**$Am_{RE}$ is the amount of DNA (ng) required to induce an oncogenic or infective event**. The gene levels required to induce an oncogenic or infective risk event were selected from animal models reported by Sheng et al. (2008) and Peden et al. (2006) as 9,400 ng and 2,500 ng, respectively. Segar et al. (1986) showed that human cells are more resistant to transformation than the animal models used for the assay of viral oncogenes; therefore, the predicted quantities are conservative for assessing the risk to humans [5, 17, 18, 19, 20].

$eAm_{RE,prd}$ is the amount of cellular DNA (ng) in a product that is equivalent to containing a single risk event gene per cell, which is compared with the amount of DNA required to induce an oncogenic or infective event: calculated as demonstrated by Sheng et al. (2009) from CBER [5, 17, and 18]:

$$eAm_{PRe,Prd} = [A_{hcDNA}] \cdot \left(\frac{S_{Re}}{S_{hc,G}}\right) \qquad \text{Equation-3}$$

**$S_{RE}$ is the size of the oncogenic or infective gene (bp).**

- For oncogenic gene size, Yang et al. (2010) reported that oncogenic DNA in humans has an average size of 1925 bp and a standard deviation (SD) of 87 bp. Therefore, as a conservative approach, the size of oncogenic DNA is selected as the average + 3 SD = 2186 bp.

- For an infective gene, the amount of gene required for inducing infectivity is adopted from an animal model study performed by Peden et al. (2006), who used a genome size of 10,000 bp from HIV retrovirus [17, 18].

**$S_{hc,G}$ is the host cell genome size (bp).**

The haploid genome size is used for oncogenic risk assessment, and the diploid genome size is used for infectivity risk assessment. For the purpose of illustration in this article, we consider HEK293 cells, which are the most widely used human cells for GT AAV production. HEK293 cells exhibit two or more copies of each chromosome, and in 30% of cells, the chromosome number is 64 (approximately three times the number of chromosomes in humans). These cells are described as hypotriploid, containing less than three times the number of chromosomes of a haploid human genome. Therefore, as a conservative approach, one human genome copy is assumed. That is, $S_{hc,G}$ values of $3x10^9$ bp and $6x10^9$ bp are good approximations for the haploid and diploid genome size, respectively [11].

**f2 is the fraction of hcDNA in the product that is larger than or equal to the size of the risk gene that causes the oncogenic or infective event.**

Krause and Lewis (2008) from CBER proposed to include fraction of DNA size greater than or equal to the size of the risk event gene in the host cell genome of the producer line, as shown in Equation-4 [5]:

- For oncogenic risk assessment, f2 is the fraction of genes ranging from the smallest oncogene size to the maximum gene capacity of the AAV capsid, 4500 bp. Yang et al. (2010) reported the average size of oncogenic DNA in humans as 1925 bp with an SD of 87 bp. As a conservative approach to incorporate the larger fraction of gene sizes, the smallest oncogene size is selected as the average - 3 SD = 1664 bp. Therefore, the f1 value for oncogenicity is the fraction of genes with sizes ranging from 1664 to 4500 bp in the human genome.

- For infectivity risk assessment, f2 is the fraction of genes ranging from the smallest infective gene size to the maximum gene capacity of the AAV capsid, 4500 bp. As a conservative approach, the smallest known human virus (hepatitis delta virus), which has a genome size of 1700 bp, is selected as the lower range for the gene size. Therefore, the f1 value for infectivity is the fraction of genes with sizes ranging from 1700 to 4500 bp in the human genome.

Figure 1 shows gene size distributions of the human genome, with $\log_{10}$ (gene size) on the Y axis and the cumulative normal frequency distribution of gene size on the X axis. The human gene size distribution shown in Figure 1 and summary statistics of human gene size distribution was created from data adopted from Whitlock, M. C., & Schluter, D. (2018) [10].

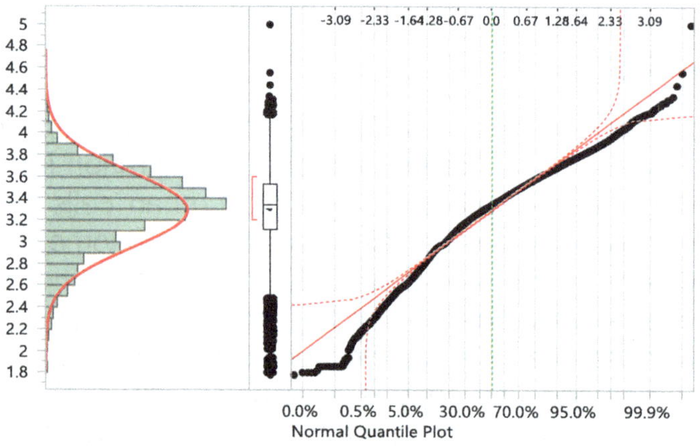


**Figure 1: Gene Size Distribution of the Human Genome.**

**Table 3: Summary Statistics of Gene Size Distribution of the Human Genome and Calculation of f1.**

| Parameter | Value |
|---|---|
| μ, Mean of $\log_{10}$(gene size) | 3.301 |
| σ, SD of $\log_{10}$(gene size) | 0.347 |
| $S_{Re,Onc}$, $Log_{10}$(1664 bp), oncogenic gene size | 3.221 |
| $S_{Re,inf}$, $Log_{10}$(1700 bp), infective gene size | 3.230 |
| $S_{Max}$, $Log_{10}$(4500 bp), infective gene size | 3.653 |
| f1 for oncogenic risk assessment: Fraction of hcDNA between 1664 and 2186 bp in the human genome | = NORM.DIST($S_{Max}$, μ, σ,TRUE) - NORM.DIST($S_{Re,Onc}$, μ, σ,TRUE) = 0.436 |
| f1 for infectivity risk assessment: Fraction of hcDNA between 1700 and 4500 bp in the human genome | = NORM.DIST($S_{Max}$, μ, σ,TRUE) - NORM.DIST($S_{Re,Inf}$, μ, σ,TRUE) = 0.425 |

### f3 is the probability of packing a functional gene in vector genome.

Risk events caused by any of the above-mentioned mechanisms, such as the integration of an activated oncogene or the integration of viral DNA, are caused by a biologically active coding sequence in a DNA impurity. Only a fraction of the genome codes for functional genes, and coding sequences are randomly scattered among non-coding DNA sequences called exons. Human genes are spaced between ≈ 3,000 to 30,000 genes over a genome size of ≈ 3 x$10^9$ bp, the predicted frequency of the packaging of any specific sequence from the host cell genome in the hcDNA is $10^{-5}$ .[1]

### Illustrative example of calculating the safety factor for the hcDNA limit

For illustration, the FR values for oncogenicity and infectivity are calculated using Equation-2.

For an oncogenic risk, FR is calculated as follows:

$$FR_{2,Oncogenicity} = \frac{[70{,}000\,ng\,] \times \left(\frac{2{,}186\,bp}{3 \times 10^9\,bp}\right) \times 0.436 \times (1 \times 10^{-5})}{9400\,ng} = 2.4 \times 10^{-11}$$

For an infectivity risk, FR is calculated as follows:

$$FR_{2,Infectivity} = \frac{[70{,}000\, ng\,] \times \left(\frac{10{,}000\, bp}{6 \times 10^{9}\, bp}\right) \times 0.425 \times (1 \times 10^{-5})}{2500\, ng} = 2.0 \times 10^{-10}$$

A quantitative risk assessment based on the methodology described in Equation-3 shows that the FR values for both oncogenic risk and infectivity risk are substantially below the FR value of $10^{-7}$, demonstrating that the assumed hcDNA limits are safe at the assumed vector dose.

## Conclusion

The mechanism by which fragments of hcDNA are packaged within viral vector capsid particles is not fully understood; therefore, control strategies in manufacturing processes have not yet been thoroughly characterized. Furthermore, as hcDNA is often encapsulated inside viral capsids, it is difficult to completely clear these residual product-related impurities out of the final purified product stream, due to their resistance to nuclease treatment and their close proximity to the product. Understanding the complexity involved in reducing residual hcDNA levels and hcDNA fragment length in a purified viral vector product, regulatory agencies have recommended to minimize the level and size of hcDNA based on risk assessment for GT products to ensure patient safety based on the nature of the host cell line used for production, the manufacturing method, and DNA fragment size. One such risk assessment methodology for quantifying the frequency of risk has been discussed and illustrated by an example in this article [1].

## References

1. Wright, J. (2014). Product-related impurities in clinical-grade recombinant AAV vectors: Characterization and risk assessment. Biomedicines,

   2(1), 80-97. https://doi.org/10.3390/biomedicines2010080

2. World Health Organisation. (2013). Guidelines on the quality, safety, and efficacy of biotherapeutic protein products prepared by recombinant DNA technology (Annex 4 of WHO Technical Report Series, No. 814).

https://cdn.who.int/media/docs/defaultsource/biologicals/biotherapeutics/trs_987_annex4.pdf?sfvrsn=d4ba378a_5&download=true

3. Vernay, O., Sarcey, E., Detrez, V., Abachin, E., Riou, P., Mouterde, B., Bonnevay, T., & Mallet, L. (2019). Comparative analysis of the performance of residual host cell DNA assays for viral vaccines produced in Vero cells. Journal of Virological Methods,

   268, 9-16. https://doi.org/10.1016/j.jviromet.2019.01.001

4. Center for Biologics Evaluation and Research Guidance for Industry. (2006). Human Gene Therapy for Neurodegenerative Diseases. Center for Biologics Evaluation and Research. https://www.fda.gov/media/144886/download

5. Yang H. (2013). Establishing acceptable limits of residual DNA. PDA journal of pharmaceutical science and technology

   ,67(2),155–163. https://doi.org/10.5731/pdajpst.2013.00910

6. What should researchers know about host cell DNA contamination risks in cell and gene therapies? (2022,March,8). STAT.

https://www.statnews.com/sponsor/2022/02/23/what-should-researchers-know-about-host-cell-dna-contamination-risks-in-cell-and-gene-therapies/

7. Sheng-Fowler, L., Lewis, A. M., & Peden, K. (2009). Issues associated with residual cell-substrate DNA in viral vaccines. Biologicals, 37(3), 190-195. https://doi.org/10.1016/j.biologicals.2009.02.015

8. Maurya, S., Sarangi, P., & Jayandharan, G. R. (2022). Safety of adeno-associated virus-based vector-mediated gene therapy—impact of vector dose. Cancer Gene Therapy, 29(10), 1305-1306. https://doi.org/10.1038/s41417-021-00413-6

9. Kaspar, B. K., Hatefiled J. M., Balleydier, J., Kasper A. A., Hodge, R. (2019). MEANS AND METHOD FOR PREPARING VIRAL VECTORS AND USES OF SAME. (W.O. Patent No. WO 2019/094253 AI). World Intellectual Property Organization.https://patentimages.storage.googleapis.com/d8/9b/b4/e932737 26559a1/WO2019094253A1.pdf

10. Whitlock, M. C., & Schluter, D. (2018). The analysis of biological data. Macmillan Higher Education.

11. Hardison R. (2021).Working with Molecular Genetics. The Pennsylvania State University.

12. Hussong, M., Bonifert, T., & Scheer, N. (2022, June 8). Reduction of Product-related Impurities during Production of recombinant Adeno-Associated Viruses. BioPharm International.

https://www.biopharminternational.com/view/reduction-of-product-related-impurities-during-production-of-recombinant-adeno-associated-viruses

13. Cellular, Tissue, and Gene Therapies Advisory committee. (2021). Toxicity Risks of Adeno-associated Virus (AAV) Vectors for Gene Therapy. Food and Drug Administration (FDA). https://www.fda.gov/media/151599/download

14. Barnes, L. F., Draper, B. E., Chen, Y. T., Powers, T. W., & Jarrold, M. F. (2021). Quantitative analysis of genome packaging in recombinant AAV vecharge detection mass spectrometry. Molecular therapy. Methods & clinical development, 23, 87–97. https://doi.org/10.1016/j.omtm.2021.08.002

15. Yang, H., Zhang, J., Yu, B., & Zhao, W. (2015). Statistical methods for immunogenicity assessment. Chapman and Hall/CRC

16. Mehta, S., & Kheer, J. T. (2007, October). Performance Characteristics of Host-Cell DNA Quantification Methods. Bioprocess International, 44-58. http://www.bioprocessintl.com/wp-content/uploads/bpi-content/070509ar06_76445a.pdf

17. Yang, H., Zhang, L., & Galinski, M. (2010). A probabilistic model for risk assessment of residual host cell DNA in biological products. Vaccine, 28(19), 3308–3311. https://doi.org/10.1016/j.vaccine.2010.02.099

18. Peden, K., Sheng, L., Pal, A., & Lewis, A. (2006). Biological activity of residual cell-substrate DNA. Developments in biologicals, 123, 45–73.

19. Sheng L, Cai F, Zhu Y, Pal A, Athanasiou M, Orrison B, Blair DG, Hughes SH, Coffin JM, Lewis AM, and K Peden (2008) Oncogenicity of DNA in vivo: tumor induction with expression plasmids for activated H-ras and c-myc. Biologicals 36:184-197

20. Sager R. (1985). Genetic suppression of tumor formation. Advances in cancer research, 44, 43–68. https://doi.org/10.1016/s0065-230x(08)60025-1

21. Temin, H. M. (1990). Overview of biological effects of addition of DNA molecules to cells. Journal of Medical Virology, 31(1), 13-17.

https://doi.org/10.1002/jmv.1890310105

22. Kurth, R. (1995). Risk potential of the chromosomal insertion of foreign DNA. Annals of the New York Academy of Sciences, 772(1 DNA Vaccines), 140-151. https://doi.org/10.1111/j.1749-6632.1995.tb44739.x

23. Keith, P. (2005, November). Issues Associated With Residual Cell-Substrate DNA [Conference session].

Made in the USA
Monee, IL
02 November 2026

67376094R00090